Sugar Spinelli's Little Instruction Book

Hrmph! I can't believe that snooty Amelia Bainbridge-Campbell showed up. What could an old biddy like her want with a bachelor? More likely, she just wants to throw her money around.... But, then again, maybe Amelia *does* need a man. Rumor has it that she's so desperate for a great-grandson, she's pushing her granddaughter to marry again! And Amelia seems to have set her sights on that sexy Marine, Nick Petrocelli. Well, the Marines do claim to enlist a few good men. But this officer's going to have to be pretty darn good to put up with the likes of Amelia....

Dear Reader,

We just knew you wouldn't want to miss the news event that has all of Wyoming abuzz! There's a herd of eligible bachelors on their way to Lightning Creek—and they're all for sale!

Cowboy, park ranger, rancher, P.I.—they all grew up at Lost Springs Ranch, and every one of these mavericks has his price, so long as the money's going to help keep Lost Springs afloat.

The auction is about to begin! Young and old, every woman in the state wants in on the action, so pony up some cash and join the fun. The man of your dreams might just be up for grabs!

Marsha Zinberg
Editorial Coordinator, HEART OF THE WEST

Nick of Time
Janelle Denison

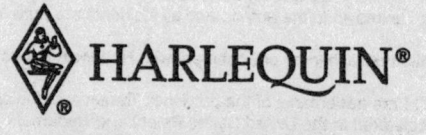

HARLEQUIN®

TORONTO • NEW YORK • LONDON
AMSTERDAM • PARIS • SYDNEY • HAMBURG
STOCKHOLM • ATHENS • TOKYO • MILAN • MADRID
PRAGUE • WARSAW • BUDAPEST • AUCKLAND

Janelle Denison is acknowledged as the author of this work.

ISBN 0-373-82597-8

NICK OF TIME

Copyright © 1999 by Harlequin Books S.A.

A Note from the Author

I have to admit, I love the idea of a series taking place around a bachelor auction, and I'm fascinated by the various reasons a woman would want to buy a sexy, gorgeous man. In *Nick of Time*, the last thing DEA officer Nick Petrocelli expects when he returns to the Lost Springs Ranch for some R&R is to be roped into his cousin's bachelor auction. If that isn't bad enough, he gets bought by Amelia Bainbridge-Campbell—a woman old enough to be his grandmother! But when he finds himself the personal assistant to Amelia's beautiful, sensual granddaughter, Samantha, what starts out as an obligation turns into a tempting attraction neither one can resist....

I hope you enjoy Nick and Samantha's story. HEART OF THE WEST is my first continuity project for Harlequin, and I was thrilled to be a part of such an exciting venture. I also write for Harlequin's Temptation series, so be sure to look for my next release, *Christmas Fantasy*, available December 1999.

Happy Reading

Janelle Denison

P.S. I'd love to hear what you think. Write to me at: P.O. Box 1102, Rialto, CA 92377-1102.

A special heartfelt thanks to my husband, Don,
for understanding when dinner didn't get made, or the
laundry didn't get done during the writing of this book.
I love you more every year.

To Jamie Denton, for always being just a phone call away.
Thank you for saving my sanity.

To my editor, Brenda Chin, for believing I *could* do this,
and to Marsha Zinberg, for taking a chance.

And to Marisa Carroll and Sarah,
for reasons they alone need to understand.

CHAPTER ONE

"RISE AND SHINE, MARINE."

Gunnery Sergeant Nick Petrocelli, late of the United States Marine Corps, rolled onto his stomach and put the pillow over his head. "Go away, Lindsay."

"Nope," his cousin Lindsay Duncan responded cheerfully. "You've slept half the day away. The auction starts in an hour and I need you out there so the ladies can get a gander at what they're bidding on."

"No way," he grumbled. Burrowing his head deeper beneath the pillow, he hoped she'd take the hint and leave him alone to sleep off the throbbing behind his temples, compliments of one too many shots of Jack Daniel's.

"Nick, you promised last night." Her feminine voice held a tinge of exasperation. "I even have it in writing, along with your signature, on a paper napkin."

He winced, remembering that he *had* promised Lindsay he'd stand in as one of her Bonus Bachelors. "It'll never hold up in court. I was drunk."

Even with the pillow over his head, Nick could sense her advancing into the bedroom, opening the curtains, flooding the room with the clear, bright sunlight of a June day. It was the same room Lindsay's parents had given him when he'd come to them twenty-two years before, a heartbroken ten-year-old whose mother had died of breast cancer just days earlier. Another lost and lonely boy that Karen and Robert Duncan had welcomed into their hearts and their home at Lost Springs Ranch for Boys. The only difference between him and the countless other boys they'd rescued was that Karen was his mother's older sister, so his ties to Lindsay and the ranch were of blood, as well as of the heart.

That spindly legged ten-year-old and that long-ago day were in the past. Still, this corner of Wyoming was the place he thought of as home, even though he'd spent precious little time here since he'd left to join the Marine Corps two weeks after he graduated from high school. He'd gone on to make a life for himself in New York, first as a cop, then a DEA agent.

This time, he was home on medical leave, recuperating from an injury he was damned lucky hadn't claimed his life. If the bullet that had grazed his left temple in the drug bust gone bad three weeks earlier had been half an inch to the right, well, he wouldn't be half-blind and temporarily disabled—he'd be dead.

His job as a DEA agent was dangerous, challenging and exciting—just the kind of occupation a solitary man with no commitments or ties thrived on. Unfortunately, he couldn't argue with his lieutenant's assessment of the situation: he'd been burning the candle at both ends for too long now. The past six months Nick had been running on pure adrenaline, and if he was honest with himself, this recent injury proved his exhaustion. He *never* should have gotten caught in the cross fire, and his carelessness and overworked mind had almost cost him his life.

Now he had a few months' leave stretching ahead of him, long, bland days filled with no purpose but to be as lazy as he wanted to be—if boredom didn't kill him first. Surviving the day-to-day monotony would be a challenge to his sanity, no doubt. He was a physical man who liked action and adventure, and he was already feeling edgy and too damned restricted.

"C'mon, Marine," Lindsay cajoled, tugging at the covers wrapped around his waist. "Duty calls."

He didn't bother grabbing for the sheet as it unraveled from his hips. Luckily for Lindsay, he'd worn his boxers to bed last night. "I'm a civilian now, remember?"

"Technically, maybe," she said from beside the bed. "But I know all about you law enforcement guys. You never really cut your ties to the military."

With a deep groan, he rolled onto his back and grimaced as the sun streaming through the window momentarily impaired the vision in his good eye and sent a sharp pain through his injured one. "I came back to Lost Springs for some R and R, not to be roped into being a bachelor for your auction." Reaching out to the side, he slapped his palm on the nightstand, searching for the black eye patch the ophthalmologist had given him to wear until they started laser treatments to restore his vision.

"C'mon, Nick," she said, putting the eye patch into his hand. "What's a weekend out of your time? It's not as though you've got anything pressing on your agenda for the next few months."

At that reminder, he scowled up at his cousin with his one good eye as he slipped on the patch. "I don't really qualify as a bachelor, Lindsay. I've been married before."

She dismissed his feeble argument with a wave of her hand. "That was over six years ago, and you've been single and available since."

"For good reason," he said, unable to forget the strain his job as a cop had put on his marriage, and that had ultimately driven him and his wife to divorce. His decision to remain single now had been an easy one, especially since his position as a DEA agent was twice as hazardous as being a patrol officer.

Lindsay crossed her arms over her chest, apparently unswayed.

He knew he was doomed to be some woman's plaything for a weekend. "There's no way I can get out of this, is there?"

"I'm afraid not. I've already passed out the flyers. You can't back out or the others will, too. You're a natural-born leader, Nick. Dad always said so."

She had to mention her dad, remind him of what he owed the founder of Lost Springs Ranch. Robert Duncan had stood in the place of the father he'd never known. Tony Petrocelli had died in Vietnam when Nick was six months old. Now Robert and Karen Duncan were dead, too, but their legacy lived on in the work their daughter was attempting to continue with at-risk boys.

"Please, Nick." Her soft voice implored him to see reason. "I really do need your help. This place is teetering on the edge of bankruptcy, and I've got a group of skittish bachelors milling around out there."

He gave a long-suffering sigh. "I'll give you every cent I've got to take my name off that flyer and leave me in peace to sleep off this hangover," he tried one last time.

"Nope. No deal," she said staunchly. "Once those women get an eyeful of you, someone like Sugar Spinelli will bid a year's oil revenues to take you home for the weekend."

A wry smile touched the corners of his mouth. Nick vaguely remembered the wife of Lightning Creek's richest man. She had a heart as big as her husband's bank account, and wouldn't miss the chance to make a sizable donation to the ranch, but she'd been an old lady fifteen years ago. "Sugar Spinelli? She's still alive?" The woman had to be eighty, at least.

"She's very much alive, and sitting in the first row." When he didn't respond to that, Lindsay continued her crusade to persuade him. "The woman who issues the highest bid isn't asking for forever, Nick, just a weekend. Surely even someone as cynical as you can appreciate that kind of no-strings-attached offer."

He mulled over her words and had to admit that the scenario did hold a certain appeal...depending on who purchased him and what they had in mind. He hadn't been on a date with a woman in what seemed like years, and since he really had nothing better to do with his time, what could a weekend spent in feminine company hurt?

"It's for a good cause, Nick."

He couldn't refute that, and figured it was time to stop teasing Lindsay. "Oh, all right," he finally relented, much to his cousin's relief. Like a lithe cat, he rolled over once and dropped to the hardwood floor at Lindsay's feet, where he started the first of two hundred push-ups. *One, two, three...* "I'll be there in thirty minutes," he promised.

She stepped back with a startled gasp. "Hey, should you be doing that?"

Thirteen, fourteen, fifteen... "The bullet grazed my temple, Lindsay," he said, effortlessly executing the daily ritual he'd established for himself years ago. "I may be temporarily half-blind, but my body is still in working order. No sense letting my forced vacation make me soft around the middle." He wanted to be in tip-top shape when he returned to the department in a few months, ready to start his next assignment.

Twenty-six, twenty-seven, twenty-eight... "Besides, there's nothing better for a hangover than the hair of the dog that bit you or exercise to sweat it out. Since I doubt you've got Jack Daniel's available, push-ups are gonna have to do."

"Whatever works."

Forty-four, forty-five, forty-six... "I forgot my tuxedo in New York," he said, sarcasm lacing his words. "And since I doubt too many women would be impressed seeing me in my favorite grunge jeans and T-shirt, what do you suggest I wear to dazzle the crowd?"

She walked across the floor toward the closet. "I've already thought of that."

Hearing the glee bubbling in her voice, he turned his head, craning his neck to keep her within vision of his good eye while he continued his push-ups. He'd lost count, but figured he must have reached the hundred mark because the muscles across his shoulders and down his back were starting to burn with the effort.

With a flourish, she opened the closet door to reveal his Marine Corps dress uniform hanging on the inside peg. The jacket and slacks were impeccably pressed, and the medals he'd earned gleamed across the front.

He groaned as the sight of the uniform flashed him back to the distant past. "You've *got* to be kidding."

"I'm completely serious. Women *love* men in uniform." She approached him, biting her bottom lip in concern. "It still fits, doesn't it?"

His push-ups grew more rapid, his breathing a bit deeper. "I'm sure it'll fit fine," he said, resigned to her scheming.

She squatted next to him so he could see her better. "Can you not wear your eye patch during the auction?"

"What?" he said in a mock tone. "You don't think it adds to the mystery?"

Her pretty eyes sparkled with humor. "Well, I hate to mix the pirate fantasy with the man-in-uniform fantasy." She blinked oh-so-innocently. "Besides, you have incredible green eyes. I'd like the women to see them... that is, if it doesn't bother you not to wear the eye patch."

Finished with his push-ups, he rolled to his back and began a series of stomach crunches. "I'll survive for ten minutes without it."

"Great!" She stood, a triumphant grin turning up the corners of her mouth. "I'll leave you to shower and dress." She headed for the door but stopped short of leaving. "You're gonna knock 'em dead, Gunnery Sergeant Petrocelli. Semper Fi." Giving him a mocking little salute, she hurried out of the room.

CHAPTER TWO

SAMANTHA FAIRMONT STROLLED leisurely behind her grandmother and aunt Kathryn as they headed toward the arena where the Lost Springs Ranch bachelor auction was being held. She found herself completely enthralled by the flurry of activity surrounding her, all for an auction of men bold and reckless enough to offer themselves for a weekend to the highest bidder.

She wondered how many hearts would get broken by the easy, cavalier attitudes of the bachelors up for auction, then told herself that wasn't her concern. She wasn't here for herself, or her aunt Kathryn, but for her grandmother, who'd insisted Samantha and Kathryn accompany her. There was no way Amelia Bainbridge-Campbell would miss the opportunity to make an appearance at one of the biggest fund-raisers in all of Wyoming, especially when Sugar Spinelli planned to be in attendance, as well.

Sugar Spinelli was Amelia's greatest rival for the title of Lady Bountiful to the residents of Lightning Creek, Wyoming, and its environs, which included the Lost Springs Ranch for Boys. Sugar had a distinct advantage in the unacknowledged competition because she lived in Lightning Creek year round and contributed to causes large and small. Amelia was only in residence six weeks a year at the ranch she'd inherited from Samantha's great-grandfather. If Sugar was bidding on a bachelor,

Samantha was certain Amelia would be, too, and the ranch would profit handsomely from the rivalry of two eccentric old women. The endless blue Wyoming sky was the limit if Amelia thought she could score points over Sugar Spinelli.

Samantha slipped on a pair of sunglasses to shade her eyes from the glare of the June sun. The sky was so blue and bright it hurt to look at it. The air was as clear as the sunlight, except for the dust stirred up by running children and excited women flocking to the showring for the start of the auction.

And what a mixture of women there was, all ages and all sizes, even a pregnant woman who clutched a bachelor auction brochure to her chest. A mom ushered her two kids along, anxious to get a good seat herself.

Enjoying the entire spectacle, Samantha slowed her steps as they walked under the shade of a towering sycamore tree. The mood was festive, and as she watched a trio of little boys running and playing nearby, she thought about how much her six-year-old daughter, Emily, would have enjoyed joining in on the fun. But Emily had asked to stay behind at the Campbell ranch house with the ranch foreman and his wife so she could play with the kittens in the barn and ride her pony. In another week, they'd be returning to Cranberry Harbor in Oregon, where they resided for the rest of the year.

Amelia stopped and turned around, leaning on the handle of the ebony cane she used but didn't really need. "Samantha, do stop dawdling. The auction is about to begin. I saw Sugar Spinelli and Theda Duckworth take their seats ten minutes ago. We need to hurry."

Kathryn, Amelia's daughter, stood to the side of the older woman, and Samantha caught her aunt rolling her eyes at her mother's competitive nature. Samantha sup-

pressed an amused smile of her own, knowing her grandmother wouldn't appreciate either of them finding humor
in what she considered very serious business.

Amelia started toward the entrance of the arena, leaving them to follow. Samantha and Kathryn fell into step
behind Amelia, both of them enjoying the scenery and
chaos surrounding them. A rich hickory scent drifted
their way from the barbecue pavilion nearby, and tables
had been set up to sell trinkets and raffle tickets for a
beautiful log cabin quilt.

"How many women do you think will find the man
of their dreams today?" Kathryn mused, glancing over
at a small group of good-looking men standing together,
a few in suits and tuxedos. They were clearly some of
the bachelors up for auction.

Surprised at Kathryn's question, Samantha glanced at
her aunt, who was nearing fifty and had never been married. She was still a very attractive woman, with generous curves that suited her tall frame. Her round face
was unlined, her complexion peaches and cream. Her
dark blond hair was threaded with silver and she wore
it in a soft knot, hidden now by the floppy brim of her
straw hat.

"Do you really think that's what these women are
here for?" Samantha asked curiously, taking a closer
look at the expressions on the faces of the women rushing toward the arena. She caught glimpses of expectation, excitement and anticipation. "To find a man to
marry?"

Kathryn gave a small shrug. "I suppose, deep down
inside, that's what most are hoping for."

The notion of purchasing a gorgeous, exciting bachelor in hopes of taming him into marriage material
seemed as reckless and foolhardy as Samantha's own

choice of a first husband had been. "Would *you* bid on a man for that reason?"

"Maybe, if he struck my fancy." A secret smile played around Kathryn's mouth, and her eyes sparkled mischievously. "But I'm too old to entertain the idea of buying one of these young men for a spouse, or anything else."

"It would have been nice if you'd settled down years ago with a husband," Amelia broke in, issuing her standard complaint that her eldest daughter had remained single. "Maybe by now I'd have myself a grandson to carry on the Bainbridge-Campbell name."

Samantha and Kathryn knew Amelia was only half joking about an heir, but took her comment in stride. The three of them were the last of the Bainbridge-Campbells, if you didn't count Samantha's wayward and disinherited mother, Lucinda, who lived in Tahiti with her fourth husband. Samantha hadn't seen her mother since she was eight, when Lucinda had dropped her off at Cranberry Harbor to live with her grandmother. Amelia never let her daughter and granddaughter forget where they came from, and how privileged they were to be one of the founding families of Wyoming. The illustrious name, impressive lineage and old money were all theirs, inherited from Amelia's Oregon timber baron forefathers. Her fondest wish was to keep the Bainbridge-Campbell name intact with a male heir, who would secure the vast holdings within the family.

Kathryn's chin lifted slightly. "When and if I find someone who accepts me for who I am, then I'll marry. And not a moment sooner."

Amelia glanced back, her expression disgruntled. "From the looks of things, I'll never get my grandson, unless Samantha quits being so stubborn and accepts a date with Tyler Grayson.''

Tyler Grayson was a well-connected, suitable man in Amelia's opinion, and she thought he would make the perfect second husband for her granddaughter, especially since she'd dated him before her marriage to Justin. "He's a nice man, Grandmother," Samantha said calmly. "But I'm not ready to date again."

"Hogwash," Amelia admonished as they headed toward the bleachers lining the showring. "It's been three years since Justin died, and it's past time you put yourself back into circulation. Tyler Grayson is a perfect match."

Samantha sighed and didn't say anything more. In a lot of ways, she knew Amelia was only looking out for her and Emily's best interests. Tyler was safe, secure and stable...everything Justin hadn't been.

Unfortunately, just like her irresponsible mother, Samantha had chosen passion and excitement over stability. She'd met Justin Fairmont at a flat-track motorcycle racing exhibition where he'd competed and won, and a girlfriend of hers had introduced them. She'd been all of twenty-one, grasping for her own sense of independence and craving the attention of this man who was sophisticated, and so very tempting. Effortlessly, he'd swept her off her feet with his irresistible charm and persuasive flattery. Against her grandmother's warnings to sever her relationship with someone so wild and impetuous, two months later she'd married Justin, believing the thrill of their fast-paced, passionate affair would ebb into a comfortable, stable marriage, with kids and a house with a white picket fence.

She'd been so very wrong, and Amelia had been so

very right in her prediction that a reckless man like Justin would only bring her grief and misery.

Justin, she'd learned, loved thrills and danger and taking risks. He lived life on the edge and didn't give much thought to his own welfare, let alone anyone else's, and she'd been naive enough to believe a child would make a difference in their marriage and the chances he took with his life. But Emily's birth hadn't tamed him. The man was drawn to danger, whether it was flat-track racing, skiing treacherous mountains or weaving through traffic at more than one hundred miles per hour on the interstate in his red Corvette.

He'd died in that sports car, in a fiery head-on crash that had reduced his vehicle to nothing more than twisted metal and ash.

Devastated, and shamed by her own imprudent choices, she'd tucked away the passionate, sensual nature that had led her astray and returned to Cranberry Harbor. For the second time in her life, Amelia had taken her in and given her a home. Her grandmother never condemned her for being as capricious as her mother, Lucinda, was, but Samantha had learned her lesson about love and passion the hard way, and she was determined to rectify the mistake she'd made in the only way she knew how—by being the dignified lady Amelia raised her to be.

Much to her dismay, the emotions and desire she tried so hard to suppress found their way into her private collection of sensuous paintings. It was the only outlet she allowed for the sensuality that seemed to be an innate part of her nature, but could never again rule her heart.

The public address system emitted a loud series of screeches and squawks as they entered the arena. The place was swarming with women, all rushing to find a seat. A lively young boy came up to them, handing a flyer to Samantha and Kathryn. He took one look at Amelia's blue-gray hair and scurried away without giving her one, obviously deciding someone as old as she was would have no use for a bachelor.

Five minutes later, they were settled in their seats a few rows above and to the left of Sugar Spinelli and Theda Duckworth. Digging the bachelor auction brochure from her handbag, Samantha flipped through the catalog of men to pass the few minutes left until the auction began. She read the bios of a cop, a cowboy, a doctor, a bull rider and even a toy manufacturer. It seemed the troubled young boys who'd spent their youth at Lost Springs Ranch had grown into successful, handsome men, thanks to the guidance and direction of the Duncans.

"What are you planning to do with a bachelor if you should win the bid on him?" Kathryn asked her mother as she gazed down at the flyer the little boy had given her. "There are sixteen of them now. They've added four Bonus Bachelors who weren't in the original auction catalog."

Amelia surveyed the colorful flyer over the gold rims of the glasses she'd slipped onto the bridge of her nose. "Good. I didn't particularly care for any of the bachelors I've seen so far."

Samantha didn't miss the way Amelia deliberately evaded Kathryn's question. "And what will you do with your bachelor?" she asked, just as curious as her aunt had been.

Amelia stared at Sugar and Theda, frowning at the way the two older women had their heads close together, as if sharing a conspiratorial secret. "I'm sure I can find something for him to do to receive my money's worth.

We do have our annual garden party coming up, you know.''

Samantha grimaced. Oh, the poor bachelor who found himself Amelia's for the weekend! The man would be expecting a fun, frivolous weekend with a young, single woman, when what Amelia had in mind was for him to slave away in her precious rose garden, pruning the bushes for their upcoming charity event.

The auction finally began, and the restless crowd quieted as the auctioneer took the microphone. Rob Carter, a doctor, was the first bachelor auctioned, and though he looked nervous and slightly embarrassed at first, he soon responded to the oohs and aahs and whistles of appreciation from the mostly female crowd. The bidding was spirited and substantial with Sugar Spinelli leading the charge. In a matter of minutes it was over. Dr. Robert Carter had been sold to the highest bidder, Sugar Spinelli, for a five-digit sum. Sugar and Theda jumped up from their seats and hugged each other, squealing in delight.

Thunderous applause reverberated through the crowd, and Samantha grinned and joined in the enthusiastic clapping. She didn't even want to speculate on what Sugar had in mind for her weekend with the handsome doctor, and from the disbelieving look on Rob Carter's face, neither did he.

Amelia tracked Sugar's progress as the other woman hurried to the cashier to pay for her purchase, and the auctioneer moved on to the next bachelor. ''That woman has always been shameless about throwing her money around.''

A ghost of a smile touched Kathryn's mouth. ''Well, how do you intend to bid, Mother?'' she asked without a hint of irony in her soft words. ''With stock shares?''

Amelia's expression turned sly. "I intend to offer a one-year scholarship to the University of Wyoming to whichever of the ranch boys graduates next spring with the highest grade point average."

"That is a generous offer," Kathryn said, truly impressed by her mother's donation, which would far exceed Sugar Spinelli's contribution to the ranch. "But hadn't we better quit talking about it and start bidding?"

The auction progressed, and among the successful bidders was Lindsay Duncan, who won a weekend with Rex Trowbridge, the ranch's director.

"What business does Lindsay Duncan have bidding on a man when she and this ranch are in debt up to their eyeballs?" Amelia exclaimed.

Kathryn shrugged. "I suppose she was saving him the embarrassment of being someone's plaything for a weekend."

Abruptly, Amelia straightened in her seat. "Who *is* that man?"

"Which one?" both Samantha and Kathryn asked at the same moment.

Amelia gestured hastily with the head of her cane. "That one. The Marine. Who is he?"

"I don't know," Kathryn replied, perusing the brochure as the Marine in dress blues mounted the stage. "I'm sure there wasn't a man in uniform pictured in the catalog."

"His name's Nick Petrocelli," Samantha offered, looking down at the flyer the little boy had given them earlier. "This says he's Gunnery Sergeant Nick Petrocelli, age thirty-two, and currently holds a position with the Justice Department."

Not that there were words powerful enough to describe this dynamic man, Samantha thought as she watched him cross the stage with a natural, lazy kind of confidence that mesmerized her.

Her stomach dipped and tumbled in a crazy kind of way when he turned and faced the crowd and she got a full-length view of him. The whistles and admiring murmurs from the crowd echoed her own appreciation. He stood straight and tall, his arms behind his back, his feet spread in a formal military stance. Medals gleamed against a broad chest that strained the coat of his well-cut uniform. The dress blues accentuated the width of his shoulders and complemented his physically fit body...making half the women in the stands crazy with lust.

The bidding began, but Samantha was too caught up in the man to enjoy the brisk rise in his purchase price. His features were lean and defined, and the sun glinting off his short dark hair revealed traces of rich auburn. Lowering her sunglasses a quarter inch down her nose, she gazed at him without any tint to obstruct her vision. His eyes, if she wasn't mistaken, were a striking, glittering green that nearly stole her breath and unfurled a startling warmth in her belly. Coupled with a devastatingly sexy smile, the man was simply gorgeous, and utterly male.

"Samantha, bid on the man."

Samantha returned to the present with a painful jolt that made her heart rate accelerate. Good Lord, had her grandmother read the thoughts that had no business being in her head? She pushed her sunglasses back up the bridge of her nose, hoping to hide the mortified flush she felt creeping over her cheeks. "Excuse me?"

Amelia's pale eyes flashed with mounting impatience. "I said, bid. He's perfect. Your grandfather was a Ma-

rine.'' When Samantha merely stared at her, she said,
''He's the only one remotely suitable. Bid on him.''

Vaguely, Samantha heard the auctioneer intoning
bids, but her mind was too hung up on her grandmother's words, *He's perfect,* to speak. Perfect body,
perfect eyes…perfect lips.

''Samantha, you're being impossible,'' Amelia
chided, then turned to her daughter. ''Kathryn, bid on
the man. Now!''

Automatically, Kathryn raised her hand, and the auctioneer pointed his mallet in their direction. ''Your bid,
madam?''

Before she could reply, Amelia stood with dramatic
importance and announced, ''I'll bid one year's tuition
at the University of Wyoming for one of the ranch
boys.''

Nick Petrocelli's eyebrows rose incredulously—
whether at the staggering donation or the elderly woman
who'd won him, Samantha wasn't sure. Heads swiveled
in their direction, and the crowd went silent for a moment, then burst into exuberant applause. Amelia nodded
regally, accepting the accolades as her due.

''That's quite a generous bid,'' the auctioneer acknowledged. ''Ladies, does anyone care to top that
bid?''

Apparently, no one did. ''The bidding is closed,'' he
announced dramatically, gazing at Amelia. ''Madam,
you've just bought yourself a Marine.''

NICK HAD BEEN AMUSED when a woman old enough to
be his grandmother had bid on Dr. Rob Carter, but being
on the receiving end of that humiliating experience
wasn't humorous at all. A petite, gray-haired old lady
with stern features had just dazzled the crowd with an

incredibly generous contribution to the ranch and had bought his presence for a weekend. What she had in mind for him he couldn't even begin to guess.

So much for two days of no-strings-attached fun with an enthusiastic beauty looking for a good time. He'd been close a few times, but unfortunately the gray-haired lady had effectively shut down all bids on him with her magnanimous offer.

He left the auction arena, grinning at the good-natured ribbing from his alumni. Most of them had fared better than he had and were spending the weekend with a young, eager female more suited to frivolous fun than the grandma who'd purchased him.

The sun was giving him a headache, right in the temple behind his left eye. He patted his coat pocket, then remembered he'd left his eye patch in his room. He thought about heading up to the ranch house to retrieve it, but before he could execute that plan, Lindsay appeared, her face beaming with excitement.

"Nick!" She flung herself into his arms for a quick hug. "A year's tuition at the University of Wyoming! I knew it was a good idea to put you up there in your uniform. Bart Campbell was a Marine. That's why she bid on you!"

"Who's Bart Campbell?" he asked, wondering if he should know the man.

"Amelia Bainbridge-Campbell's husband. The woman who bought you. He's dead now, but obviously your dress blues did the trick!" She squeezed his hand, her smile as bright and glorious as the June day. "I'm beginning to think this auction is going to work. If we can bring in enough money today to satisfy the creditors, I can get this ranch back on its feet. And I have you and all the other guys to thank for that."

"I'd do anything for you, Lindsay," he said, speaking the truth. He'd been giving her a hard time this morning, but he wouldn't hesitate to auction himself off three times over if it meant saving the ranch. "Your mom and dad gave me a home and a family, and I owe them every bit as much as the other guys here."

She stood up on tiptoe and gave him a quick kiss on the cheek. "They loved you like a son, Nick. Truly, they did."

"Sergeant!"

Nick dropped Lindsay's hand and automatically snapped to attention, answering the voice of authority. It had been more than ten years since his stint in the Marines, but some habits died harder than others. "Yes, ma'am," Nick replied crisply, staring down at the petite woman with the voice of a drill instructor.

She looked him over, as if checking the authenticity of his dress blues. "I'm Amelia Bainbridge-Campbell," she said, introducing herself with a curt nod. "This is my daughter Kathryn and my granddaughter, Samantha Fairmont."

Nick shook Kathryn's hand first. She was tall and heavy-set, with kind blue eyes and a ready smile. "Ma'am," he acknowledged.

She blushed ever so slightly and murmured, "Sergeant."

He turned toward the granddaughter, expecting someone equally as sweet and unassuming as Kathryn. For the most part Samantha Fairmont did come across as reserved, but there was a light in the depths of her pale blue eyes, a spark of something alluring that made him think of soft, silky skin and warm tangled sheets.

That brought him up short. His thoughts were, without a doubt, inappropriate...especially since she gave no outward sign that she'd been struck with the same intense awareness.

She was a natural beauty, the kind of woman who possessed wholesome, girl-next-door looks and, if she chose to, could take advantage of those pretty features and be a real head-turner. A quick, visual sweep confirmed she had the body of a siren, though she tried to downplay her flattering curves and full, rounded breasts beneath a simple cotton summer dress in a pale shade of pink. What she couldn't hide, though, were those long, slender legs of hers.

He dragged his gaze up, focusing on safer territory. Her hair, which she'd pulled into a practical French braid, was what most would technically call "blond," but he thought the thick strands were more the color of rich butterscotch. He couldn't help but wonder what her hair would look like down.

He inclined his head, reminding himself of his manners. "Ms. Fairmont."

She didn't offer her hand, which made him suspect she was more aware of him than she'd let on. "Hello," she replied, her voice husky-soft.

His gut tightened, and his traitorous gaze landed on her mouth, which was full and soft-looking—ripe for slow, deep kisses.

"Sergeant Petrocelli," her grandmother broke in again, demanding his attention.

Nick turned to the older woman. "Please, call me Nick. I'm not a Marine anymore."

"Nonsense," the woman scoffed. "Once a Marine, always a Marine, Sergeant. Lindsay—" Amelia turned her penetrating gaze on his cousin "—I've got a deal for you."

"A deal?" Lindsay shot Nick a quick questioning look. "What kind of deal?"

"I will increase my scholarship donation to the ranch fourfold if Sergeant Petrocelli agrees to come to my home in Oregon and act as my personal assistant for two weeks."

"What the hell?" Nick bit back a groan of disbelief, wondering once again why he couldn't have been purchased by some young woman...like Samantha.

Lindsay's eyes widened at the extravagant, and much needed, four-year scholarship. Kathryn's expression reflected her surprise at her mother's outrageous request. And amusement teased the corners of Samantha's lips.

"Oh, come, come, Mr. Petrocelli. You heard me," Amelia said. "I'm willing to offer a full scholarship. Four years' tuition, books, room and board to one of the ranch students if you will agree to come to my home in Oregon and act as my personal assistant for two weeks to help with the planning of my annual garden party."

Beside him, Lindsay was all but bursting with the chance to grasp that scholarship, but she said nothing.

"I'm afraid I don't know much about being someone's personal assistant," Nick said. In his line of work he dealt with criminals, and he sure as hell didn't cater to any of them, or anyone else for that matter. He'd been alone for so long, depending on no one but himself, and hadn't a clue what to do to please another person, let alone assist them in day-to-day tasks.

"Oh, it's not at all difficult," Amelia said vaguely, raising Nick's suspicions. "And since you're on leave, I'm sure your time at Cranberry Harbor won't interfere with your job."

His gaze narrowed. "How did you know I'm on leave?"

Her thin shoulders lifted in a nonchalant shrug, but Nick wasn't fooled. "I asked Rex Trowbridge about you a few minutes ago. Since your ties to Lost Springs Ranch are of blood as well as the heart, I'm sure you won't say no to my offer."

Ties of blood as well as the heart. Exactly the words he'd used himself to describe his attachment to Lindsay and the ranch. There was no way he'd ever renege on a deal to his cousin, not when so much was at stake.

He looked down at the tiny woman before him and held out a white-gloved hand. "You have a deal, ma'am," he said, executing a mock bow. "You've bought yourself a personal assistant."

CHAPTER THREE

Two weeks later

HE WAS ARRIVING TODAY. A combination of nerves and anticipation fluttered in Samantha's belly, which seemed to happen every time she thought of the dark-haired, green-eyed, sexy Marine.

This morning at breakfast Samantha's grandmother had reminded Kathryn and her of Nick Petrocelli's arrival, and announced that he'd be occupying the east-wing suite opposite Samantha's on the third floor. Amelia and Kathryn shared the second-floor suites, so the arrangement was logical. A grand staircase spiraled up to each landing, then a long hall split the floor into two separate sections. It was like having your own apartment, and Samantha cherished the privacy it afforded her.

Now she'd be sharing the third floor with a man who made her too aware of herself as a woman, and that knowledge was enough to make her feel nervous.

Picking up her sketch pad and black pencil, Samantha sat on the window seat of her third-floor bedroom. In an attempt to burn some of her restless energy, she sketched an image of her daughter—the way Emily had looked that morning while playing tea party with her dolls. Samantha's gaze alternated between the open bedroom window, which faced the front of the house, and her developing picture.

Normally, she preferred to draw in her sitting room across the hall, whose balcony overlooked the Pacific Ocean. But Amelia had instructed her to greet Nick when he arrived, and this vantage allowed her to keep an eye on the driveway. Her grandmother's imposing house dominated a low bluff off their private stretch of beach an hour's drive outside Portland, Oregon. But the property was so secluded it could have been in a world all its own. Her great-grandfather Bainbridge had had the enormous house built as a wedding gift for his bride in the early twenties, and Amelia had been born in this very room.

Amelia's daughters, Kathryn and Lucinda, had also grown up in this house. While Kathryn had grown into a prim and proper woman befitting the Bainbridge-Campbell name, Samantha's mother, Lucinda, had run off with a boy from the wrong side of the tracks to join the Summer of Love in San Francisco and had never looked back. She'd married the boy, Samantha's father, but he was long gone from her life by the time Samantha turned two. And after him came an endless procession of boyfriends, lovers and ex-husbands. So many that Samantha lost count.

Lucinda hated being tied down by a child, so Samantha had spent every summer in this house and came to live with Kathryn and Amelia for good when her mother married for the third time and moved to Paris when her daughter was eight. Samantha had remained at Cranberry Harbor until her tempestuous marriage to Justin Fairmont. When he'd died, she'd returned to the only home she'd ever known with Emily in tow. She had spent the past three years raising her daughter in a nurturing atmosphere, while restoring the respectability she'd lost with her impetuous choice of husband. She owed that to

Amelia, and Emily deserved a mother who didn't make
rash decisions based on frivolous whims or the forbidden
lure of passion and excitement, as Samantha's own
mother had.

But for all the outward decorum Samantha had established since Justin's death, deep inside, she feared she
was too much like Lucinda, who embraced the thrilling
rush and temptation of what she perceived as love, and
had spent her adult life searching for that elusive emotion with countless men.

Samantha wouldn't, *couldn't* follow that destructive
pattern. And the only way she knew how to control her
urges was to paint her sensual pictures, providing an
outlet for all those pent-up emotions.

Sighing deeply at those troubling thoughts, she looked
out over the manicured lawns and the huge rose gardens
that were Amelia's pride and joy. She spotted Victor
Kislenko, a Russian immigrant her grandmother had em-
ployed for the past four years as chauffeur, mechanic
and general overseer of Cranberry Harbor. He was a tall,
balding man in his mid-fifties, with a fierce mustache, a
marvelous smile, and a way with roses and cars. Samantha also suspected the older gentleman fancied her
aunt Kathryn. As she watched, he walked among the
rose beds, supervising the progress of three part-time
gardeners as they worked to ready the area for her grandmother's upcoming garden party.

A black sports utility vehicle caught her attention as
it slowly wound its way up the long, curving drive from
the main road. Guessing it was Nick Petrocelli, she stood
and put her sketch pad away. Since she'd been appointed
his welcoming committee, Samantha decided to enlist
one more person for extra support, and headed to her

daughter's bedroom, where she was still playing with her dolls.

Samantha smiled as Emily handed her fuzzy bear a plastic cookie and held an imaginary, animated conversation with him. She hated to interrupt the precious moment. "We have a guest to greet, Emily."

Emily glanced back at her, blue eyes wide with excitement. "Maybe they'd like to come to my tea party!"

Samantha envisioned Nick folding his large, solid frame into one of Emily's tiny wicker chairs and drinking from a dainty teacup. The thought was ludicrous. Besides, she had no idea how Nick might feel about a precocious little girl who craved the attention of a father figure.

Samantha held her hand out for Emily to hold. "He's here to help Grandmother, sweetie."

"Oh." Emily's expression reflected her disappointment, and Samantha made a mental note to spend the afternoon with her out on the playground situated in the side yard.

Together, they headed downstairs, and by the time they opened the massive carved cedar doors leading to the front of the house, Nick had already parked his Blazer next to the ostentatious dolphin and mermaid fountain dominating the center of the circular drive. He slid from the vehicle, reached in for a black leather duffel on the passenger seat, then shut the door. He approached them, that lazy confidence of his apparent in his easy stride. Samantha experienced surprise at the black eye patch he wore over his left eye. It hadn't been there at the auction. But that one green eye seemed to miss nothing.

"Mama, he's a pirate!" Emily announced, her voice infused with fascination.

"He certainly looks like one," she agreed.

All traces of the uniformed Marine her grandmother had purchased were gone, and in his place was a casually dressed bachelor in faded jeans and a T-shirt with the name of a New York pool joint, Paradise Billiards, slashed across the front. He looked more suited as a handyman than a personal assistant, and Samantha was pretty certain his blue-collar attire would be one of the first things her grandmother exchanged for something more dignified and appropriate for his position.

"I never met a pirate before!" Emily exclaimed as Nick stopped a few feet away from them, the width of his shoulders blocking them from the glare of the sun. "Mister, are you a pirate?"

His mouth curved into a rogue grin that could have belonged to Blackbeard himself. "Well, I suppose I could have descended from a crew of buccaneers," he said, feeding Emily's active imagination.

Emily stared up at him in awe. "Wow."

While her daughter digested that adventurous thought, he turned his megawatt smile her way. She noticed a small puckered scar on his left temple that she hadn't noticed at the bachelor auction, and wondered what had happened to him.

He inclined his head at her. "Ms. Fairmont, isn't it?"

His deep, rich voice was more personal than the amused tone he'd used with Emily, and the resonant sound made her skin tingle. He held out his hand for her to shake. At the auction, she'd managed to avoid touching him, but to ignore his gesture now would be rude.

She slipped her hand into his, and her pulse raced. His palm was so large, his fingers so long they swallowed up her slender hand in a startling, but pleasant, warmth. "Please, call me Samantha."

"Only if you'll call me Nick." He let go of her hand, very slowly, and turned to Emily. "And who is this pretty little girl?"

Samantha smiled as Emily peered up at him with sudden, uncharacteristic shyness. "My daughter."

"Oh." His surprised gaze flickered to Samantha's left hand, the fingers of which were threading through Emily's silky blond hair, then back up to her face. "You're married, then?"

She shook her head. "No. I'm widowed."

He offered a sympathetic smile. "I'm sorry."

"I'm Emily," Samantha's daughter announced, seemingly over her short bout of bashfulness. "I'm six years old."

Another dazzling grin from Nick. "Hello, Emily." Reaching out, he brushed his fingers along Emily's ear and a quarter magically appeared in his hand. He looked at the coin with a perplexed frown, as if he couldn't understand where it had come from. "Hmm, you must not have washed behind your ears last night."

Emily's gaze grew as round as the quarter Nick handed her. Samantha laughed, and Nick winked conspiratorially at her.

"Wow, you're a pirate magician!" Emily said, completely enthralled by Nick's sleight of hand. She hugged the quarter to her chest. "Are you staying at Cranberry Harbor?" she asked hopefully.

"Yep," he confirmed. "For two whole weeks."

Samantha gently touched Emily's shoulder. "He's not here to play, Emily," she said, heading off her daughter's mistaken belief that she'd just discovered a new, fun playmate. "He'll be grandmother's personal assistant, and he'll be too busy to entertain you."

Emily frowned in disappointment at that, then her features suddenly brightened. "I'm gonna go tell Aunt Kathryn and Grandmother that Mr. Nick found a quarter behind my ear!"

Once she was inside the house and Samantha was alone with Nick, his mouth curved into one of those devastating grins that made her feel as if she'd lost her breath.

"So much for hoping I might be able to enjoy part of my two-week stint as Amelia's bachelor, huh?" he asked humorously.

For a man who'd been bought by a fastidious old lady instead of a fun-loving younger woman, he'd accepted his unfortunate luck extremely well. "I'm afraid Amelia likes to get her money's worth, and though I don't know exactly what she has planned for you, I can guarantee she'll keep you occupied."

From the corner of her eye Samantha saw Victor heading their way from the rose gardens. "Is there something you need me for, Miss Samantha?" he asked in his low, accented English.

Nick turned toward the other man, who'd been approaching from his left side, and Samantha made the introductions. "Victor, this is Nick Petrocelli. He's agreed to act as Grandmother's personal assistant for the next two weeks."

Victor's bushy gray brows rose at that announcement, but he merely held out his hand and said, "Welcome to Cranberry Harbor Cottage."

Their grips locked for a moment. "Thank you, but where I come from, this pile of stones isn't a *cottage*," Nick said, nodding toward the monstrous estate looming behind them.

Victor's mustache twitched with bemused agreement. "It was built by Miss Samantha's great-grandfather, and to a man of Alistair Bainbridge's vast wealth, it did qualify as a cottage. The monstrosity is truly decadent. The architect must have been drunk or crazy."

"Or both," Nick added humorously.

Samantha glanced at the only real home she'd ever known, seeing it through their eyes. The mansion *was* decadent. Towers sprouted from every corner of the crenellated roofline, dormers abounded. There were chimneys everywhere. The Gothic windows were diamond paned and oversize. When she was little she'd thought of it as a fairy princess's castle. Now the place had become a haven for her.

"Would you like me to park Mr. Petrocelli's vehicle in the garage?" Victor asked, interrupting her thoughts.

Shoving her hands into the pockets of her shorts, Samantha returned her attention to Victor and their guest. "Yes, please. I need to show Mr. Petrocelli his room, then take him to Grandmother's library, where she's waiting for him."

With a nod, Victor caught the keys Nick tossed his way, then was off to do her bidding.

"Right this way, Mr. Petrocelli," she said, and started for the carved front doors.

He caught her arm, stopping her. His touch was light, and not at all intimidating, but everything within her went on alert as a tantalizing heat spread up her arm and her breath hitched in her throat. Her breasts grew heavy, tingly and she was appalled at her unexpected response and everything it implied.

Their gazes met, and she hoped, prayed, he didn't notice her reaction.

"I thought you agreed to call me Nick," he said, while his thumb stroked the soft, sensitive skin in the crease of her elbow.

"I..." Her voice faltered, as did her heart. His touch was incredibly sensual, the brush of his fingers oddly tender, making her mind spin. She wondered if he felt the connection between them, too, or if she was making more of it than it warranted.

His handsome face revealed nothing. "I'm not much into formality, and going by Mr. Petrocelli makes me feel like an old man." He smiled. Just a simple smile, but it made him more gorgeously male, and so very tempting. "Say it, Samantha."

She swallowed the thick knot that had lodged in her throat. *"Nick."* The one word soughed out of her and seemed to zap her of energy.

Pleasure touched his features. "Very good," he murmured, his voice low and silky. "Let's try and keep it that way." Releasing her arm, he shifted his duffel in his hand. "Now, you'd better take me to Amelia before she thinks I stood her up and puts out a warrant for my arrest."

A tentative smile curved Samantha's mouth, and though she suspected his humor was an attempt to dissolve the tension between them, she appreciated it just the same.

AFTER A QUICK TOUR of the Cranberry Harbor estate and the luxurious suite of rooms he'd been appointed, Nick followed Samantha to the opposite side of the manor and Amelia's private library. The extravagance of the interior of the house far exceeded anything he'd ever seen. Thick, lush carpets lined the halls and entryway, and expensive-looking antiques graced small tables and ornate fireplace mantels. Chippendale and French provincial furniture abounded. Some of the furnishings were just as gaudy as the exterior of the house, though he didn't doubt that every piece had cost a small fortune.

As they passed yet another room filled with more period pieces in immaculate condition, Nick wondered how a six-year-old child managed to be playful and care-free when surrounded by such stuffy elegance. The furnishings certainly wouldn't welcome sticky fingers, muddy shoes or dusty clothes.

The accommodations at the Lost Springs Ranch where he'd grown up had been modest, but more important, the ranch had felt warm and welcoming. Although his aunt Karen had tried to instill in her foster boys a sense of cleanliness and responsibility, inevitably someone tracked the more unpleasant odors and grime of ranch life into the house. But Karen and Robert Duncan's ordinary home had been filled with extraordinary love, daily doses of affection and good-natured ribbing, and the dirt that accumulated became inconsequential. Instilling a sense of worth in the boys had been more important to the Duncans than maintaining an immaculate house.

Now, surrounded by this formal elegance, Nick appreciated his humble upbringing all the more.

"Here we are," Samantha announced as they entered an immense marble-floored foyer with a crystal chandelier hanging from a beveled-glass dome in the center of the ceiling.

As Nick glanced up in stunned disbelief at such flagrant extravagance, the sun came out from behind a cloud, and the chandelier's crystal prisms caught and refracted the sun's light into a thousand rainbows. There were marble statues of classical figures in niches along the wall, and a huge table in the center of the room with an arrangement of at least two dozen pale pink roses.

Real roses, Nick thought as he caught their scent drifting across the vast space.

He let out a low whistle under his breath and turned toward his tour guide with a grin. "I think I'll keep my hands firmly placed in my pockets and hope to God I don't trip. I figure I'd have to spend the rest of my life just trying to work off that crystal vase."

He was joking, of course, trying to prod a smile from her. Ever since their brief contact outside she'd been very stiff, her manner reserved, and he wanted to set her at ease.

His strategy worked, to a degree. He watched her bite the inside of her cheek to keep from smiling, but her eyes sparkled with merriment. She knew from various teasing comments he'd made that he found all this opulence excessive, and surprisingly, he'd concluded from her responses that she agreed.

She waved a slender hand toward a pair of carved pocket doors. "She's waiting for you, right through those doors."

He shuddered, feigning mock fright. "You're abandoning me to go in there by *myself?*"

The smile she'd been holding back slowly pulled up the corner of her mouth, and something low in his belly coiled tight. "I'll let you in on a little secret. Amelia may come across as a lioness, but she's really a pussycat."

Nick saw the deep devotion and respect for her grandmother in Samantha's gaze and smiled back. "I'll see you later, then?"

Mischief colored her blue eyes. "Hmm, that depends on what Grandmother has in mind for you, and whether she allows you to fraternize with the family." She waggled her fingers at him, then headed for the branching mahogany staircase fit for a baronial hall. Over her shoulder, she called, "Enjoy yourself."

Oh, he did, at least for the minute it took for her to climb up those stairs to the second landing. She'd worn shorts today, giving him a gander at her small, rounded bottom and showing him just how long, slender and beautifully shaped her legs were. Her T-shirt revealed the lush curves the dress she'd worn at the auction had concealed. She had nice, full breasts that would fill his large hands perfectly. Her hips swayed with sublime grace with each step she took, reminding him that she was way out of his league. Reminding him, too, that he had no business thinking about her in terms of a no-strings-attached affair, which he'd been flirting with in the back of his mind. She was the kind of woman who'd no doubt expect commitment and forever, and he guaranteed neither, not with his line of work.

On that thought, he turned and faced the pocket doors that led to Amelia's private library. It was time for him to face the pussycat in her den.

CHAPTER FOUR

AMELIA BAINBRIDGE-CAMPBELL sat in a large wing chair before a massive marble fireplace in her private library. Emily sat on the edge of the cushion next to her, the little girl's animated chatter captivating her great-grandmother's attention.

Nick listened from just inside the doorway as Emily went on about the way he'd discovered a quarter behind her ear, and she had no idea how that could have happened because she was pretty certain she'd scrubbed behind her ears last night. Then the little girl looked up at Amelia expectantly, waiting for her to offer an explanation.

Amelia thought about it for a moment. "I'm truly baffled."

"I keep feeling behind my ear, but there's nothing there." Emily sighed and glanced at the silver coin in her hand. "I wonder how long this quarter was there."

"Probably not long," Nick said, attempting to appease the little girl's curiosity.

Emily glanced over her shoulder, her expression brightening when she saw him. "Maybe you can find a quarter behind Grandmother's ear."

Amelia's appalled expression suggested otherwise. While Amelia might indulge her great-granddaughter's inquisitive nature, she clearly had no desire to be part of Nick's antics.

Nick let her off the hook. "The trick only works on little girls."

Emily slid off the seat and hurried over to him, her eyes hopeful. "Could you check the other ear, just to be sure there's not a quarter there, too?"

He lightly brushed his fingers behind her ear and came up empty-handed. "Nope. No quarter behind that ear."

A frown creased her delicate brow, and he could almost hear her little mind trying to figure out a logical explanation for the coin he'd found earlier.

"Emily, I need to speak with Mr. Petrocelli," Amelia said, her tone soft but undeniably firm. "You may go and play."

"Yes, Grandmother." Emily looked up at Nick. "I hope I see you later." With an impish grin, she slipped around him and out the door, closing it shut behind her.

"That little girl has an insatiable curiosity," Amelia said with a shake of her head, though there was affection in her eyes. "She'll talk your ear off if you let her. She's just like Samantha when she was that age."

The Samantha he'd encountered was so composed, Nick found it difficult to imagine her being as gregarious and inquisitive as her daughter. He briefly wondered what had happened to diminish that affable, open quality Amelia mentioned.

"Emily is a sweet little girl," he replied.

"You've certainly managed to win over her affections."

"It's amazing how that quarter trick breaks the ice with kids." He moved deeper into the room to where she sat, his gaze taking in the impressive surroundings. The parquet floors gleamed, and floor-to-ceiling shelves of leather-bound books towered over him, the titles picked out in gold leaf. The bindings shimmered softly in the subdued lighting that found its way through the multipaned windows dominating the far end of the long room.

Since she hadn't asked him to take the seat opposite her, he affected the same stance he had on the bachelor auction stage—straight and tall, hands behind his back, feet braced apart.

The older woman seemed to appreciate the formality. "I trust you had a good drive from Wyoming?"

He gave a slight inclination of his head. "I did."

"You're wearing an eye patch," she observed out loud. "Is your injury bothering you?"

"My eye is healing quite well, though I need to wear the patch until I begin laser surgery next month to restore my vision."

She nodded, but didn't linger on personal issues. "Did Samantha show you your room, and around the estate?"

"Yes, ma'am."

"Good." Her pale gaze flickered down the length of him. "Are all your clothes the same quality as those you're wearing?"

The corner of his mouth twitched with a smile, but he didn't dare show his amusement. "Yes, ma'am."

Her gnarled, beringed hand tightened on the head of her cane. "They aren't suitable for your duties here."

The last thing he'd expected when he'd left New York and headed to Wyoming for some R and R was to be someone's personal assistant. He'd packed for comfort, not an executive position. "Jeans and T-shirts are all I have with me."

"Unacceptable. Victor will take you into town tomorrow and help you purchase suitable garments. I will, of course, pay for them."

He lived in jeans and T-shirts. He wasn't one to wear

a suit unless he was attending a funeral or wedding, and though he knew his threadbare denims were on the shabby side, he couldn't see himself trussed up in a coat, tie and slacks. The woman would have to settle for a compromise.

"And my duties for the next two weeks are?" he prompted, wanting to know exactly what she expected of him.

"Oh, this and that," she said vaguely, then went on, her next pronouncement far more straightforward. "Mr. Petrocelli, I have another proposition for you."

Nick affected nonchalance, but his insides tensed at the sudden change in Amelia's demeanor. "Go on," he said.

"What would you say to my endowing the scholarship I'm providing for the ranch on a permanent basis?"

"That's a very generous offer," he acknowledged. "One I'm sure Lindsay would appreciate."

"And that's a very cautious answer." Something akin to respect entered her pale gaze. Releasing a long-suffering sigh, she motioned to the chair across from her. "Sit down, Mr. Petrocelli. You're giving me a pain in my neck looking up at you."

He sat in the wing chair opposite hers without comment.

"The scholarship would be endowed in the name of your aunt and uncle. Do you think that's a fitting memorial for them, Mr. Petrocelli?"

"Yes, I do." He blinked lazily and smiled. "The question remains. Why would you do it?"

"No beating around the bush. I like that in a man." She leaned forward slightly, resting her weight on the head of her cane. "Would you be willing to do something for me in return for that memorial?"

He lifted a brow. "That depends on what you're asking of me."

"Do you consider yourself an honorable man, Mr. Petrocelli?"

Nick didn't dignify that question with an answer. The woman wouldn't have chosen him for whatever she had in mind if she didn't believe he was honorable.

She smiled with satisfaction. "You don't need to say anything. I already know the answer. Duty. Honor. Country. The code you live by. The code my late husband lived by."

"Lindsay told me he was a Marine."

"Yes. He died fifteen years ago. I miss him every day I live." The briefest hint of nostalgia entered her eyes, but before the emotion could fully develop, it was gone and she was back to business. "But that's beside the point. You live by the same code he did. Therefore, I know you're the right man for the job."

He shifted in his stiff seat and thought of his comfortable, broken-in recliner waiting for his return at his apartment back in New York. "Which is?"

"Samantha loves children. She needs more of them. And I would like a great-grandson. I had no sons, my daughter Kathryn never married, and Samantha is my only grandchild by my other daughter, Lucinda, who never had any more children. I'm seventy-five years old and my time is growing short."

Nick stared at Amelia in stunned disbelief. She couldn't be suggesting he make love to Samantha Fairmont to give her a child? The notion was impossible. Ridiculous. Intriguing.

He pulled his wayward thoughts up short. "I don't see what any of this has to do with me."

"I want Samantha to marry again," Amelia stated.

"I've already picked out a suitable man for her second husband. Tyler Grayson is very well-connected, his social status is impeccable, and he's dated Samantha in the past, so they have something of a history. He's practical, and more important, stable, which is what Samantha needs. Samantha, unfortunately, wants nothing to do with him."

"And this is where I come in?" he guessed, unsure what she expected of him.

"Exactly." She sat back in her chair, hesitating, seemingly mulling over her words before speaking them. "Maybe I should explain the situation more clearly. Samantha refused a proposal from Tyler and married her first husband for all the wrong reasons. Justin Fairmont was wild and rebellious, and I suppose to a young, impressionable woman of twenty-one, all that recklessness seemed very enticing. Her marriage was rocky and filled with heartbreak and misery. But it was a lesson she had to learn on her own." Her voice was quiet with resignation, as if she regretted the fact that Samantha had to endure such grief. "Unfortunately, that experience has made her very cautious when it comes to men and her own judgment of them. It's been three years since Justin died, and she still refuses to consider another relationship, even to a man who'd proposed to her once before."

Nick silently digested all that, understanding Samantha's reserve a bit more. Yet earlier when he'd grabbed her arm outside, he'd had a fleeting glimpse of a warm, sensual woman...albeit a wary one.

"What Samantha needs is a sedate, harmless love affair," Amelia continued. "A way to get her back into the swing of things, so to speak, and see Tyler Grayson in a more favorable light."

Sedate didn't equate *love affair* in Nick's mind. No,

when he thought of an affair, he envisioned heat, anticipation, illicit trysts shared by two anxious lovers who
couldn't keep their hands off each other. He was certain
Amelia would be shocked to learn his definition of the
word didn't resemble hers in the least.

"I think you bought the wrong bachelor," he said
bluntly.

"Hear me out, Mr. Petrocelli," she said patiently, obviously believing otherwise. "I'm not proposing that you
act unworthily toward my granddaughter. In fact, if you
were not who you are, and what you are, I wouldn't
have dared suggest such a thing."

What he was was just a mortal man with a healthy
sex drive and baser male needs that seemed to come
alive whenever he was near Samantha. His attraction to
the woman wasn't as noble as Amelia believed it to be.
He'd be better off walking away from this harebrained
scheme of Amelia's instead of tangling himself in the
middle of something potentially dangerous.

Yet there was no way he could refuse the permanent
scholarship she was offering, or explain to Lindsay his
reasons for forfeiting the endowment, which would go a
long way in helping many underprivileged boys.

"I'll assign you as Samantha's personal assistant to
help her with the planning of the upcoming garden party.
You will make yourself available to her at all times, and
stick close to her side." He said nothing, just waited
until she laid out all her terms. "All I'd like from you
is to be kind and attentive to Samantha. To court her a
little, and flatter her. Most important, build her confidence as a woman so that when she hears from Tyler
again she will be inclined to view him in a more favorable light and reconsider his original proposal."

Still he remained silent, not sure he wanted to tangle himself up in Amelia's plan.

With a sigh, she stood and walked over to a shelf holding an assortment of small framed pictures. Picking one up, she returned to Nick and held it out for him to see. "This was Samantha a few months before she met Justin. She was a vibrant woman, and was a bit impetuous herself, which is what got her into trouble with Justin. The excitement he represented appealed to her, but it also nearly destroyed her. She lost all sense of security and what was important to her...until Justin's recklessness killed him and she realized the importance of stability. Now Samantha struggles to keep her more impulsive, passionate nature under control, for herself as much as for Emily."

Nick stared at the photograph of Samantha, her eyes full of sparkle and life and an innate zest for life—so different from the sedate woman he'd met.

"I care for my granddaughter and Emily very much, and only want the best for them." She replaced the picture, then returned to stand in front of the massive marble fireplace. "Tyler Grayson is a decent man, and he'll offer Samantha and Emily a secure future. And he won't threaten her more impulsive nature. But before that can happen, Samantha needs to feel confident about herself as a woman, and trust her emotions again, so she can fall in love."

Nick understood Amelia's motives, which were all in Samantha's best interests. Flirting with Samantha was the simple part; keeping things from crossing that very fine line to something more emotional would be a bit trickier. Essentially, he'd be prepping her for another man to take over where he left off.

"It really is the perfect arrangement," Amelia said,

confident of her plan. "You'll be Samantha's personal assistant for the garden party. You'll spend time with her, compliment her, make her feel as a woman should. A little harmless flirtation is all she needs. After two weeks you'll be gone, and she'll be more willing to give Tyler Grayson the chance he deserves. It's all very simple, really."

Nick scrubbed a hand through his close-cropped hair and leaned forward, his gaze on hers. "And in return for me paying attention to your granddaughter for the next couple of weeks, you'll endow a permanent scholarship in my aunt and uncle's memory?"

"In perpetuity," she acknowledged with a nod. "Will you accept my offer?"

The way he saw things, he had two choices. One, he could refuse Amelia's proposition and give up the scholarship, which wasn't an option at all. Or two, he could enjoy the next two weeks with Samantha and have fun flirting with her and bolstering her confidence. No Strings Attached was his motto, and Amelia was offering it to him on a silver platter with a lucrative return.

"You have yourself a deal," he heard himself say, and stretched his hand toward her to seal their pact.

"Excellent." She shook his hand, a relieved smile curving her lips. "There are great depths to Samantha, Mr. Petrocelli, but they're for Tyler Grayson to discover and explore. All I want of you is what we've already discussed."

He nodded his agreement. Two weeks of seduction, and then he'd be gone. The arrangement suited him perfectly.

NICK FOUND HIS UNSUSPECTING pupil outside sitting on a redwood lawn chair beneath a huge shade tree, her attention focused on the sketch pad in her lap and the strokes of her pencil along the paper. Following the brick pathway toward Samantha, he passed a state-of-the-art play yard with a sandbox and wooden jungle gym, complete with a fortress, bridges, swings and slides.

Emily stood in the fortress, looking through a wooden telescope, which she'd trained on him to watch his progress across the yard. "Hi, Mr. Nick," she called gaily, waving wildly at him.

"Hey, Emily." He grinned and waved back. "Looks like you and I are going to be spending some time together, after all."

"Maybe we can play pirates together!" she cried excitedly.

"Aye, matie," he said, playing the part of pirate for her. "Sounds like fun, but later, okay?"

"Okay." Happy with his promise, she went back to searching the yard through her telescope, singing, "Yo-ho, yo-ho, a pirate's life for me."

Nick cut across the lawn toward Samantha. As he neared, she folded the cover over her sketch pad, as if hiding her private thoughts, but left the tablet on her lap.

Her speculative gaze met his. "You can't mean that."

"What? That playing pirates would be fun? I think it'd be a blast, and Emily could be my first mate." Folding his frame into the redwood chair next to hers, he summoned a roguish grin. "Of course, I'd need a female captive to be a legitimate pirate. You interested in playing the part?"

A becoming shade of pink flushed her cheeks. "I'm talking about you spending time with Emily."

"Oh, that," he said mildly, but didn't elaborate. Clasping his hands over his belly, he stretched out his long legs.

"Yes, that." Her voice was tinged with exasperation, and a smile. "I'm sure kid-sitting isn't in your job description here at Cranberry Harbor." Her blue eyes took on a mischievous twinkle. "Speaking of your job, shouldn't you be working your way through a list of tasks, or has Grandmother fired you already?"

He laughed. "Nope, I got a promotion."

She tilted her head and tucked back a stray strand of hair that had escaped her French braid. "Really?" she asked, intrigued.

"Yep. Amelia liked me so much, she assigned me to be *your* personal assistant."

The light moment between them shifted, and her expression turned guarded. "I'm sure you misunderstood my grandmother."

"Oh, I'm sure I didn't," he countered easily. "She made her request *very* clear."

"Mr. Petrocelli—" She cut herself off when he lifted a brow at the formal address. "Nick," she amended, obviously not wanting to chance him touching her again. "I don't need a personal assistant."

"She seems to think you do."

Her brow creased into a perplexed frown. "Whatever for?"

"To help plan the garden party, to run errands, to watch Emily if you need me to." *To flatter you and build you up for another man.* Dismissing that bothersome thought, he spread his arms wide. "I'm at your command. Whatever you want or need, I'll do my best to provide."

Her gaze flickered over him, down his chest to his thighs, awareness swirling to life in the depths of her eyes. When she realized where her gaze had wandered, she turned her head away, looking toward the jungle gym and her daughter, who was playing on one of the swings. She touched her tongue to her bottom lip in a nervous gesture.

"So, what do you think about having your own personal assistant, Samantha?"

After a hesitant moment, she glanced back at him. "I appreciate your offer," she said in a polite manner that didn't completely conceal the more tenacious, strong-willed emotion that had suddenly flared in her eyes. "But I don't need a personal assistant. I can handle everything on my own."

"I don't doubt that for a minute," he said, rethinking his strategy. "But I've got two weeks to work off in exchange for a scholarship, and I'm counting on you to keep me busy so I won't get stuck polishing the silver, or waxing the cars, or preparing the meals. I'm a horrible cook, so it would be to your advantage to keep me otherwise occupied so your grandmother doesn't think I'm slacking on my duties and decide to reassign me to a job I'm really awful at."

With an indecisive sigh, she shifted in her chair, crossing one tanned leg over the other. Her finger absently slid down the edge of her sketch pad, still lying protectively in her lap. "I really am sorry about all this."

"All this?" he asked, not sure what she meant.

"You having to be my personal assistant during your stay here. It's quite ridiculous." Her expression turned apologetic. "My grandmother can be a bit…eccentric, and when she bid on you, she did so to upstage Sugar Spinelli, which put you in the middle of a silly rivalry between the two women."

"Ah," he said in understanding, though he'd received a deeper insight into Amelia's motivations earlier, and they had nothing to do with any competition between her and Sugar. "You know, when your grandmother bought me, I thought at first I got the raw end of the deal, since all the other bachelors, other than Rob Carter and myself, were purchased by young, enthusiastic women who wanted a man. But I'm beginning to think I got extremely lucky."

She rolled her eyes at that. "You must have lost your mind somewhere between Wyoming and Oregon."

He knew his comment sounded like a come-on line, but he meant it sincerely. "I like you, Samantha Fairmont. And for the next two weeks I'm yours, so let's have fun and enjoy the time together, okay? And I promise to make sure Amelia thinks you're working me to the edge of exhaustion and she's getting her money's worth."

"All right," she said, relenting with a tentative smile. "I just hope I don't bore you to death before the next two weeks are out."

"Boredom isn't even a remote possibility. I won't allow it," he promised, just as a screen door off the side of the house banged shut, putting an end to their conversation.

Samantha watched her aunt Kathryn approach them, grateful for the reprieve her presence provided. Her head was still spinning from the fact that this man would be her companion for the next two weeks. She'd thought it bad enough that he'd be occupying the same floor as her, now she had to deal with all that gorgeous male magnetism surrounding her ten hours a day.

Kathryn smiled as she neared. She was dressed in a cotton summer dress and her favorite floral apron, which she used when baking. In her hands, she carried a silver tray with refreshments. "I saw you two sitting out here and thought you might enjoy some fresh-squeezed lemonade and just-out-of-the-oven cinnamon sugar cookies.''

"Thank you," Samantha said as Kathryn set the tray on the ground in between the two redwood chairs. "You'll never believe what Amelia did."

Kathryn straightened and smoothed a hand down her apron, looking from Nick to Samantha. "Try me," she said wryly.

"She assigned Nick as *my* personal assistant."

Kathryn's brow rose, and her eyes sparkled with silent humor. "Well, you could use the extra help with the garden party arrangements. Every year the event seems to get bigger and bigger. How many guests are being invited this year?"

"Nearly two hundred," Samantha admitted.

Emily skipped up to them, her expression eager as she spied the tray of refreshments. "Can I have a cookie, too, Aunt Kathryn?"

"As soon as you wash your hands and face, munchkin," Kathryn said, affectionately swiping at a streak of dust on Emily's cheek.

Emily inspected her hands with a frown. "Do I have to wash up? I only got a little dirty and I won't lick my fingers."

Samantha suppressed a grin and noticed that Nick did, too. "Yes, you need to wash up, Em."

"I'll tell you what," Kathryn said, smiling softly at the little girl she'd come to adore. "Wash those grubby hands of yours, and I'll make sure you get a fresh, warm cookie straight from the oven. And when you're done eating it, you can help me make strawberry preserves."

Emily's expression lit up at the prospect of cooking with her aunt, something she loved to do. "Okay!"

Without another complaint, she raced toward the house to clean her hands and face.

Samantha shook her head at her daughter's enthusiasm. "At least someone in the family will acquire your culinary talents."

"Don't be so modest, Samantha," Kathryn chided gently, her gaze dropping to the sketch pad resting against her niece's thighs. "You have your own talents and they far exceed my culinary skills."

Samantha stiffened at her aunt's mention of her artistic ability—a personal, *private* hobby she'd shared only with Kathryn and Amelia. Even at that, her grandmother wasn't aware of the provocative slant to her artwork.

The sensual paintings she created in the privacy of the attic weren't up for public speculation and never would be. Her exclusive art was an escape for her, a way for her to release all the reckless passion she'd suppressed since Justin's death. Samantha glanced at Nick. Though he sat quietly beside her, his intense expression told her he'd analyzed the brief conversation between her and Kathryn and sensed the undercurrents of something deeper in her aunt's words.

Unnerved, she looked away.

"Well, I'd better get back to the kitchen before Emily gets into trouble by herself," Kathryn said, breaking the silence.

Samantha managed a smile. "Don't forget to bake an extra batch of these cinnamon sugar cookies for Victor," she suggested, promoting the attraction she'd seen between her aunt and the Russian gardener. "He told me they're his favorite."

"Um, yes, I know," Kathryn said, seemingly flustered by Samantha's suggestion. Without another comment, she turned and headed toward the house before Samantha could say anything more.

Picking up the crystal carafe, Samantha poured them each a tumbler of the fresh-squeezed lemonade. "Help yourself," she said to Nick, motioning to the cookies.

He picked up two and bit into one, his expression reflecting his appreciation. "These are fantastic. I can't remember the last time I had a homemade cookie."

A true bachelor, Samantha thought, reaching for a cookie of her own. "If you think these are good, Kathryn makes the best meat loaf you've ever tasted. There's something she puts in the mixture that makes the meat melt in your mouth."

"Ah, two weeks of home-cooked meals and time spent in the company of a beautiful woman." He released a long, contented sigh that sounded ridiculously sexy to Samantha's ears. "I do believe I got a fabulous deal, one I wasn't expecting when I decided to head to Wyoming to recover from my eye injury."

His one good eye twinkled with too much male satisfaction. "You don't live in Wyoming, then?" she asked curiously.

"No. I live in New York." He filched two more cookies, enjoying the treat. "I moved there after my stint in the Marines, and I've been there ever since."

New York...a world away from Oregon, physically and culturally. "You weren't wearing the patch on the day of the auction," she commented, trying to find a tactful way to find out what had happened to him.

"Lindsay asked me not to, but my ophthalmologist suggested I wear it as much as possible until my appointment for laser surgery next month."

She wondered about that tiny scar on his temple, a slight puckering of skin she had the urge to touch. A battle scar of some sort. "Do you mind me asking what happened?"

He gave a shrug that appeared nonchalant, but was contradicted by the hardening of his jaw. "I made a stupid mistake during a drug bust and got caught in the cross fire. A bullet grazed my temple and damaged some nerve endings in my eye." A wry grin tipped the corners of his mouth. "All in all, I'm lucky to be alive. And I have to admit, the forced vacation is long overdue. I pushed myself to exhaustion and wasn't thinking straight during the bust. A burned-out, frustrated cop is ripe for the pickin', and I nearly got myself killed, not to mention endangered other people's lives."

Despite the pleasant warmth of the day, a shiver chased down her spine. He'd defied death, just barely, which reminded her too much of Justin's obsession with danger and compelling, life-threatening dares. By day, he'd been a junior executive at an advertising firm, but in the evenings and on the weekends he'd taken unnecessary risks just for the thrill of it…despite her objections.

Nick's job demanded that he put his life in jeopardy in the name of justice, but still it paralleled her late husband's life-style. Justin Fairmont had also gambled with his life on a daily basis.

She imagined this solid, muscular man wielding a gun and fearlessly chasing down bad guys. Living out at Cranberry Harbor, she was removed from the crime that was so much a part of most cities, and she found his choice of career disturbing.

She took a long swallow of the lemonade, letting the tart taste linger on her tongue for a moment. "Is the damage to your eye permanent?"

"No, thank God." He looked dismayed at the thought

as he brushed cookie crumbs from his jeans-clad thighs. "Laser surgery should restore my vision and I could be back on the force in a few months, if I don't go completely insane in the interim from lack of activity."

He seemed anxious to return to his job, the energy rippling from him nearly tangible. His only impairment was his sight—his finely tuned body was still primed and equipped for action. "You like what you do, then, despite the danger?"

"I love it," he admitted without hesitation. "I thrive on the adrenaline rush that comes from being right in the middle of a risky assignment. Put me at a desk job and I'd wither and die."

"And how does the woman in your life deal with you putting yourself in the line of danger on a daily basis?" The inquisitive, personal question was out before she could stop it.

He flashed her a grin. "I don't have a 'woman,' not a steady one, anyway. I date occasionally, but I learned early on that my choice of profession and marriage don't mix real well."

So, in essence, the man had no commitment or ties, other than to himself, and expended all that virility and ambition on his job.

Samantha conjured up an image of Tyler Grayson, and in her mind's eye saw his cool, polished demeanor, the complete opposite of Nick's earthy, physical maleness. One man thrived on risking his life and had adopted a solitary attitude, and the other offered the kind of security most women craved. Yet Samantha was drawn to the bad-boy cop who clearly didn't fit into her life, or her future, and would never give her the kind of healthy, stable environment she needed for herself and Emily.

He was the kind of man who threatened emotions she'd spent the last three years denying.

He reached out and rubbed his thumb along the corner of her mouth, startling her out of her musings. Her skin caught fire from his unexpected touch, making her pulse race and her breasts tingle...beckoning to her wilder, sensual side. Unsettled by the tantalizing sensations invading her body, she jerked back, belatedly realizing how uptight that made her seem.

A lazy grin teased his lips. "Sugar from your cookie," he explained in a soft-as-velvet murmur. Instead of wiping his finger on a napkin, he brought it to his mouth, using his tongue to lick off the granules.

Heat pooled in her belly, and her lips parted to draw in a breath. His gesture was as intimate as a kiss—as if he were tasting her that way. The coiling need he evoked inside her grew unbearable...all from a brief caress. She struggled to retain her composure.

As if he hadn't just turned her inside out with a reminder of a long-denied pleasure, he reached for the last cookie on the plate and eyed the tablet on her lap. "Enough about me. What do you say you show me what's on that sketch pad?"

She dragged in a steadying breath. Though she welcomed the change in subject, she had no intentions of sharing her work with him. "Just a drawing," she said vaguely.

A dark brow lifted. "Of?"

The man was too persistent. "Emily."

"May I see it?"

There was honest interest reflected in his gaze, and she reasoned that her sketches weren't nearly as intimate or revealing as her sensual paintings. She opened the cover to show him the sketch of Emily's tea party she'd started that morning. He leaned closer to get a better look, and she caught a faint spicy scent.

"Kathryn was right," he said, lifting his gaze from the picture. "You're very talented."

Her cheeks warmed at the compliment. "Thank you."

"I take it you don't hear that very often."

"I don't share my work with many people," she admitted.

He looked genuinely disappointed. "Keeping all this talent to yourself is a real shame."

She thought of the collection of paintings she'd finished that lay dormant in her makeshift studio in the attic. "It's just a hobby," she said, knowing her landscapes and seascapes would never see the light of day. Exhibiting her provocative artwork wasn't an option for her. Such an idea bordered on frivolous, not to mention the possibility of exposing the Bainbridge-Campbell name to scandal with her "lovers."

She'd disgraced her grandmother once before with her marriage to Justin. She wouldn't risk disappointing Amelia again.

CHAPTER FIVE

SAMANTHA CONSULTED the growing garden party "to do" list in her appointment book as she ate breakfast with Kathryn and Emily the following morning. Slathering butter on half of a warm apple spice muffin, she searched for a project that would require two people working closely together, yet wasn't so glaringly obvious that her aunt Kathryn would suspect her ulterior motives in moving along the budding romance between her and Victor.

More than anything, Samantha wanted to see her unmarried aunt happy with a man who'd appreciate the sweet woman she was, and lately Victor had been expressing his interest in subtle ways that made her aunt blush like a schoolgirl. Unlike Lucinda, Kathryn had lived her entire life at Cranberry Harbor being a responsible, reliable daughter to Amelia, helping to raise Samantha when she was a child, and sacrificing her own dreams of opening a bed-and-breakfast inn. Though Kathryn had never seemed unhappy or complained about her single status, Samantha wanted her aunt to find that love she'd spent a lifetime searching for.

Samantha casually glanced up at Kathryn, who sat across the table from her. "Would you be able to get together with Victor this week about the outdoor setup of tables and chairs for the garden party? I need a diagram of twenty round tables so I can start working on the seating plan.''

Kathryn carefully set down her fork. She appeared surprised at the request. "I suppose Victor and I could arrange to do that, but aren't you and Nick working on everything?''

"Oh, there's plenty to keep us busy. A few last minute invitations that need to be sent out, the florist, the caterer,'' she said, ticking off only a few of the tasks she needed to attend to. "You and Victor are most familiar with the rose garden, so I thought together you'd be able to figure out the most strategic way to place all those tables.''

Kathryn nodded, and took a sip of her hot tea.

"Besides, I know how much you enjoy being a part of the planning, too.'' Samantha bit into her muffin, pleased with her matchmaking attempt.

A smile softened Kathryn's features. "Oh, I do.''

"Good, then it's settled.'' Picking up her pen, she made a notation on her list.

"What can I do to help, Mama?'' Emily asked from beside her.

Samantha thought for a moment, wanting to include Emily in the preparations, too. "Well, I know we'll have favors for everyone, and when the time comes, you can help make them.''

Emily's eyes lit up. "Something pretty with candy and bows?''

Samantha smiled. "Probably.'' She jotted down a few notes about finalizing the menu with the caterer, unable to believe the garden party was only a month away.

"Where is Nick this morning?'' Kathryn asked.

"I don't know,'' she answered, not looking up from her appointment book, grateful that the mention of Nick didn't send her pulse racing. She'd spent last night painting in her studio in an attempt to clear her head and banish that dangerous awareness he'd stimulated yesterday afternoon. Thank goodness her brand of therapy had worked, she thought in relief. "I went to his room before coming down for breakfast and he wasn't there. Grandmother mentioned that Victor would be taking him to Portland today to purchase some pants and shirts to wear."

"Victor mentioned that, too," Kathryn acknowledged.

The kitchen door leading out to the side of the house opened, then shut. "Good morning, ladies."

Three female heads turned in unison at the sound of the deep voice greeting them, and Samantha gave a small gasp of appreciation. Standing in the archway separating the kitchen from the bay area was an Adonis of gorgeous male perfection.

"Oh, my," Kathryn breathed.

Samantha silently echoed her aunt's sentiment, and she cursed her insidious pulse for fluttering when she'd believed she had her reaction to this man under tight control. Other than that roguish grin and eye patch of his, Nick wore nylon jogging shorts and a tank shirt that revealed more bronze skin than it concealed. The pumped muscles of his arms, chest and thighs glistened with clean male sweat, attesting to physical exertion.

Despite her stern lecture to herself last night about keeping her relationship with Nick strictly business, the artist in her wished for her sketch pad and an hour alone with him, just the way he was at this moment. He was virility at its most tempting—wholly sexual, solidly built with sleek, beautiful muscles unlike anything she'd ever encountered.

Her thoughts were dangerous, reckless and completely

inappropriate, but much to her dismay, she couldn't stop them from entering her mind.

"Hi, Mr. Nick," Emily said, breaking the silence that had settled over the room. She wrinkled her pert little nose at him. "How come you're all sweaty?"

"Yes, please enlighten us," Kathryn added, her eyes sparkling humorously. "I didn't think your duties to my niece would be so strenuous."

"I jog five miles every morning," he explained with a slight shrug of those broad shoulders. "No reason why that should be any different here. It gets your blood pumping, clears your head and reduces stress." He rubbed a hand over his flat stomach. "And it keeps me in shape. Judging by all this delicious home-cooking I'll be eating, that's something I need to keep on top of."

Kathryn smiled at his compliment, and Nick turned toward Samantha. "So, what's on today's agenda, boss?"

"For you, according to Amelia, a new wardrobe." Closing her appointment book, she popped a small bite of muffin into her mouth.

He propped his hands on his hips and sighed. "I suppose that's unavoidable."

"I'm afraid so." Grabbing Emily's napkin, Samantha wiped the milk mustache clinging to her daughter's upper lip. "I don't have much to do for the garden party today, so you're free to spend the day shopping."

He moved closer to where she sat at the table, surrounding her with his scent. His thigh brushed the back of her arm as he reached into the basket of fresh muffins and grabbed one, and she managed, just barely, not to flinch at the heat he generated. He examined the muffin for a second, then took a big bite and chewed with an appreciative "mmm" that rumbled along Samantha's nerve endings.

Once he swallowed the muffin, he returned his attention back to her. "You sure you don't need me here for something important, like polishing the silver?"

His statement was testimony to just how much he disliked shopping. She laughed lightly, desperately trying to release the provocative tension inside her. "Nope. I suspect it might take a couple hours to get fitted for a few suits, so take your time."

He feigned a shudder that rippled those marvelous muscles of his. "I don't do suits, but I'll do my best to find something appropriate." With a slow, unmistakable wink, he turned and headed out of the kitchen, his stride lazy, giving Samantha plenty of time to enjoy his backside view, which was equally as impressive as the front.

NICK DROPPED AN ARMLOAD of bags on his four-poster bed, all from a ritzy department store he'd never set foot in again in his lifetime. He had gone with casual clothing for the most part, a compromise between his standards and Amelia's, and nearly had a heart attack when his purchases totaled more than a month's salary. Without a blink, Victor had signed the sales slip to charge Amelia's account, then led a stunned Nick back out to the Rolls-Royce he used to chauffeur Amelia and run errands.

They'd stopped for lunch at an outdoor café, and Nick ordered a beer to relax and chase down his cheeseburger—both of which tasted heavenly. He'd enjoyed the time with Victor, and the two of them developed an easy, friendly rapport that led to the discovery that they had a lot in common. Surprisingly, Nick learned Victor hadn't been a blue-collar worker back in Russia, but had held a position with the Russian military intelligence. After losing his wife and family in a bombing incident, he'd defected to America eleven years ago in hopes of starting a new life for himself and erasing the pain of the past.

With a heavy sigh, Nick sorted through his new, expensive garments. He knew what it was like to lose a wife, though not the way Victor had. He'd made plenty of mistakes with his own wife, Camille, who'd suffered emotional pain and frustration because his dangerous, threatening job had consumed so much of his life and ultimately destroyed their marriage.

What Camille had wanted had been simple, really—a husband who came home on a nightly basis, and a family. Stability of some sort. Yet Nick hadn't been able to give her any of that. The lure of his job had been too enticing for him, sometimes making him forget about the woman waiting for him at home. He'd get so caught up in an undercover assignment or a hot lead that it wasn't unusual for a day or two to pass without talking to Camille—leaving her to wonder if he was alive or dead.

The strain and stress of his job had been excruciating, on him and his wife. The frequent arguments and demands that ensued had driven a wedge between them. Then came the ultimatums, and finally, the divorce. In the end it had been a relief for both of them.

Hanging five pairs of black jeans in the cavernous walk-in closet, Nick grabbed more hangers for his new shirts, his mind still lingering on the past. He hadn't really given much thought to it until now, when he had too much time on his hands.

He never blamed Camille for wanting out of their marriage, but now that he was older and wiser, he often wondered if he'd given up too easily. There were men on the force who were happily married, but it took a special kind of woman to understand the long hours, the daily threat of never seeing her husband again. That had been his and Camille's biggest conflict—she hadn't understood his commitment to his job, and he hadn't taken the time to reassure her or work through her fears and insecurities.

He'd been a lousy husband. He would have made a worse father. Children needed a full-time dad to guide them through life, not a part-time parent who wouldn't be around for ball games or ballet recitals. He'd learned the importance of stability as a kid from his aunt and uncle, and was smart enough to realize his job didn't allow a child that kind of security.

He knew he'd made the right choice by giving Camille the divorce she asked for, but there had been times lately when he'd walk into his small, quiet apartment and be swamped with an overwhelming sense of emptiness. Especially after his accident, when he no longer had an assignment to occupy his mind and restless body. That discontent had been part of the reason why he'd taken off for Wyoming and the Lost Springs Ranch. The solitude of his tiny apartment had nearly driven him crazy, but it had also induced an odd craving for the warmth of home and family. He knew he could find both at the ranch where he'd grown up.

He supposed his brush with death had been responsible for that bit of melancholy. It was the only explanation that made sense.

Once he'd put away his new wardrobe, Nick rubbed the taut muscles at the back of his neck and tucked away his disturbing analysis of his personal life. He attempted to conjure up more pleasant thoughts, and wasn't completely surprised when Samantha Fairmont filled his mind, with her soft blue eyes and sweet smile. He wondered where she was in this monstrosity of a house, and if she'd welcome his company.

"Emily, wait up for me."

As if he'd cast a personal spell, her sweet, lilting voice drifted through the window he'd left open that morning. Moving to the window, which was at the back of the cottage and faced the ocean, he glanced outside and found Samantha and Emily heading along a wooden walkway toward the beach, Emily in the lead by at least ten yards.

The exuberant child turned to her mother. "You're a slowpoke, Mama."

Samantha laughed, the warm, affectionate sound stirring something deep within Nick. "Well, if I didn't have to carry all your sand toys, along with my things, I'm sure we'd be at the beach by now."

"Last one there is a rotten egg," Emily announced gleefully, and skipped the rest of the way to the end of the wooden planking. Once there, she stopped and waited for her mother to catch up.

Leaning against the wall, Nick crossed his arms over his chest and continued to watch the pair—more specifically, Samantha—as they chose a spot on the sand to spread out their blanket and unload their beach paraphernalia. She wore a prim pink cover-up that reached her knees, and he waited patiently for the unveiling.

A few minutes later, she peeled the outer garment up and over her head, revealing a simple one-piece swimsuit in a plaid design of bright turquoise, hot pink and purple. Though the suit was modest and demure by his standards, and just what he'd expect from Samantha, the spandex displayed her curves to their fullest advantage.

The plaid material clung to generous breasts, skimmed the dip of her waist and flat tummy, and outlined the gentle flare of her hips. The sexiest part of the suit was the leg openings cut high on her thighs, nearly to her hips, which made her legs look incredibly slender and impossibly endless.

That damnable awareness rumbled through him, luring him to join her, to be with her, yet he hesitated.

He watched her with Emily. She was a good mom, lavishing her daughter with plenty of attention and patience, her unconditional love obvious in every smile or touch. Emily seemed to blossom in that love. There was a bond between mother and daughter that was deep, solid and impenetrable. He guessed Samantha's unstable marriage to Justin was part of the reason why she was so doting and protective of Emily; she'd lacked that security in her relationship with her husband.

Nick thought about his meeting with Amelia yesterday and the things he'd learned about Samantha. Outwardly, she appeared strong, sensible and sedate, but he wondered about the impetuous woman Amelia had mentioned, and what she'd been like. He'd briefly glimpsed that fire and passion, but he'd also seen how wary she was of those emotions—as if she feared not being able to subdue them. For all her strength, she was extremely vulnerable and uncertain of herself.

And that's where he came in. Samantha was his to enjoy, to flirt with, and he would boost that feminine confidence of hers. A friendly, fun relationship with a woman, without any emotional entanglements, was just his style, he reminded himself.

So why was he standing here hesitating when the beach, relaxation and two beauties beckoned?

THE JULY SUN WARMED Samantha's skin. Sitting in her beach chair, she rubbed suntan lotion on her thighs and legs, smiling as she watched her daughter carry a pail of wet sand to the creation starting to take form a few feet away from the blanket. Tipping the bucket upside down, she tapped it with her shovel, then lifted the container, revealing a cone-shaped sand formation, half of which was still stuck inside the pail.

Emily looked from the bucket to her mound of wet sand and frowned unahppily.

"What'cha making, sweetie?" she asked, squirting a cold line of coconut-scented lotion down her right arm, then smoothing it in.

"A castle. With a dragon. And a prince and princess." She mashed the inception of her fortress with her fingers, her frustration evident. "But it's not working."

"We've got all afternoon, Em," Samantha said gently, switching to her other arm and shoulder. "Why don't you make a farm with your animal molds, and in a little bit I'll help you with that castle." She finished slathering her skin with suntan lotion, all except for her back, which she couldn't reach. "Em, will you put some of this lotion on my back?"

"Okay."

Samantha cringed as Emily wiped her hands down the front of her suit to remove the damp sand clinging to her fingers. She imagined those gritty granules mixing in with her lotion and decided to forgo her back. "Uh, never mind, sweetie."

"I'll do it for you."

At the sound of Nick's voice behind her, Samantha's heart leapt in her chest, then began an erratic pounding behind her breast. She turned and looked at him through her sunglasses, and found herself staring at his knees.

He was a tall man, which made the journey up his well-built body a pleasantly long excursion. If she thought he'd looked gorgeous this morning in jogging shorts and a tank shirt, then he was magnificent now, wearing only a pair of light blue swimming trunks.

"Oh," she said, the one word expressing her breathless rush of surprise at seeing him.

"Hi, Mr. Nick," Emily said cheerfully, quick to garner his attention. "I'm making farm animals out of sand."

He stepped over to Emily's play area and examined what she'd made so far. "And doing a heck of a job, too."

Emily beamed and picked up one of the molds. "I'll make you a pig. Or do you want a horse?"

"How 'bout both?" he suggested with a smile.

Once Emily was busy filling his request, he turned back to Samantha, and she seemed to lose her breath all over again as his gaze stroked along her bare skin. Her entire body felt warm and flushed, and it had nothing to do with the sun and too much to do with the appreciative way Nick looked at her.

She found her vocal cords. "You're back already?" she blurted out, desperate to redirect his attention.

"*Already?* Are you kidding?" He sat next to her, making the blanket shrink in size. "That was the longest three hours of my life!"

She casually set the suntan lotion aside, hoping he'd forget about her back. "I take it you'll be appropriately dressed?"

"I don't do suits or slacks unless it's a dire circumstance." His eyes crinkled at the corners as he grinned. "Black jeans and collared polo shirts will have to do."

Samantha smiled. "I'm sure you'll pass muster just fine."

He drew his legs up and rested his forearms on his knees. "And while I wasn't looking, Victor tossed in some slacks, dress shirts and a few ties, 'just in case,' he insisted."

"It never hurts to be prepared, especially where Grandmother is concerned." Rummaging through her canvas bag, she withdrew the romantic suspense novel she was reading. The thought crossed her mind that he'd joined her and Emily out of obligation. "You know, you don't have to spend the afternoon down here with us. You're free to take the rest of the day off and do as you please."

"This pleases me just fine," he assured her, his deep voice rumbling with sincerity. "And so would rubbing suntan lotion on your back."

She went completely still. To refuse his offer would make her look silly, but the thought of those large hands touching her so intimately, caressing her flesh, made her experience a combination of apprehension and excitement.

Before she could fabricate an excuse, he reached around her and grabbed the bottle, pouring a generous amount of lotion into his hand. He rubbed his palms together, warming the slick substance.

"Turn around," he urged.

Swallowing her protest, she did as he ordered. She pulled the end of her French braid over her shoulder, determined to keep this incident in proper perspective.

The moment his strong, slippery hands smoothed over her shoulders and down her back, her muscles quivered in response, and she bit back a groan of pleasure. Letting her head fall forward, she closed her eyes, conjuring up the list of garden party tasks in her mind to distract her from his sensual rubdown.

It was no use. He pressed his callused fingers to the taut tendons on either side of her spine, making them ache in a wonderful kind of way. Despite her best efforts to remain immune to his touch, her long-denied body grew restless, aroused.

His thumbs found more drawn muscles along her shoulders, and his fingers kneaded gently, working out the kinks. His hands slowed near the nape of her neck. "You have freckles on your shoulders, did you know that?"

"Yeah." The man noticed too much and made her too aware of the needs and desires she'd suppressed the past three years in her attempt to be the decorous lady Amelia raised her to be, and a dependable mom for her daughter.

Nick threatened the barriers she'd erected, made her realize just how much she craved to taste the passion he stimulated, to be impetuous and just a little bit wild. *Again.* The recklessness was still there, simmering beneath the surface. She feared it always would be. Knowing how destructive those emotions could be, she forcibly pushed them from her mind. *She had to.*

She swallowed to ease the sudden dryness in her throat. "I've had those freckles since I was a little girl."

"I like them. Especially this cluster right here that's in the shape of a heart." His finger traced the pattern on her slick skin, and she managed, just barely, to restrain a shiver.

Then his hands were gone. "Return the favor?"

She turned and looked at him, an instinctive refusal leaping to her lips. But there in his glittering green gaze was the hint of a dare beckoning to her.

She glanced at Emily, who was playing happily and carrying on a one-sided conversation with her imaginary farm animals, then back at Nick, who held the suntan lotion out to her, waiting.

Refusing to let him believe she was a prude, she took the bottle from his hand, determined to get the deed done quickly. Kneeling behind him, she coated her palms with the lotion. His back was broad, his skin already a toasty brown, and just as warm when she slicked her hands across his shoulders. Nick was all hard muscle, his flesh firm beneath her touch.

His muscles rippled as she stroked her fingers along his shoulders and down his back. Unable to help herself, she absorbed the feel of him beneath her hands. The scent of coconut swirled around her, and she grew dizzy from the essence of hot male skin and tropical lotion. Nick said nothing, but judging by the rise and fall of his shoulders, indicating his own shallow breathing, she guessed he was just as affected as she was by all this rubbing, touching and stroking.

Heat suffused her cheeks. Mortified that she'd allowed things to get so out of hand, she stopped. "Um, you're done." She moved away, rubbing her sticky hands down her thighs. Her palms were still warm from his skin and held his scent. The knot in her stomach tightened.

"Not quite," he muttered in a gruff, strained voice. He whipped off his eye patch and tossed it aside on the blanket. "I'll be right back." Jumping to his feet, he jogged down to the cool water, dived fluidly into a cresting wave and executed a series of laps.

Settling back into her beach chair, Samantha fought to regain the composure that had shattered the moment Nick touched her. What had just transpired on this blanket went beyond the stirring of awareness that had been simmering between them since yesterday. There was no denying the attraction was mutual, and on the verge of spinning out of control.

It was a scary thought, and an impossible situation.

She had no business letting reawakening desires run rampant, not with a man who was only in her life temporarily. A man who would make her no promises nor give her the things she and Emily needed in their lives—like the security and stability Tyler had to offer.

But, oh, how she wished Tyler aroused her half as much as Nick did.

Finally, Nick strode out of the ocean, ran his hands through his hair to wring out the excess water, then let the rest sluice off his body as he approached them. When Emily pinned those adoring blue eyes on him and asked him to help her build a castle, the man caved in to the little girl's whim with little resistance.

Now that everything was back to normal, Samantha pushed her sunglasses up the bridge of her nose, opened her book and tried concentrating on her story. She couldn't. Though she pretended interest in the novel, her gaze kept straying to Nick, who was helping Emily tote pails of wet sand to the smooth surface they'd made for their castle's foundation. He wasn't the type to lie lazily in the sun. He had too much energy for that. So he expended that energy by playing with Emily, who flourished like a budding flower beneath all his attention.

Together, the two of them created a magnificent sand castle, complete with a sculpted dragon with razor tail and a prince and princess who looked more like snowmen. But Emily was enchanted, nonetheless. Nick played ball with her on the sand, joined her in a snack of pretzels and apple juice, then put her into a life jacket and took her out for a swim, allowing her no farther than where the water reached her hips. They spent at least an hour frolicking in the waves, laughing and splashing each other.

The man was a huge marshmallow when it came to children, and Samantha enjoyed every moment of watching them. Justin had never taken an interest in his daughter, and other than Victor, Emily had little male influence in her life. As for Tyler, Samantha had no idea how he felt about kids, and wondered if he'd be as lively and outgoing as Nick was with her daughter.

Eventually Nick coaxed Samantha to join in on the fun, threatening her with a drenching if she didn't comply. By the time they arrived back at the house that afternoon, they were all exhausted from the sun and playing in the ocean. Nick helped Samantha put the beach paraphernalia away, then went to his wing of the third floor to shower. Samantha did the same, bathing Emily first and washing her hair. Changed into a pretty dress, her cheeks glowing with sunshine and health, Emily scampered off, leaving Samantha alone to shower.

Half an hour later, feeling more refreshed, Samantha descended to the first floor in search of Emily. Usually she could find her affable daughter by following the sound of her voice, but the house was quiet.

She entered the kitchen and found Victor and Kathryn together. They didn't hear her at first, probably because they were too caught up in each other. Her aunt was standing on a step stool, reaching up into one of the high cupboards for a bowl.

"I'll get that for you," Victor said, lightly touching Kathryn's hip and holding out his fingers for her to step down.

A faint blush stained Kathryn's cheeks, but she took his hand and allowed him to steady her down the three steps. "I'm perfectly capable of getting it myself, Victor," she said softly.

"I'm certain you are," he agreed, affection coloring his accented English. "But I will do it for you, then with any luck I will be invited to eat whatever wonderful thing you are going to make in it." Effortlessly, he grabbed the bowl she needed.

"It's just ordinary meat loaf," she said, and laughed, the lilting tone sounding flirtatious to Samantha's ears.

A smile twitched the corners of Victor's mustache. "Ah, there is nothing at all ordinary about your meat loaf, my dear."

"I have to agree with Victor, Aunt Kathryn," Samantha said, finally making her presence known before the pair said or did something they'd rather keep between the two of them. "I've already bragged to Nick how good your meat loaf is, so make plenty to feed two hungry men."

Kathryn's hand fluttered to her throat, guilt shading her features. "Samantha, I didn't hear you come in."

"I'm sorry to interrupt," she said easily. "I'm looking for Emily or Nick. Have you seen either one of them?"

Kathryn busied herself, putting distance between her and Victor. "I think I saw them go out on the back porch."

"Great. Thanks." Samantha left the two of them alone and headed toward the back porch. She came to a sudden stop, catching the screen door before it slammed shut and awakened the sleeping occupants in the hammock strung between two sturdy columns.

Her heart snagged in her chest at the precious scene before her. Nick was sprawled in the hammock in a relaxed pose, his long, gorgeous body stretched out with one leg draped over the side, the toe of his sneaker touching the floor for support. One arm rested behind his head and the other curled protectively around her daughter, who'd climbed into the netting to join him and had snuggled up to his side. Both were napping from their fun-filled day, and Nick's peaceful, content expression struck a chord deep within her, making her yearn for something so impossible she chided herself for allowing the thought to enter her head.

Samantha didn't waste any time retrieving her sketch pad, wanting this priceless moment down on paper. While the sun set over Cranberry Harbor, she duplicated the image for her own private collection of sketches. She knew she'd remember this day, and this man, long after he left their lives and returned to his dangerous job, and she made the right, *safe* choice...with Tyler.

CHAPTER SIX

FINISHED PAINTING for the evening, Samantha eyed the landscape she was currently working on, viewing it critically. It was a country scene, with a riot of bright wildflowers surrounding an old dilapidated barn. A huge oak tree shaded one side of the structure, and a wooden swing blew gently in the breeze that swept across the deserted prairie.

The barn doors were open, revealing her trademark silhouette inside the rundown building. To someone casually glancing at the painting, the shadows seemed a part of the picture's charm. To someone with knowledge of Samantha's whimsical addition to her landscapes and seascapes, the nebulous figures took the form of lovers entwined in a provocative embrace.

She'd only shared her secret with one person. Kathryn was the only one who knew of her sensual lovers camouflaged in strategic shadows. As for Amelia, she inquired about her paintings often, even ventured up to her studio on occasion to see what she had in the works, but Amelia had no idea her granddaughter was so artistic. Samantha had no intention of enlightening her grandmother, either, and shocking her with the provocative pictures.

Kathryn delighted in discovering those clandestine couples, and even encouraged Samantha to pursue the possibility of exhibiting her artwork. Samantha refused—everything about these paintings revealed too much of the reckless, passionate woman who'd nearly allowed her frivolous choices to ruin her life, and Emily's.

Thankfully, Samantha had learned to curb the instinctive urges she'd inherited from her mother...until Nick. Yesterday down at the beach made her realize that despite the sedate life she'd led the past three years, that sensual part of her still existed—and sparked and sizzled whenever he touched her. Nick was the kind of trouble she knew she should avoid, yet she was drawn to him in a way that made her want to experience that exhilarating rush of abandon one last time before she agreed to a comfortable, and possibly loveless, marriage.

They were foolish, dangerous thoughts she had no business entertaining.

She'd managed to keep her physical distance from Nick today while they'd worked on arrangements for the garden party. She consciously avoided any excuse for them to touch, but that hadn't stopped him from flirting with her, and making her laugh and smile and even enjoy his company. The thing was, she really *liked* Nick—his personality, his innate honesty, and just being with him. Even when he was quiet, she found his mere presence exciting.

Releasing a sigh, she glanced at her watch. It was a quarter past nine, and though she'd put Emily to bed more than an hour ago, she wasn't at all tired. She'd taken a two-hour nap that afternoon, which was obviously why she was so wide awake.

The deep restlessness stirring within her was another matter altogether.

Grabbing her sketch pad and pencil, she flipped off the lights in the studio and crossed to her sitting room, planning to spend the next hour or so capturing Nick's sensual expression on paper. She would be able to enjoy looking at the portrait long after he fulfilled his obligation to Amelia.

Setting her tablet on the round mahogany table in the corner of the room, she turned the radio on low to an all-music station to break the silence, then opened the French doors leading to the balcony for fresh air. In the distance, she could hear the crash of waves on the beach, the sound soothing her. Returning to the table, she relaxed in one of the cushioned chairs, flipped open her sketch pad and immersed herself in her own private thoughts and images.

A light knock sometime later made her glance up. Her pulse fluttered at the sight of Nick standing in the doorway she'd left open. He was wearing a pair of crisp black jeans and a beige knit shirt that did wonderful things for that solid chest of his and made his green eye sparkle with specks of gold. In his hands he carried a silver serving tray holding one of Kathryn's china teapots, a matching cup and saucer, a can of soda and a plate of Kathryn's double-chocolate fudge brownies.

Frowning, she closed her pad and set it aside. "What is all this for?" And how had he known she sometimes enjoyed a cup of tea in the evenings?

"You. Us," he responded vaguely, strolling toward her with a grin. Setting the tray on the table, he reclined his long body in the chair across from hers. "I took a walk on the beach, and I saw your light on when I came back and thought you might like some company. Do you mind me visiting?"

"No." The answer was honest. She didn't mind at all, which should have caused her more worry than it did, considering her attraction to the man.

He grabbed the can of soda and popped it open. "Is there something going on between Victor and Kathryn?"

Reaching for the china cup and saucer, Samantha wondered what had prompted his question. "I have my suspicions."

A devilish light entered his eye. "They've been confirmed."

She raised a brow at that announcement. "Oh?" Raising the china pot, she poured the fragrant tea into her cup. It was her favorite blend, she noted.

Setting the pot back on the tray, she glanced up to see Nick grinning at her. "I went to the kitchen to get myself a soda, and caught Victor and Kathryn in a compromising position."

"You didn't!" Samantha couldn't contain her glee.

"I did. I had to clear my throat before they realized they weren't alone." He traced a finger around the rim of the soda can, the gesture reminding Samantha of how those fingers had felt sliding on her skin. "Kathryn took one look at me and went on about how she was getting herself a cup of hot tea, and that you enjoy a cup in the evenings, too, and that I ought to bring you one. Before I knew it, she'd loaded up the tray and was pushing it into my hands, anxious for me to be on my way."

Amused at her aunt's creative diversion, Samantha took a sip of the steaming tea. "I don't know how long things have been going on between Victor and my aunt, but there does seem to be a romance on the horizon. I'd love to see Kathryn get married and be happy with a man who genuinely cares for her."

"Amelia mentioned that she's never been married."

"No," she verified. "I suppose I'm partly to blame for Kathryn not getting out and dating like she should have when she was younger."

Confusion touched his dark brow. "How are you responsible for that?"

"Kathryn spent those young adult years helping Amelia raise me." Settling back in her seat, she drew her legs up onto the chair, curling them to the side. "In a lot of ways, I'm like the daughter Kathryn never had, and she's been more of a mother to me than my own ever was."

He took a drink of his soda, seemingly digesting her words. "Where are your parents?"

Samantha hesitated, reluctant to dredge up her personal family history, which was less than sterling. But he appeared genuinely interested, and he didn't seem the type to judge her. "My mother, Lucinda, was the black sheep of the Bainbridge-Campbell family, the quintessential wild child," she said with a small smile. "Though she grew up in this house with Kathryn, she wasn't one to conform to my grandfather's ideals and rules, or listen to Amelia's advice. She left Cranberry Harbor and was out on her own by the age of eighteen, and had me before she turned nineteen."

"I'm definitely intrigued," he said, reaching for a brownie. "Tell me more."

Because Nick made her feel as if every word mattered, she found herself spilling the details of her unstable childhood. It had been years since she'd talked about it to anyone. "My father left Lucinda by the time I turned two, and after that there were two more husbands, and more boyfriends than I can remember. My mother didn't stay in one place long, either. We went from San Francisco to Texas to New York, and a dozen other states in between."

"Your mother sounds like a free spirit," he commented.

Samantha silently disagreed. Her mother had been flighty, irresponsible and selfish, thinking of no one but herself and her desires. And for the first eight years of her life, Samantha had been dragged along for the rocky ride. More often than not she'd been ignored or barely tolerated. It had been a painful experience, one she never wanted Emily to experience.

She took another soothing drink of tea to calm her, and Nick waited patiently for her to continue. "My mother didn't like to stay in one place long, that's true, but she forgot about the fact that she had a little girl to think about and care for. Every summer, she sent me to Cranberry Harbor to live, more for her own freedom than a vacation for me. But I loved it here, because for those three short months I never had to worry about waking up one day with the fear of moving on to someplace new and leaving everything familiar behind. This is the one place where I've always felt safe and secure."

Her chest grew tight at the memories, but with Nick listening so intently, she went on. "Every fall, when Lucinda came for me, Amelia would try and talk her into moving back and staying here. My mother refused, of course, because she found this place too restrictive and not exciting enough for her. When I was eight, she sent me here for the summer while she ran off to Paris and married her third husband, and she never returned for me. Amelia and Kathryn raised me, and I owe them both for giving me the love and security my mother never did."

She summoned a halfhearted smile for the man watching her across the table. "Last I heard, Lucinda is living in Tahiti with her fifth husband," she said, without emotion for the woman she spent more time resenting than loving. "She's never seen Emily or made any attempt to contact either one of us."

Nick's brows rose in stunned disbelief. "That's a shame. Emily's a bright, beautiful little girl."

His praise touched a deep chord within her. "Yeah, I think so, too. And she deserves a better childhood than the one I had."

"From what I can see, you're giving her that."

"I'm trying, but her life didn't start out so stable." He tilted his head inquisitively, and she worked up the nerve to admit that she hadn't made the right choice when she'd married Justin Fairmont, but had allowed their passionate affair to influence her decisions. "Justin, Emily's dad, wasn't the responsible, nurturing type. He was reckless and liked living on the edge, and that kind of life-style didn't include doting on a child, or settling down with a wife." She refrained from telling Nick just how much Justin's wildness had enticed her, the same kind of alluring traits that had attracted her mother to the men she'd pursued.

There was no doubt in Samantha's mind that deep down inside, past the respectability she'd established over the past three years, she *was* Lucinda's daughter. If it hadn't been for Amelia's caring and understanding after Justin's death, she could have easily gotten caught up in that vicious cycle of men—just as her mother had.

"I'm determined not to make that same mistake again with the next man I marry," she said resolutely.

Understanding flickered in the depth of his gaze. "At least the experience didn't completely turn you off marriage."

"No." But it had made her more cautious, and wary of her judgment of men. The next time she considered marriage, wild passion would remain out of the equation—which made her think of Tyler Grayson. Safe, secure Tyler had never inspired reckless emotions.

Reaching for the teapot, she refilled her cup. "I would like Emily to have siblings someday, and the best way to do that is with a reliable husband who'll make a good father."

"That's true," he agreed.

Before he could ask any more questions, she switched the conversation to him. "Now that you know more about me than you probably ever wanted to, what about you?"

He shifted his shoulders and rested his clasped hands over his stomach. "What about me?"

"Well, about the only thing I *do* know about you is that you're a bachelor—"

"A confirmed one," he added with one of his bad-boy grins.

She smiled back. "And according to Victor, you're more comfortable with a gun than a hammer."

He winced, looking adorably sheepish. "He told you about me trying to help him fix that broken hinge on the pantry door, huh?"

She laughed, the light, humorous sound helping to take her mind off the oppressive recollections she'd shared with him. While it had felt good to talk about parts of her past, there was so much more she kept bottled up. "Yeah, he said you missed the nail about as many times as you hit it."

He groaned in embarrassment. "I confess, I'm not much of a handyman. And I do have to admit that I've felt naked without my weapon these past few weeks." He smiled ruefully. "I can't seem to remember a time when I didn't have a gun in my hand or somewhere on my person. Even as a young boy, when I was living at

Lost Springs, I used to play cops and robbers. I was the good guy, of course, and I had this small wooden gun I'd carved from a thick maple branch that I used to catch the bad guys.'' His gaze glimmered with the fond memory. ''I guess I was destined to go into law enforcement.''

Samantha imagined him as a young boy, full of mischief and energy. From what she knew of Lost Springs Ranch, it had been a haven for troubled foster boys, but Nick appeared so well-adjusted, it prompted her curiosity. ''I hope I'm not being too personal, but how did you come to live at Lost Springs?''

The question didn't seem to bother him at all. ''My father died in Vietnam when I was just a baby, and when my mother passed away from breast cancer when I was ten, I went to live at Lost Springs. Karen and Robert Duncan were my aunt and uncle, and Lindsay is my cousin. Karen was my mother's older sister,'' he explained, setting a plate with a brownie on it in front of her, silently urging her to sample the treat. ''Since they were the only family I had left, they took me in and raised me like one of their own.''

She watched him take another brownie for himself and bite into it, chewing appreciatively. ''It must have been hard, growing up in a house with so many boys.''

''Naw,'' he said with a slight shrug. ''As unruly as most of us were, Karen and Robert kept us in line. Their rules were strict, but they doled out so much love and affection you couldn't help but want to please them and make them proud. Of course, there were a few who were beyond reforming and caused some trouble, but for the most part, all of us got along like brothers.''

Breaking off a corner of her brownie, she popped it into her mouth and let the rich chocolate melt on her tongue. She'd always wished for a sibling to play and share secrets with, and envied Nick that he'd been surrounded with so much camaraderie. "What made you decide to join the Marines?"

"I never knew my father, but he was a Marine, and I wanted to be just like him." His face was etched with earnest respect for the man who'd given his life for his country. "Two weeks after graduation I enlisted, and spent four years working my way up to gunnery sergeant. By the time my stint in the service was over, I had my sights on being a cop. I joined the police academy, and a few months later I got married."

Surprise rippled through her at that admission. "It didn't work out?" she guessed, considering he'd admitted to being a confirmed bachelor.

He absently rubbed the scar on his left temple. "No. Camille and I divorced four years later. She couldn't handle the pressure of being a cop's wife, and I admit I had a tough time juggling our relationship and my goals."

"Which were?"

"I wanted to be more than just a street cop, and in order to pursue a higher field in law enforcement, I needed my degree in criminal justice. I worked the streets of New York by day and spent my evenings attending college. I graduated at the top of my class, but by then it was too late for me and Camille. We'd grown apart. She wanted more than I could give her. After we divorced, without any obligations or commitments to tie me down, I applied to the Justice Department for a place with the DEA, went through fourteen rigorous weeks of training and received the position I wanted."

The casual conversation gave Samantha a greater insight into Nick. Special Agent Nicholas Petrocelli was a good, honorable man, but he'd learned he wasn't the settling-down type. He struck her as being fiercely independent, and needing no one. Judging by the resignation she heard in his voice, she surmised that he had no intention of marrying again, and preferred to remain single and uncommitted. He liked the action and pure adrenaline rush his job provided too much, and refused to expect any woman to tolerate his erratic schedule, the late nights and perilous assignments that consumed so much of his life.

As much as Samantha appreciated Nick's honesty about his inability to nurture a relationship, she felt a twinge of sadness for certain things he'd never experience. He was a natural with kids. Considering his playful manner with Emily, she was certain he would have made a good father, yet he clearly had no intentions of having a family of his own.

An unexpected yawn sneaked up on her, and they both laughed. She glanced at the clock on the wall, surprised to discover more than two pleasurable hours had passed since he'd arrived.

Nick stood, stacking the plates and her teacup and saucer back on the tray. "I think I've stayed way past curfew."

Samantha stood, too, wishing he didn't have to leave. "Don't worry, Amelia doesn't do bed checks." As soon as the words left her mouth, she blushed at the underlying connotation.

"I'll keep that in mind," he murmured, one of those mischievous grins curving his lips.

Her heart fluttered, and she quickly stifled her reaction. "I really enjoyed your company tonight." She couldn't remember the last time she'd felt so relaxed and comfortable with a man.

He glanced up, meeting her gaze. "I enjoyed yours, too," he said sincerely. Picking up the tray, he headed for the door, but stopped and turned before leaving. "Maybe we could do this again?"

The hopeful note in his deep voice warmed her belly. She nodded, too eagerly, and didn't dare analyze the anticipation she experienced at the thought of spending more time alone with him. "I'd like that."

CHAPTER SEVEN

SITTING AT THE TABLE in the cozy bay area just off the kitchen, Nick licked and stamped the envelopes holding invitations for Amelia's upcoming garden party. The bulk of the invitations had already been mailed, Samantha had told him, but a few people had been added at the last minute at her grandmother's request.

His assistance really wasn't necessary for the simple, mundane task—Emily could have sealed and stamped the envelopes just as easily—but Nick enjoyed watching Samantha as she addressed each invitation in gold calligraphy. She had beautiful, graceful handwriting, and made the fancy script seem effortless.

Affixing a floral stamp to an envelope, he set it on top of the pile to be mailed and reached for another. "Eight down, five more to go," he said wryly.

She cast him a sidelong glance, and the tail end of her French braid slid over her shoulder to curve along the collar of her blouse. "Feeling a little antsy and bored, Special Agent Petrocelli?" she teased.

Her low, husky voice drizzled over him like warm honey. "Actually, I'm feeling very relaxed, which is surprising considering I'm used to always moving and doing something. Usually, sitting for any length of time makes me fidgety."

"Sounds like Emily," she commented lightly. "Am I going to have to bribe you to sit still the same way I have to bribe her?"

His gaze flickered to her mouth, shimmering with a pale pink gloss that made him think of cotton candy, then lifted back to her eyes. "Depends on what you're bribing with."

Her lips parted enticingly, and awareness flared in the depth of her gaze. He watched her struggle to subdue that tempting spark between them, and understood her internal battle perfectly. It was beginning to reflect his own. Samantha evoked something deep within him—a hunger and need he instinctively wanted to deny. The hunger wasn't something he could satisfy with Samantha, and the need, well, that was an emotion he had no use for. Needing meant depending on someone. Needing meant losing sight of what was important to him, which was his job.

He hadn't needed anyone since his mother died. His aunt and uncle had given him a home, and love, and while he'd loved them in return for their generosity, he'd always relied on his own abilities to make his way in life. He'd known from the moment he'd arrived at Lost Springs that there were boys who required his aunt and uncle's undivided attention and guidance more than he did. At the age of ten, he'd made the decision to be tough and independent so he could always survive on his own, regardless of the circumstances.

Then why was he so tempted by this woman? Maybe it was the combination of strength and vulnerability he'd glimpsed last night when she'd talked about her mother's abandonment and her marriage to Justin—and her resolve not to repeat past mistakes for the sake of her daughter. Or maybe it was that latent sensuality she tried so hard to suppress that lured him to discover just how passionate she truly was. Despite her demure facade, that craving shone in her eyes…like now.

"M&M's," she said on a breathy whisper.

Pulling his mind back to the present, he tried to remember the question he'd asked. Bribing. With M&M's. He concocted a lazy smile. "I'd behave for M&M's. The peanut ones."

Looking away, she released a slow breath and concentrated on dipping the tip of her pen into the well of gold ink. "I'll make sure to buy a one-pound bag the next time I'm at the store." She began addressing the next envelope, her hand steady and sure.

"So, what's left on our to-do list for the party?" he asked, switching to a safe, uninspiring subject.

Apparently grateful for the reprieve, she warmed to the shift in topic. "We need to go over the menu so I can firm up things with the caterer, and we need to decide what kind of centerpieces we should use for the tables. Amelia loves roses, but I was thinking of going with something different, like tulips."

He shrugged, feeling totally out of his element. "All flowers look the same to me."

Smiling, she handed him another addressed invitation. "There's a big difference between roses and tulips. Whatever floral arrangement I decide to go with, it needs to be elegant and elaborate, since they'll be raffled off at the end of the afternoon."

He took a drink of his iced tea to wash down the bitter taste lingering from the envelope flaps. "What, exactly, is the purpose of this annual garden party?"

"Mainly, to raise money for the various charities that Amelia supports. She invites the crème de la crème of Oregon society, hosts the spectacular bash and collects tens of thousands of dollars, which she awards to a selected charity. It's quite a lavish affair."

He lifted a brow, silently agreeing. "Sounds way out of my league, and beyond my casual attire."

She laughed, the sound light and relaxed. "It's definitely a suit-and-tie affair."

He feigned a shudder. "Thank goodness my obligation to Amelia will be over before the party."

Her smile gradually faded, as if she remembered that his assignment at Cranberry Harbor was temporary, and he'd be gone soon. He didn't want to be affected by her sudden cheerless expression, but he discovered that the thought of returning to his empty apartment in New York made him feel equally depressed, which was absurd. He gave himself a hard mental shake—all this forced time off was turning him soft and too damned contemplative.

Without another comment, she bent her head and resumed her calligraphy. In the background, the phone rang, and a few moments later Kathryn entered the room, a cordless unit in hand. "Samantha, there's a call for you. It's Tyler Grayson."

Samantha's gaze widened in surprise. Setting her pen aside, she reached for the phone. "Thank you, Aunt Kathryn."

Before Samantha connected the call, Kathryn said, "Just so you know, Francis picked Amelia up, and she'll be spending the afternoon at her place. Victor and I are heading into town to run some errands, and I don't expect we'll be back until after five."

Samantha smiled. "Have a good time." Standing, she moved toward the windows overlooking the landscaped side yard, took a deep breath and clicked on the phone. "Hello?" Her voice was soft, and very hesitant.

Nick knew who Tyler was from Amelia. He probably should leave the room to afford Samantha some privacy with her potential beau, but he found he didn't want to leave. He'd never met the other man, but he was experiencing an odd sense of protectiveness that tightened his gut. With a frown, he reminded himself that his job was to *encourage* a relationship between Tyler Grayson and Samantha, not hinder it.

"Tomorrow evening?" Samantha said after a few quiet seconds had passed, her shoulders tightening. "I'm not sure I'll be available. We have a guest staying with us, and I'd hate to leave him alone for the evening."

Nick suppressed a grin when he realized she was using him for an excuse to decline Tyler's date. She was polite enough on the phone, but obviously uncertain about spending the evening in Tyler's company.

"Yes, I'll call you if I change my mind. Goodbye, Tyler." She executed a graceful departure and quickly disconnected the call.

When she turned back around and saw that he'd heard her conversation, she offered him a faint smile. Without comment, she returned to her seat and quietly resumed her task.

"So, who is Tyler Grayson?" he asked casually. He wanted to hear Samantha's opinion of the suitor Amelia believed would make her granddaughter happy.

"He's a friend of the family," she said vaguely, not looking at him, and leaving out the important fact that Tyler had once proposed to her.

Samantha's reluctance to talk about Tyler was palpable. Since she wasn't openly offering information he needed to capitalize on, he pried for it. "Did he ask you out for tomorrow night?"

Flipping the page in her address book, she dipped her pen into the ink well. "Yes, but I declined his invitation."

"Not on my behalf, I hope."

Her brow puckered as she concentrated on writing the name "Whitley" in her scrolling script. "You're a guest here, and it would be rude of me to leave you alone while I go out on a date.''

Another excuse that was his responsibility to waylay. "I'm a big boy, Samantha. Call Tyler back and tell him yes. I'll stay here and spend the evening with Emily.'' Picking up the cordless phone on the table, he handed it to her before she could argue. "Go on, call him before he makes other plans.''

Wiping her palms down the shorts of the culotte outfit she wore, she tentatively reached out and took the phone from him. Locating Tyler's number in the address book in front of her, she punched it in. A few moments of awkward silence settled between them while she waited for someone to pick up the line.

"Hello, Tyler, it's Samantha,'' she finally said, her voice fabricating a brightness he knew she was far from feeling. "I'm free tomorrow night, after all.''

Nick listened as Samantha decided on a time and they firmed up their plans. He should have been relieved that she'd accepted Tyler's dinner invitation, but he wasn't. A part of him regretted pressuring her into a situation she seemed unsure of, yet having Samantha accept Tyler's date served two very valid purposes. It prompted Samantha to consider the safe, secure man Amelia had in mind for her next husband, and it doused any notions that there could be anything more between them besides a flirtatious friendship.

So why was he feeling so bothered by the thought of another man touching her, kissing her and tapping into all that fire and passion simmering beneath her reserved facade?

EMILY SET HER GREEN CRAYON on the table, propped her chin in her hand and heaved a huge sigh. "Mama, I'm bored.''

Samantha bit the inside of her cheek to keep from grinning at her daughter's theatrical display. "Are you done coloring that picture for me already?"

"Yes, see?" Sitting across the table from Samantha and Nick while they worked on the menu for the garden party, she lifted the piece of paper for them to inspect. "Do you like it?"

Samantha's heart thumped in her chest. For a six-year-old, Emily drew exceptionally well, paying attention to detail, color and design. Without asking, Samantha knew the child in her drawing was Emily herself, flanked by Samantha and Nick, the three of them holding hands like a happy family. There was a dog beside them, and they stood in front of a small house with a big tree and a swing and a white picket fence. The picture was simple, but held a wealth of meaning—Emily craved a family of her own, and the father she'd never known.

Samantha didn't look at Nick, hoping he realized Emily's picture was just a child's whim. His presence at Cranberry Harbor and his attentiveness with Emily had obviously had a profound effect on her daughter.

"It's lovely, sweetie," Samantha said with quiet sincerity.

Putting her crayons back in the box, Emily looked up at her with beseeching eyes no mother could resist. "I want you to play with me, please?"

"Sure, I'll play with you." Samantha set the caterer's list of appetizers back in the menu folder and started stacking other notes together. "I think it's time we call it a day on our planning, anyway."

Her daughter needed attention, and she desperately needed a diversion. Ever since her conversation with Tyler, her stomach had been in knots. She knew agreeing to have dinner with him was smart and practical, and something she could no longer avoid because of her own uncertainties. Witnessing her daughter's yearning for a family in the picture she'd drawn was proof that she needed to start dating again, and thinking about marriage. Despite her reluctance, she knew Emily deserved a secure future, siblings to enrich her life and a dependable father figure who would offer her everything her real dad hadn't.

In a lot of ways, she was grateful to Amelia for making this transition fairly easy for her, and persuading Tyler to pursue a relationship with her again. Eight years ago she'd refused Tyler's marriage proposal because she'd thought him staid and boring. Now she found all that predictability reassuring. He was someone who wouldn't inspire or tempt her wild, capricious nature, as Justin had. Marriage to Tyler would be pleasant, and comfortable, and the right thing to do.

Pushing those thoughts from her mind, she gave her daughter the attention she sought. "What would you like to do, Em?"

"I want to play hide and seek," she said with a huge grin.

Samantha glanced out the window. The morning had dawned overcast, and during the past few hours, dark, menacing clouds had rolled in. "It looks like a summer storm is heading our way."

"We can play inside," she suggested brightly. Before Samantha could protest, Emily flashed those baby blues on their guest. "Would you like to play hide and seek with us, Mr. Nick?"

Nick looked Samantha's way, giving her one of those slow, sexy winks that made her nerve endings tingle. "I can't think of anything I'd like better," he drawled.

Emily scrambled around the table, grabbed his hand and tugged him up from his seat. "You're 'it' first, Mama."

"All right." Samantha stood, and before Emily could drag Nick off, she set down the rules and boundaries, restricting the game to the public rooms on the first floor only. The coatrack in the entry hall was the free zone, and there was absolutely no running allowed in the house.

While Nick and Emily scurried off to find places to conceal themselves, Samantha counted to twenty-five, then started her search. She spotted Emily right away, ducking behind an end table in the family room. Not wanting to spoil the fun so soon, Samantha pretended not to see her and continued her hunt.

Just as she exited the family room, Emily darted past her to the free zone, yelling "I'm safe, I'm safe!"

Samantha propped her hands on her hips and summoned a frown. "Where did you come from, Em?"

Emily grinned gleefully, looking pleased with herself and her secret hiding spot. "I was in the family room."

"Well, you certainly had me fooled," Samantha replied, shaking a finger at her daughter. "Next time don't hide in such a hard place."

Emily laughed and twirled around. "You still have to find Mr. Nick."

Samantha set off on her search again. Nick was tougher to locate, and she was amazed that he'd managed to camouflage that large, wide-shouldered body of his so easily. Walking into the sitting room, she glanced around and almost left, when she noticed that the heavy velvet draperies had a suspicious lump in the folds.

Sneaking up to him, she whipped back the curtain and tagged him. "Gotcha. You're it."

A gracious loser, he laughed good-naturedly. "I feel like a kid again."

She grinned at him over her shoulder as they walked

back to the free zone. She had to admit that she was having a good time, too.

Nick faced the wall and began counting while Samantha and Emily scrambled for inconspicuous places to hide. This time, Samantha made it to the free zone and called safe, and Nick had no choice but to tag Emily as they nearly collided when she rounded a corner to escape him.

With Emily being "it," Samantha and Nick went their separate ways to find their own hiding spots. Samantha found a few places, but discarding them all as too obvious, she continued looking. When she heard Emily counting to nineteen, twenty, twenty-one, and realized she was running out of time, she did the obvious and slipped into the small closet in the sitting room, closed the door quietly…and backed into a hard male body.

She gasped as an instantaneous heat radiated along her spine. She was too stunned by this unexpected surprise to breathe. Even her heartbeat seemed to falter in her chest.

"Out of all the hiding places in this house, you had to pick *this* closet?" Nick's voice rumbled with good humor.

"I could say the same of you!" she whispered fiercely, finding nothing amusing about their predicament. It was pitch dark in the closet, increasing her awareness of the man behind her. Her senses sprang to life, and when she dragged in a deep, steady breath, the warm masculine scent that filled her head evoked a startling sensual hunger she couldn't deny.

She had to get out of there, and away from him.

"I'll go find another place to hide," she said, fumbling to find the doorknob in front of her. Just as she turned the handle, Emily's footsteps echoed off the floor somewhere nearby.

Nick's hand found her arm in the dark, and his fingers slid down, encircling her wrist. A tingling sensation spread upward, touching the tips of her breasts and settling in her belly like a warm shot of brandy.

He lowered his head near her ear, his breath hot and damp against her neck. "Stay put," he murmured huskily. "If Emily finds us now, your daughter is going to ask questions I'm not prepared to answer, if you know what I mean."

She swallowed hard. Oh, she knew exactly what he meant. The man was aroused, and just as affected as she was by their close proximity.

He wanted her. That knowledge sent a thrill through her, causing her to experience a rush of feminine daring that tossed every demure, ladylike lesson she'd ever learned to the wind. There was something about Nick Petrocelli that made her feel desirable, and reckless, and just a little bit wicked.

And because she knew she would most likely never encounter this kind of undeniable chemistry with another man again, and certainly not with Tyler, she wanted to experience it with Nick. If she didn't take a little risk now, she reasoned, she might miss her last opportunity to sample passion.

The temptation was too great to resist.

Slowly, she turned around and reached her hand out until her palm flattened on his hard, muscular chest—right over his thundering heart. The frantic beat matched her own, and gave her the fortitude to release the sensual side of her personality that she'd nearly forgotten existed.

Secluded in the dark, she couldn't see, yet every other sense was vividly alert. The subtle scent of his cologne surrounded her, as did the incredible heat he generated.

She ached to touch him, to feel and linger over every part that made him intrinsically male.

He tensed when her other hand joined the first, but said nothing—probably too stunned by her bold move. His honed body fascinated her, prompting her to discover more. With her fingers, she traced the contours of his chest through his knit shirt, then slowly skimmed lower, exploring the lean lines of his taut belly.

A jolt of pure excitement spiraled through her, deliciously compelling. When her fingers brushed the waistband of his jeans, he swore, and encircled her wrists to halt their progress.

His breath rushed from his lungs, sounding harsh and ragged in their cramped quarters. "You're asking for trouble, sweetheart."

He wasn't refusing or rejecting her, just issuing a warning she refused to heed, not when she was emboldened by a sexual confidence long denied. It had to be the dark, she reasoned, but knew the man was equally responsible for the bright, hot need swirling within her.

Moving closer, she pressed her lips to the warm, fragrant skin of his neck. "What if I want your brand of trouble?" she asked, not even shocked by the throaty quality of her voice.

His body shuddered, and with a deep, guttural groan he lifted his hands, found her face and brought her mouth to his. He slid his lips warmly, damply over hers, taking things slow and easy when she wanted something fast and wild. He dragged his tongue across her bottom lip, making her ache to taste him.

On a soft moan, she parted her lips, inviting him inside, wanting to taste the hot male flavor of him. With a lazy, provocative stroke of his tongue, he coaxed her to join in the sensual foray. With a shiver, she surrendered to the glorious sensation.

What had begun as a tentative, exploring kiss turned swift and searing. Tongues stroked and tangled, delving deep. She slid her arms around his neck, arching into him, straining closer. Without asking, he seemed to know what she wanted.

His touch.

Like a phantom lover, his hands roamed in the velvet darkness, sliding down her back, meshing her body with his. One palm splayed low on her spine, his fingers branding her. The other hand skimmed up over her waist and found her breast, gently kneading the swollen, aching flesh.

She moaned into his mouth as shock waves of pleasure shot through her. She shuddered when he rubbed his thumb over her stiff nipple through the sheer bra, and her knees threatened to buckle.

Feeling her slip, he effectively grasped her hips and slid a thigh between hers for support, which touched off a whole new realm of sensations. Tantalizing heat. Electrifying desire. Sizzling lightning through her veins.

It had been so long since she'd felt this alive. And it felt good, so good.

She couldn't think straight, couldn't focus on any one thing because there were too many sensations clamoring for her attention. His lips and tongue seduced her mouth with deep, drugging kisses, her breasts grew excruciatingly taut, and an insatiable need grew to startling proportions within her. Her belly tightened, and her thighs clenched around his.

She wanted…she needed…*something completely forbidden to her.* A frustrated sob escaped her, and it was that desperate sound that shattered the dark, mysterious tension that had pulled both of them into its tempestuous grip.

With a rough growl that rumbled up from his chest,

he dragged his lips from hers and set her as far away from him as their restricted space allowed. They both panted for breath, the sound intensely erotic to her ears.

"This is crazy," he said, his voice gruff, agonized. "Dammit, Samantha, I can't do this. *We* can't do this."

At the moment, she wanted to refute his statement. She licked her swollen bottom lip, tasting him, wanting him more than she wanted her next breath. He'd roused that deep, dark desire within her, making her ache for more....

Shock and shame mingled, and she wished she could see Nick's face, his expression.

"Nick," she whispered, trying to find the words to assure him that none of what happened was his fault, but hers.

"Don't say anything, Samantha," he said. "You need to get out of here—now—before we do something we'll regret later."

She knew all about regrets. She harbored a dozen. But a part of her was beginning to believe that she wouldn't even remotely regret what had happened with Nick, not when he filled the gaping void within her. Instead of arguing, she found the knob and opened the door, welcoming the rush of cool air against her heated skin and flushed face.

She could hear Emily calling for her from the other side of the house. Relieved that her daughter was far enough away, she risked a quick glance at Nick, and knew by the glimmer of longing in his gaze that their encounter had been more than a sexy, provocative tryst in the dark. He'd been just as swept away as she had.

"Go," he said, the single word a warning.

She did, but she couldn't escape the terrifying realization that haunted her.

She'd almost given in to the powerful longing within

her. Next time, she wasn't sure she would be able to resist.

"HOW ARE THE ARRANGEMENTS for the garden party coming along?" Amelia asked that night at dinner as the various dishes were passed around.

"Just fine," Samantha replied, glancing across the table at her grandmother. "The extra invitations you needed me to send were put in the mail this afternoon."

Amelia smiled her approval and accepted the bowl of wild rice from Kathryn, who sat to her left. "And did you get a chance to plan the menu?"

Samantha nodded, taking a portion of pot roast from the serving plate in front of her before passing it on to Nick.

She refrained from looking in his direction; her evasiveness frustrated the hell out of him. But he understood her reserve, too, considering how abrupt he'd been with her that afternoon. She obviously didn't realize just how close his restraint had come to unraveling with her. How close he'd come to pinning her against the back of the closet door and giving her body the release it hungered for as she'd clung to him.

He was a man who prided himself on control and having a level head, but it seemed he had none where Samantha was concerned. She'd proved to be a weakness he couldn't afford to indulge in—for both their sakes.

"What did you decide on?" Kathryn asked, genuine interest in her voice.

Samantha smiled at her aunt while spooning mashed potatoes onto Emily's plate. "I thought the glazed chicken crepes with a wild mushroom sauce would please most people. Nick seemed to think so, too."

Amelia lifted a brow his way, and he shrugged off

Samantha's comment. "When it comes to food, anything sounds good to me," he said, not wanting to take any of the credit for what Samantha had essentially done on her own. His input had been minimal.

"And for dessert?" Kathryn prompted, cutting a piece of her meat.

"I went with the lemon-and-white-chocolate cheese-cake." Samantha passed the rolls to Nick, and when their fingers brushed, she nearly dropped the basket in his lap. Quickly regaining her composure before anyone commented on the odd incident, she added, "I also decided on having an orchestra during cocktails and dinner, and a band for dancing afterward."

"You make quite the hostess, Samantha," Amelia said, the pride in her voice unmistakable. "Many men appreciate that skill in a wife, along with running a large household, which you do equally well."

She spread her napkin on her lap, giving the task more attention than it warranted. "Thank you," she said, quietly accepting her grandmother's compliment.

Amelia took a drink of her wine, then dabbed at her lips with her napkin. "I hear Tyler called for you today, Samantha."

Samantha stiffened, a subtle gesture Nick immediately noticed. The dread etched on her expression dissolved into hopeless resignation by the time she met her grandmother's gaze. "Yes, he did. We have a date for tomorrow evening."

"Splendid." Amelia glanced at Nick as if bestowing her approval on him for any part he might have played in Samantha's acceptance of the invitation, but he refused to acknowledge his participation in the older woman's romantic ploy.

As much as he was coming to resent this socially acceptable man he'd never met, he knew Samantha was

better off with a stable guy like Tyler, instead of someone like him, who didn't make promises and couldn't
give her what she ultimately needed. He had a job waiting for him—a dangerous, risky, demanding job that
didn't allow time in his erratic schedule to nurture a
relationship or a marriage.

He *knew* that, had lived by that bachelor creed for the
past six years, so he couldn't understand why he felt so
possessive, so protective when it came to Samantha. Her
life, her future weren't his responsibility, and he was
hoping like hell her date with Tyler would put things
into proper perspective for both of them, and make him
forget about that searing kiss they'd shared that afternoon.

"We've also been invited to a dinner party this Saturday evening at Tyler's estate." Amelia set her fork
and knife on her plate. "I'm sure Tyler will mention it
on your date tomorrow night, so please confirm that the
three of us will attend."

"Yes, Grandmother," Samantha responded, absently
pushing her food around on her plate.

Kathryn shook her head, frowning. "Mother, I have
no interest in attending Tyler Grayson's dinner gathering."

Amelia looked at her daughter. "I was referring to
Mr. Petrocelli. I assumed you'd stay home with Emily."

Kathryn's brief smile was one of relief. "Perfect."

The matriarch of the family turned those pale eyes on
him. "Mr. Petrocelli, I would like you to escort us both
to the dinner party, if you would, please."

"It would be my pleasure," he drawled pleasantly.

"It's a suit-and-tie affair. Did you buy something appropriate to wear when you went shopping with Victor?"

"Yes, ma'am," he said with a nod. "When I wasn't

looking, Victor made sure he slipped in a few dress shirts, slacks and ties during our shopping expedition.''

Amelia smiled faintly at his wry humor, then turned her attention to her granddaughter. ''Samantha, dear, are you feeling all right? You seem quiet this evening.''

''I just have a lot on my mind.'' She offered Amelia a reassuring smile, one that didn't quite reach her eyes. ''I'll be fine.''

Nick had a feeling their provocative encounter in the closet was responsible for her preoccupation. Their kiss, and the warm, open way Samantha had responded to him, had certainly consumed *his* thoughts for the better part of the afternoon. As had the stricken look on her face when she'd opened the door and light had flooded inside the small cubicle. She'd appeared to be completely appalled by her uninhibited behavior.

Since she'd done her best to avoid him in the hours since the incident, he needed to put things back on track with them. Last night in her sitting room, they'd spent a comfortable evening with easy conversation.

Tonight would be no different. And before the night was out, he'd see her smile, and hear her laughter, and everything would return to status quo.

It couldn't be any other way.

CHAPTER EIGHT

NICK GLANCED at his wristwatch for the sixth time in the past half hour, noting the time: 9:20 p.m. Tyler Grayson had arrived precisely at five to pick Samantha up for their dinner date, and in Nick's estimation, they should have been back an hour ago.... Unless Tyler had taken her to a fancy-schmancy restaurant that took its time serving a five-course meal. Or Tyler had taken her out to a movie, or dancing, or somewhere equally romantic.

He didn't want to care about any of that, but found he couldn't help himself. Last night, as he'd planned, he'd gone up to Samantha's sitting room for conversation and to reestablish the boundaries of their friendship. He'd made her smile, laugh and relax, which had been his goal. Except he couldn't forget about that damnable kiss in the closet, the tantalizing sensuality she'd allowed to surface for that brief time in the dark. How he ached to taste her again, to feel her soft hands on his skin, and encourage that exciting passion she suppressed.

He wanted that, and more. The intense need she'd ignited within him wreaked havoc with his normally sane mind, and had him in a state of emotional and physical frustration.

One hot, rapacious kiss and he was a jealous man. Over a woman who was completely off limits...except to Tyler Grayson.

Frowning irritably, he scrubbed a hand along his jaw

and forced himself to relax on the sofa and keep his mind off Samantha and her date with Grayson. On the family room floor in front of him, Emily lay on her stomach, chin propped in her hands, absorbed in the *Sleeping Beauty* video she'd picked out for them to watch after a dinner of cheese pizza and root beer.

Despite wanting to dislike the man, Nick had to concede that Grayson was a decent guy, if a little prissy in his appearance and demeanor. His light blond hair had been styled and sprayed, not a strand out of place. His dress shirt had been impeccably pressed, and amazingly wrinkle-free even after the drive over in his meticulously detailed BMW. His slacks had been creased with a sharper line than Nick's dress blues, and the luster on his wing tips had been shined to a high gloss.

Their introductory handshake was a gesture Nick had initiated, but wasn't anxious to repeat. Grayson's hand had been too smooth, his grip too soft.

But the man was as staid as they came, which was what Amelia believed her granddaughter needed. Nick couldn't help but think that Grayson would never appreciate all that Samantha was, and could be, or encourage all that latent passion. The man probably kissed as immaculately as he dressed, and made love quickly, with minimal fuss and mess.

Nick liked lots of fuss, and lots of foreplay. He liked it even better when things got a little messy, especially when it involved deep, wet kisses and slick, aroused flesh beneath his fingers…

"When is Mama coming home?" Emily asked, pulling him back from his erotic thoughts. The movie was over, the credits were rolling, and Samantha's daughter was looking up at him with a forlorn expression. "She's been gone a long time."

Nick was feeling just as restless as Emily. Blowing out a harsh breath to release the stress gathering across his shoulders, he stood and smiled at Emily. "What do you say you and I go and make a chocolate sundae?"

Emily's eyes lit up. "With whipped cream, nuts and a cherry?"

He angled his head toward the kitchen and waggled one brow. "Two cherries if you like."

She slipped her hand into his trustingly, her tiny fingers wrapping around his heart just as warmly. He tried not to analyze too closely the tug of emotion he experienced.

Together, they headed to the kitchen, where they spread out a smorgasbord of ice cream, hot fudge, whipped cream in a can, crushed nuts and a jar of cherries. He let Emily have free rein to make her own dessert because it was so much fun to watch her. She smothered her vanilla ice cream in so much gooey chocolate it overflowed down the sides of her dish. They laughed, and she scooped up the dollop with her finger and licked off the sweet confection, leaving a streak of chocolate on her hand. Without thinking, she wiped her sticky palm down the front of her shirt.

Nick groaned. He should have put an apron on her. "You're gonna need a bath after this, kiddo."

She grinned up at him. "Okay. Can I have some whipped cream, please?"

He shook the can for her, but Miss Independent insisted on topping her ice cream by herself. The white, foamy stuff came out fast, creating a mountain of whipped cream that leaned precariously to the side. Using her tongue, she lapped up the excess before it slid off her sundae, then looked cross-eyed at the blob on her nose.

Nick chuckled as he wiped off the cream with his finger, unable to remember when he'd enjoyed being with a child more. He didn't have much experience with kids, but Emily made it all so easy. She was bright, adorable and incredibly sweet. He tried not to think of how her future might turn out if her mother married Tyler.

It wasn't any of his concern, he told himself.

"Nuts?" he asked, passing her the bowl.

"I'm not nuts, *you* are," she teased, and laughed at her own silly joke. She sprinkled the crushed walnuts and pecans on top of her creation with a flourish. "And now for the cherries. Two of them, like you promised."

He executed a mock bow. "As you wish, madam." He gave her two juicy red maraschino cherries to garnish her sundae.

"Ta-da! I did it!" Giggling impishly, she grabbed her spoon and dug into the dessert with gusto. Just as she'd finished her treat, they both heard a car pull into the circular drive.

Like radar, Emily perked up, cocking her head to the side. Two car doors slammed shut, and her eyes widened in delight. "Mama's here!"

She scrambled from the stool and hit the ground, running toward the foyer before Nick could clean her messy hands and face, which were smudged with chocolate and whipped cream. He shrugged, figuring it wouldn't be a bad thing for the meticulous Grayson to see what he was getting himself into with a child as exuberant and mischievous as Emily.

He headed toward the front rooms at a slower pace, not wanting to seem as anxious as Emily, but he was counting on the little girl to interrupt a good-night kiss on the porch, or a little touchy-feely before it happened.

She didn't disappoint him, and he made it just in time to enjoy the show.

Emily flung open the door, startling the two on the other side of the threshold during what looked to be a very serious moment. Grayson jerked back, a flicker of annoyance crossing his features as he stared at the little urchin who'd aborted his end-of-the-evening plans. Samantha's features reflected a mixture of relief and gratitude.

"Mama, you're finally home!" Emily launched herself into Samantha's arms and buried her sticky face into the midsection of her tailored dress. "I missed you so much!" she said, her words muffled against the folds of material.

Laughing at her daughter's dramatic display, Samantha stroked her hand over Emily's soft hair, thinking nothing of the face-print and smears the little girl was leaving on her dress. "I missed you, too, sweetie."

Emily beamed up at her. "I made myself a hot fudge sundae," she announced importantly.

Grinning, Samantha rubbed her thumb over a dried splotch of chocolate stuck on Emily's chin. "I can see that."

Tyler looked on with a frown. "It looks like you got more on your face than you did in your mouth."

If Tyler meant to be humorous, his attempt fell flat. Emily's smile drooped, and her childlike enthusiasm deflated like a popped balloon. She burrowed closer to her mother, instinctively seeking comfort.

The fun moment turned strained, and Nick strove to fill the awkward silence with other conversation. "So, did you two have a nice evening?"

Tyler glanced back at Nick. "It was quite enjoyable. We had dinner at the Windsor House, and we were lucky enough to get a window seat overlooking the ocean,'' he replied, as if Nick should have known the elite place, or at least been impressed by their seating arrangements.

He wasn't. The pizza he'd had delivered for dinner was more his style. "How about coming in for an ice cream sundae?" He opened the door wider in invitation. "Emily just practiced on hers, and I'm sure she'd be glad to make you one, too."

The very idea of eating a messy sundae created by a six-year-old seemed to appall Tyler, and he took a safe step back. "I, uh, we had dessert at the restaurant."

Samantha stepped inside the foyer with Emily, which also effectively extinguished any possibility of Tyler stealing a kiss. "I think I should take Emily upstairs for a bath and get her ready for bed." She looked at Tyler. "Would you like to stay for coffee?"

He glanced from her to Nick. Obviously deciding that three would be a crowd, he shook his head. "I should be going. I have an early game of golf in the morning."

"All right. I'll see you Saturday evening at your dinner party, then." Samantha touched Emily tenderly beneath her chin, a maternal, loving caress. "Emily, say good-night to Mr. Grayson."

Very reluctantly, and with her gaze downcast, Emily obeyed her mother. "Good night, Mr. Grayson."

Tyler gave the little girl a polite nod. "Good night, Emily."

Samantha turned her daughter to face Nick. "And how about Mr. Petrocelli?"

Nick hunkered down to Emily's level. Wanting to end their fun evening together on a happy note, he touched the back of her ear and magically retrieved a silver coin, as he'd done the first day they'd met. "Hey, you be sure to wash behind those ears. I found another quarter."

He pressed the money into the palm of her grubby hand, and she smiled at the shiny coin, still awed that he had the ability to find quarters behind her ears. Without warning, she wrapped her arms around his neck and hugged him tight, then gave him a sticky kiss on his cheek. "Good night, Mr. Nick."

He rubbed her back, unable to dismiss the strange emotion tightening his chest and filling up that empty part of him he'd lived with for so long. Since Camille, he'd faced the fact that he'd never have kids or a family of his own, and he'd been okay with that realization—until this moment, when one little girl made him too aware of just how incomplete his life really was.

"Sweet dreams," he said as he let her go, refusing to dwell on so complicated a thought. "I'll see you in the morning."

Samantha and Emily headed up to the third landing, and Tyler departed, too. Nick went back to the kitchen to clean up. He stacked the plates, glasses and utensils from dinner into the dishwasher, and wiped down all the counters, not wanting Kathryn to deal with the mess he and Emily had made.

He smiled at the thought of Samantha's aunt. Around six, the older woman had claimed she was off to dinner and the movies with a friend, but Nick found it more than a coincidence that Victor had also left the house not five minutes after Kathryn. No doubt the two were enjoying an intimate date.

When he'd finished straightening the kitchen, he realized a hot fudge sundae sounded mighty good, especially since it appeared he'd be spending the rest of the evening alone. He dragged out all the ingredients again, and was just scooping vanilla ice cream into a fountain glass, when Samantha joined him.

"My freshly bathed gremlin is down for the count," she said, sounding tired herself. Her gaze took in the fixings for a sundae, and her eyes lit up. "Mind making one for me, too? I need more of a boost than hot tea tonight."

He grinned. After her date with Grayson and the episode in the foyer, he hadn't expected her to come back downstairs, but he was glad she had. She'd changed into a pair of red leggings and an oversize flannel shirt. Her hair was still in the French braid she'd worn all day, and he had the fleeting thought that he'd yet to see all that rich, silky butterscotch hair flowing free.

"One or two scoops?" he asked, retrieving another fountain glass from the cupboard.

With a heavy sigh, she slipped onto the bar stool across the counter from him. "Two scoops, and extra hot fudge and whipped cream."

"Hmm, must have been some date," he teased, and nearly laughed when she grimaced. Sensing her need to release some tension, he asked more seriously, "Wanna talk about it?"

Propping her forearms on the counter, she gave a half-hearted shrug. "There isn't a whole lot to talk about. My dating Tyler pleases my grandmother, and Tyler is interested."

Nick filled her glass with ice cream and drizzled lots of hot fudge over the top. "Do *you* like the guy?"

"He's...nice," she said, without the enthusiasm that should have accompanied a woman who was renewing a new romance with an old beau.

"Nice?" His eyebrows rose at the bland adjective. "So is a hot fudge sundae."

"No, a hot fudge sundae is *decadent*." Her eyes glittered with devious pleasure, and she licked her bottom lip as he piled her dessert with a mountain of whipped cream. "With extra hot fudge and whipped cream, it's *sinful.*"

He could think of a few other things that qualified as sinful, like that full, sensual mouth of hers, those soft breasts and the long, slender legs that had clenched his thigh so temptingly yesterday afternoon in the closet.

Pushing those distracting thoughts from his mind, he tossed nuts onto both their sundaes, added a cherry on top and pushed one glass across the counter to her. "I guess there's no comparison between Tyler and a hot fudge sundae, huh?"

She grinned. "Nope." She took a big bite and groaned in appreciation. Her eyes momentarily closed as she savored the flavor on her tongue, making him wish he had the right to pull her across the counter and taste her cold, sweetened mouth for himself. He'd never been one to play with his food, but he suddenly had the urge to dip his finger into his hot fudge and trace a line from her breasts to her belly and her thighs...and follow the path with his tongue.

After a few spoonfuls, she continued their conversation about Grayson. "I've known Tyler for years, actually. He's the son of one of Amelia's friends, and comes from a respectable family. We dated before I met Justin, and he even proposed to me, but I've always just considered him a friend." More quietly, and with obvious reluctance, she added, "Amelia is hoping that things work out between Tyler and me, and that I'll marry him. This date is the beginning of our courtship, so to speak."

The uncertainty swimming in her eyes prompted him to ask, "Have you told Amelia how you feel?"

A resigned smile touched the corner of her mouth. "It

doesn't make any difference how I feel or what I want. Marrying Tyler is the right thing to do.''

A slow burn of irritation stirred in his belly. He knew his purpose for being at Cranberry Harbor was to cast Tyler in a favorable light, as well as build Samantha's self-esteem, but a part of her gaining confidence also meant that she take charge of her future, as well…which might not belong with Tyler.

"Samantha, this isn't the Middle Ages. You have every right to marry who you want, not who you feel is suitable or respectable.'' He kept his voice low. If Amelia heard those words coming out of his mouth, he was certain she would send him packing and revoke her scholarship endowment.

"It's not that simple, Nick,'' she said softly, meeting his gaze. "I married who I wanted once before, someone who was highly unsuitable, and I ended up miserable. I won't disappoint Amelia again by making the same mistake twice. Besides, I have to think of Emily, and what's in her best interest.''

"And you think that's Tyler Grayson?'' he asked, trying to remain impartial.

"Maybe,'' she said, not sounding completely convinced. "She does need a father and a stable environment, and I want a family of my own, and siblings for Em.''

"The man was hardly comfortable with Emily tonight.'' So much for remaining unbiased.

"He's not used to kids. He told me that tonight at dinner.'' She pushed her half-eaten sundae aside. "It'll take some time for them to get used to each other.''

Nick flattened his hands on the counter, keeping a tight rein on his growing annoyance. "So, you'd marry

Grayson, even though you don't love him? Even though there are no obvious sparks between you two?"

Her expressive eyes flashed defensively. "There's more to a marriage than just chemistry."

Frustrated that he wasn't making headway with her, he didn't hold back his thoughts. "In my opinion, sexual chemistry is an important part of most relationships, and passion is elemental to a marriage."

She laughed, but the sound lacked humor. After a quiet moment passed, she said, "I married my first husband..." With a shake of her head, she cut herself off and glanced away. "Never mind. I'm sure you don't want to hear the boring details."

All he knew of her marriage was what little she'd divulged during their conversation a few nights ago. He wanted to know more. He wanted to know everything about her, and what had happened to shape her into the reserved woman she'd become, so unlike the vibrant young woman in that photograph Amelia had shown him.

Slipping his fingers beneath her chin, he lifted her face back up and saw the torment in her gaze, the need to release burdens she'd carried for too long. "You haven't bored me yet, sweetheart. You could talk to me all night and I'd never get tired of listening to you."

A tentative smile touched her mouth, and after a moment she began to speak. "I married Justin when I was twenty-one, against my grandmother's advice, and after declining Tyler's marriage proposal. Justin was twenty-four, and while he held a job as an advertising executive, that's where respectability, and his responsibility, ended. He was reckless, daring and lived life as if today was all that mattered."

Her gaze held his, as if she needed that emotional

anchor, and he waited patiently for her to continue. "I was young and impressionable, and when someone as exciting as Justin pursued me, I fell for him. I thought he was everything I was missing in the quiet, routine life I led here at Cranberry Harbor, and he made me feel equally impulsive and reckless. I was too flattered by his attention to realize what I was getting myself into."

"Which was?" he prompted.

"A marriage neither one of us was ready for." She absently traced the grooves at the bottom of her sundae glass. "I wanted a family, and he wanted someone to share his life-style—the flat-track racing, back-country skiing and other risky stunts."

"But you got pregnant." Irony laced his voice.

She nodded. "Emily wasn't planned, but I was thrilled once I knew I was going to have a baby. I hoped a child and having a family would make Justin stop taking chances with his life. Although my mother wasn't a daredevil, she possessed the same kind of capricious, 'please yourself' kind of attitude, and I knew what it was like to grow up without the security of knowing if she was going to be there from one day to the next. I was determined to give my child that kind of security, and two parents she could rely on. But the more I tried to rein Justin in and keep him from being so negligent with his life, the more reckless he became. He'd thumb his nose at danger, as if to prove he was invincible."

She grew quiet, and the lapse gave Nick too much time to contemplate his own marriage, and how similar his situation had been to Samantha's relationship with Justin. Camille had issued her own demands, none of which had made any kind of impact on his decision to pursue a career in law enforcement. His goals had been single-minded, and as a result he'd lost sight of his relationship, and the marriage dissolved under the pressure and strain of his job.

While he had a healthy respect for life and didn't deliberately tempt fate as Justin had, he did put himself at risk every time he strapped on his holster and accepted a potentially hazardous assignment, like infiltrating a narcotics ring. His job was just as ominous as Justin's lust for danger had been. And as he well knew, the adrenaline rush of narrowly escaping death could be just as irresistible as being hooked on an addictive substance. Once you tasted the thrill, it was difficult to give it up.

"What happened?" he asked.

"Justin was far from invincible," she said with a faint smile. "One night, he was driving his Corvette on the interstate. According to witnesses and the police report, he was weaving in and out of traffic, and he lost control of his car. He passed over the center divider and hit a truck head-on. The police were fairly certain that he died instantly, considering there wasn't much left of his Corvette or him."

Absently, Nick rubbed at the scar on his left temple, thinking about his own brush with death. Hearing Samantha's story made him realize how fortunate he'd been, and that next time he might not be so lucky. That was the reason why he preferred to remain uncommitted and independent. What right did he have to put a wife and kids through that kind of constant worry?

"His death was devastating," she continued, "but my marriage to Justin taught me a valuable lesson. I was attracted to him for all the wrong reasons, and I let my skewed judgment of what I thought I *wanted* cloud my mind to what I *needed,* and I suffered the consequences during the four years that we were married. The naive, hopeful part of me believed we'd have this wonderful marriage based on love and respect, but I was wrong. I never had either.''

"So now you feel you have to punish yourself for one youthful mistake?''

"You don't understand," she said, shaking her head, a touch of desperation in her voice.

"Then explain it to me," he said gently, wanting to know what, exactly, she feared.

"I *liked* that excitement that surrounded Justin," she said, her tone angry. More at herself than him, he suspected. "I *liked* that reckless feeling, the thrill and passion I tasted with him. Those feelings and urges are still there, and I struggle with them all the time, Nick. Just like my mother, I'm tempted to be wild and impetuous. But unlike my mother, I won't sacrifice my child's needs for it. And I *will not* disgrace my grandmother again, as her own daughter has done too many times to count.''

In a stunning moment of revelation, Nick suddenly understood her struggle to be reserved and responsible, and *why* she tried so hard to suppress her innate sexuality. She'd unleashed that passion once before with Justin and it had cost her emotionally. The thought of doing so again obviously frightened her. It was easier for her to hide behind that cool facade than face the truth that Samantha Fairmont was a very sensual and sexy woman.

"You're settling for less than you deserve with Tyler." He sounded ruthless, but didn't care. He wanted better for her than a marriage based solely on stability with a man who would not appreciate all that she had to offer.

"I've never experienced real love, so I suppose I can't miss something I've never had. This time, I'm making the decision with my head, and not my emotions. This time I won't be so swept up in a passionate affair that I lose sight of what's important to me. Emily deserves that."

And Tyler wouldn't threaten that reckless part of her, because he didn't touch her emotions in a passionate, exciting way. "So marriage to Tyler will be comfortable and predictable, and you'll never have to worry about the temptation that clouded your judgment with Justin."

"Yes," she whispered, her voice pained.

Nick ached to reach out and touch her, to chase away the vulnerability in her eyes. So many insecurities brought on by one youthful mistake.

But he could offer her one assurance he hoped she'd remember long after he was gone from Cranberry Harbor. He touched her then, tenderly stroking his knuckles down her soft cheek. He wanted her to experience gentleness, and longing, so she'd know what to hold out for in her relationship with Grayson, or any other man.

Her eyes widened, the heated awareness sparking between them instantaneously. It took all the willpower he possessed not to lean across the counter and kiss her, to show her exactly the kind of passion she should demand from a relationship, regardless of what she perceived as her own weakness.

Knowing he'd never be able to stop at one kiss, he settled for the next best thing, and traced his thumb over her bottom lip. "You're a beautiful, desirable woman. Don't let anyone cheat you out of the kind of marriage you deserve."

She exhaled on a sigh, and managed a tremulous smile. "I'll keep that in mind."

IT WAS PAST MIDNIGHT, and though Samantha was emotionally drained from her date with Tyler and her ensuing conversation with Nick, sleep eluded her. She'd tried reading, but couldn't concentrate on the story. She'd taken a warm bath, and though that had helped to relax her, she was still restless.

Slipping into her robe, she checked on Emily, who was sleeping peacefully, then climbed the stairs to the attic. She flipped the lights on in her studio and glanced around, drawing comfort from the familiar sights and smells of her paintings.

She hadn't come up to her studio to paint, but to think. Her mind wouldn't leave her alone. Neither could she forget the haunting words Nick had spoken to her.

You're a beautiful, desirable woman. Don't let anyone cheat you out of the kind of marriage you deserve.

Her heart twisted in misery. Her soul was in equal turmoil. Nick made love sound so easy, so attainable, yet her greatest fear wasn't that she'd never fall in love, but that she'd waste her life looking for something that didn't exist.

So many struggles warred within her, especially the fact that she'd made the most important decisions of her life on impulse. And after Justin's death she'd adopted a complacent and obedient manner because that had been the safest, most responsible route. From the time she'd returned as a widow to Cranberry Harbor with Emily, she'd gladly forfeited something elemental—the right to be her true self.

How did she go about regaining what she'd lost? How did she go about taking control of her life and pleasing herself, without making wrong choices again? She had no idea, no direction other than the one Amelia suggested. More and more she was realizing she wanted that independence and freedom, yet she feared the repercussions.

If it was just her, she would have struck out on her own after Justin had died. But she had Emily to think about, and Amelia had offered her a safe haven at Cranberry Harbor.

Approaching her current painting, she stared at the dilapidated barn and smoothed her fingers over the silhouette of lovers within, wanting the passion and emotional connection those illusive couples shared. But she also found comfort in knowing she'd never experience that kind of abandon with Tyler. An agonizing ache squeezed her chest, even though she knew she was doing the right thing, making the practical choice.

She bit her bottom lip, feeling torn and confused. She suspected her future would be with Tyler, but before she committed herself to a loveless marriage based on familial expectations and her own craving for security, the need to be a little bit daring, brazen even, called to her. To experience that rush of excitement and the thrill of passion one last time.

She wanted it with Nick. Considering the attraction they were both fighting, and the way they burned when they kissed or touched, he'd be perfect for a brief, no-strings-attached affair. He wasn't the committing kind, he'd told her, and she wasn't asking for forever. Not with a man intent on risking his life. Just a few nights of mindless pleasure, to experience everything Nick had to offer, and do a little exploring of her own.

And once Nick was gone, she'd resume her monotonous life and accept her duty as Tyler's wife.

CHAPTER NINE

NICK ENTERED AMELIA'S library and found the old woman sitting in her wing chair by the fireplace, waiting for him. "You asked to see me, ma'am?"

"Yes, I did." She motioned to the chair across from her. "Have a seat, Mr. Petrocelli."

Once he'd folded his frame in the chair across from hers, she got down to business.

"I'm very pleased with your progress with Samantha," she said, a satisfied smile gracing her lips. "Obviously you managed to convince her to go out on last night's date with Tyler."

"It seemed like a very strained date to me," he said, not bothering to hold back his assessment of the situation.

She stared at him for a moment, not quite sure what to make of his direct approach. "She's taking a step in the right direction, and that's all that matters. After a while, when they grow comfortable with each other again, she'll realize marrying Tyler is the right choice for her. It's what she should have done when he'd proposed to her years ago."

She looked thoughtful for a few seconds, then went on. "I do have to say Samantha has blossomed since you've been here. She smiles more often and seems to have acquired some confidence. It's nice to see, but I want you to be careful not to overencourage her."

"Excuse me?"

She sighed, her gaze softening. "Mr. Petrocelli, as much as I appreciate you flattering Samantha and building her self-esteem, I don't want her to let all your attention go to her head. Though she's a sensible young woman, she's very easily influenced, and I don't want her thinking foolish thoughts that might hinder her progress with Tyler. She's been very practical since returning to Cranberry Harbor, and I'd like her to remain that way."

He understood Amelia's concern, because it echoed the same fears Samantha had divulged last night. Yet in the short week he'd been there, he'd seen subtle changes in Samantha, a definite struggle between being the responsible, dependable woman she'd become since Justin's death, and allowing deeper desires to surface. Somehow, someway, she had to find a common ground between the two, or else she would never truly be happy.

Amelia rested her hands over the head of her cane. "I think you've found a neutral balance with Samantha that's working, so stick with it."

"Yes, ma'am. Is there anything else?" he asked, anxious to be on his way.

"No. Just keep up the good work." Standing, she headed toward an antique rolltop desk. "I have things I need to attend to, so you are excused. Please shut the door when you leave."

Agitated by the entire situation, and his part in it, Nick left the library and went in search of Samantha to find out what was on the afternoon's agenda. It was Friday, and they needed to head into town to pick up a few things for the garden party. Maybe he'd take Emily and Samantha to lunch at the café he'd gone to with Victor.

He could use the time away from Cranberry Harbor, and he suspected Samantha could, too.

Strangely enough, this morning at breakfast there had been an odd tension between the two of them. She'd kept glancing at him nervously, as if she had something on her mind but wasn't ready to discuss whatever it was. Maybe a more relaxed atmosphere would make her more comfortable and get her to open up about whatever was troubling her.

She wasn't downstairs, so he headed up to the third floor. He found Emily alone in her room playing with her dollhouse.

He smiled at the little girl. "Hey, Em, do you know where your mom is?"

"I don't know," she said with a shrug. "Maybe she's in the attic where she paints."

He knew Samantha enjoyed sketching, but Emily's bit of news surprised him. He didn't realize Samantha also painted. Intrigued, he located the door at the end of the hall that concealed the stairs leading to the final floor of the mansion.

"Samantha?" he called as he climbed the stairs, not wanting to startle her.

There was no reply, and when he finally entered the loft, he was completely unprepared for the sight that greeted him. The room had been transformed into a private studio, with an array of canvases stacked against the walls. A workbench off to the side held cans of different-size brushes, tubes of paint, rags splotched with oils, and various painting paraphernalia he didn't recognize. An easel and small table were propped near the diamond-paned, oversize windows that allowed sunlight into the room, and a sheet covered whatever work she had in progress.

Spotting her sketch pad on the workbench, he opened it, and received yet another shock. The first few pages were filled with drawings of him, mainly portraits she must have created from memory, but the details were incredible. He slowly thumbed through the pages, and stopped abruptly when he came across a drawing of him and Emily sleeping in the porch hammock. He remembered the day, recalling how content he'd felt when Emily had curled up beside him so trustingly. But he never could have known just how peaceful and perfect it had been for him if Samantha hadn't captured his expression on paper. It was as though this was where he belonged, with Emily, with Samantha.

The wave of yearning he experienced threw him off-kilter. His heart pounded so hard it hurt. It was as if everything that had been missing from his life for so long crashed over him at that moment, overwhelming him with emotions he would have sworn he didn't want or need. But he did want, and he did need, and that powerful realization shook him up.

After his divorce, he'd resigned himself to remaining a bachelor and never having a family of his own. He had no time or room in his life for a wife and kids. His job was all he needed to be satisfied, he firmly reminded himself. He *knew* that, dammit!

His heart told him differently. In a week's time, mother and daughter had crawled under his skin, nestled close to his heart. Without his job to hide behind and force him to keep the ruthless pace he'd grown accustomed to, he'd allowed a woman to breach the emotional barriers he'd erected after his divorce.

He wanted Samantha, not because of Amelia's scheme to have him flirt with her, but because she represented too much of what was missing from his life. Warmth, laughter, companionship...and a gentleness that countered all the hard edges he'd developed over the years.

He already cared for both of them more than was wise. They lived in separate worlds, and neither of them belonged in the other's environment. He wouldn't—*couldn't*—expect Samantha to adapt to his life-style, and he sure as hell couldn't survive living here.

Forcing those troubling thoughts from his mind, he closed the sketch pad and moved away from the workbench. Totally enthralled by this hidden side to Samantha, he roamed around the room and looked through the finished paintings stacked against the wall. Many of them were of Emily in various stages of growth—from a happy, cooing baby lying on a white fur rug, her bottom bare, to a toddler with a frilly dress holding an Easter basket filled with colorful eggs. Then there was a more recent portrait of Emily picking a bouquet of flowers, a mischievous glint in her eyes.

The collection of landscapes and seascapes were breathtaking, enticing the viewer's eye. They were full of color, warmth and passion...and something else that eluded him. He found himself fascinated by the paintings, but couldn't pinpoint why. All he knew was that Samantha's creations had the ability to stir something deep within him.

"Nick?" Her tentative voice drifted up from the stairs.

"I'm in here," he said, unable to pull his gaze from a painting of a charming cottage surrounded by a deep blue lake. There was something about the picture that made him feel as though he was missing something important, but try as he might, he couldn't figure out what.

Hearing her soft footsteps behind him as she approached, he glanced over his shoulder and smiled.

"Emily said you might be up here," he told her, attempting to explain why he'd invaded what was clearly her personal turf.

Her uncertain gaze flickered to the canvas he held in his hands. "I was, earlier."

He knew he should apologize for going through her work, which she obviously considered private, but he couldn't just dismiss what he'd discovered. "Samantha..." He struggled for the right words. "These paintings are incredible."

She bit her lower lip at his praise, looking hesitant and hopeful at the same time. "Do you really think so?"

He shook his head incredulously, unable to believe she could doubt her talent. "Sweetheart, it's a crying shame that you keep them up here, covered in sheets. These paintings need to be displayed in an art gallery."

Her light laughter held an odd tightness. "No."

The one word was indisputable. "Why? Even you have to appreciate your talent."

Samantha remained stubbornly quiet.

Setting down the painting he was holding, he regarded her thoughtfully. "Well?" he prompted.

She stared at him for a long moment, indecision and longing warring in her blue eyes, as if she harbored a secret she wasn't sure she wanted to share. He waited patiently, giving her time to decide whether or not she could trust him.

Finally, she moved away from him to another stack of canvases nearby. Lifting a painting, she tilted it toward him to view. "What do you see?"

He glanced at her, a humorous grin canting his mouth. "Is this a trick question?"

She grinned back, and he was gratified to see that she

was finally relaxing with him. "Yeah, in some ways it is."

"Okay, I'll play along." Standing beside her, he narrowed his one good eye and examined the landscape. "I see a greenhouse, with exotic plants and flowers." Something more nebulous beckoned to him, and he tried to grasp what he was missing, but failed. "There's something else in this painting..."

She pointed to a row of blooming orchids, directing his gaze. "It's right here, in these shadows."

He stared, forcing his gaze to relax and discover what Samantha saw. The shadows gradually formed into an image that took him by surprise. "Is that what I think it is?"

"What do you think it is?" she asked, not giving anything away.

He rubbed the back of his neck, wondering if maybe his own gaze was deceiving him and making more of those shadows than what was actually there. "It looks like, well, lovers in a clinch."

"That's it exactly." Her mouth remained unsmiling, her eyes filled with dismay. "All of the paintings I've done recently have these illusive lovers somewhere in the picture."

He looked at her in amazement, but she seemed more upset than enthusiastic about her clever illusion. "I'll be damned. Show me another one."

She introduced him to her collection of artwork, and he searched for the shadowed lovers concealed within her paintings. This was the passionate side he knew Samantha tried to conceal. She might struggle to be practical and demure, but her sensual, impetuous nature radiated from the landscapes and seascapes she created, and the camouflaged lovers within.

These paintings could very well be her ticket to stability, Nick thought—if she believed in herself, and her talent. Instead, she was using them to hide behind.

Just as he hid behind his job...

He dismissed the thought as quickly as it entered his head. "You need to find an art gallery to show your collection," he said.

"It's just a hobby, Nick," she explained quietly. "That's all it can ever be."

"Your paintings are unique." Frustration flared within him at the way she retreated. "Any art dealer could see the potential in your work. What harm can there be in pursuing the idea?"

"A lot, unfortunately." She arranged the canvases against the wall, not looking at him. "Going public with my work..." She shook her head at the thought, as if it pained her to finish it.

He jammed his hands on his hips. "Going public would what?" he demanded, more forcefully than he'd intended.

Straightening, she cast him an angry glance. "It would prove that I'm just as reckless and impulsive as my mother. Those lovers represent everything I *can't* allow myself to be in public. That's why they're private. My paintings are an outlet for my emotions and feelings, and they reveal who and what I really am."

"Which is a passionate, sensual woman."

"Yes," she admitted, unable to deny the truth. "I've spent the past three years rebuilding my reputation after my destructive marriage to Justin. I've achieved that respectability, for myself as much as for Emily, and I won't jeopardize it because of a careless impulse. And there's Amelia to consider as well. She knows I paint, but she has no idea just how inappropriate my pictures are.''

His mouth thinned in frustration. ''Amelia would survive.''

''I can't do it, Nick.'' Her eyes held a wealth of sadness. ''I'd never disgrace her that way, not after everything she's done for me.'' She gave a feeble shrug. ''Besides, I doubt anyone would have an interest in a collection of paintings so eccentric.''

He smiled, though he felt a little sad himself. ''If you don't take a little risk, you'll never know that for certain.''

A LITTLE RISK. Although Samantha wasn't quite willing to take chances with her unconventional paintings, she *was* working up the nerve to take a big risk with the man sitting across from her, studying the cards in his hand as they played their third round of gin rummy. Emily was in bed, Amelia and Kathryn had retired for the night, and she and Nick were in her sitting room. Alone. The night stretched ahead of them, along with endless possibilities.

She took a drink of the passion fruit iced tea she'd opted for over hot tea, trying to calm the flutters in her belly. Now that she'd made up her mind to have an affair with Nick, she admitted she was a bit nervous about how to approach him with such an outrageous proposition.

All I want is a night of anything-goes sex. Can you accommodate me? The words sounded ridiculous in her mind, and then there was always the possibility he'd refuse her flat out, the humiliation of which didn't bear thinking about.

''Your turn, Samantha,'' he said, his deep voice pulling her back to the game at hand.

She lifted her gaze and summoned a slow, sultry smile. *That* snagged his attention and made his gaze linger on her mouth a fraction longer than normal before he glanced back to the cards in his hands. The perplexed frown creasing his brow did a good job at concealing the flare of desire she'd glimpsed darkening his gaze.

She drew the last card she needed for her run of spades and laid down her hand. "I'm out. Again."

Considering she'd claimed victory on all three games, Nick was an extremely good sport. Tossing his cards on the table, he allowed one of those sexy grins to make an appearance. "I'm used to playing a *man's* game of cards," he grumbled good-naturedly.

"Really?" She shuffled the deck of cards at a leisurely pace. "And what do you consider a *man's* game?"

Leaning back in his chair, he laced his fingers behind his head in a pose that was relaxed, but also emphasized the taut muscles across his chest and abdomen. "Poker, of course."

She touched her tongue to her bottom lip, dampening it. To her delight, he noticed. "Then teach me, and we'll play your *man's* game," she said, her voice low and throaty.

From across the table, he studied her intently. "Poker isn't exactly the kind of game I should be teaching a woman like you to play."

A woman like her. Samantha suddenly resented the stereotype she'd created for herself. A good girl. Refined. Virtuous. A well-bred lady who didn't indulge in any kind of activity that might sully her reputation or remind anyone that she was Lucinda's daughter.

"Teach me to play." She placed the deck of cards on

the table in front of him. "As my personal assistant, I insist that you do."

He sat up straighter, bracing his elbows on the table, his expression reluctant. "We have no chips or money to play with."

"I'm sure we can improvise somehow."

An impossibly wicked grin slashed across his mouth, daring and bold. "I suppose we could play the good old-fashioned way…for articles of clothing."

Heat spread through her, drawing her nipples into tight, hard peaks against the lacy webbing of her bra. She knew he was purposely trying to shock her into recanting her request, to call off the game he'd just turned into a sexy, forbidden sport between lovers. The staid, respectable Samantha should have been shocked. The passionate, tempestuous Samantha was ready to up the stakes.

Ever since the day in the closet, she'd craved more of his deep, delicious, erotic kisses. Had dreamed and fantasized about them. Wanting to store up enough of those drugging kisses for a lifetime without him, she embraced the reckless suggestion flirting with the fringes of her mind.

"How about we play for kisses?" she countered.

He stilled, her proposition surprising him. He hesitated before answering, his gaze holding hers, something akin to intrigue glimmering within. For a heart-stopping moment she thought he'd refuse, or laugh at her request, and she'd experience that humiliation she dreaded.

"All right, we'll play for kisses." His long fingers curled around the deck of cards and began shuffling them. "But I've got a stipulation to add."

She drew a deep breath, knowing she couldn't back

down now, no matter what condition he attached to the game. "And that is?"

"Whoever wins the hand calls the shots and decides where and how those kisses will be delivered."

Her body pulsed with thrilling awareness. With a stipulation like that, there was no way she could lose. Folding her hands primly on the table, she smiled. "Let the game begin."

WHAT THE HELL was Samantha up to?

She'd boldly called his bluff, and now he had no choice but to teach her to play poker and collect payment, or pay up, in kisses. Slow, deep kisses, or wild, devouring ones. The choice belonged to the winner of each hand. Either way, he was certain his sanity and libido would be shot by the end of the night, and no amount of push-ups would relieve his physical pain.

What had he been thinking to demand such an idiotic stipulation? The answer was too easy. He'd been thinking about Samantha, and kissing her again—no holds barred. He'd been thinking about all that sexy confidence surrounding her tonight, and wanting it for himself.

Dangerous, foolish thoughts. Yet he couldn't bring himself to deny either one of them what they both seemed to want. Kisses were relatively harmless, and a whole lot safer than playing strip poker, he reasoned.

She was a quick learner, and it took only a few hands for her to grasp the concept of the game. She even managed to beat him the first go-round. She laughed giddily, her eyes glimmering mischievously.

Her request was a surprisingly shy one. "I want a chaste kiss, on the lips. No time limit."

They both stood and leaned across the table, meeting halfway. Since she'd won the hand, it was up to her to instigate the kiss and control it. Considering she'd asked for one that didn't require his mouth to be open or his tongue to participate, there wasn't much for him to do but enjoy the feel of her soft lips pressing against his.

Their mouths were less than an inch away, and he could feel her warm, passion-fruit-scented breath on his lips. Anticipation spiraled low in his belly as he waited for her to seal the scant distance between them.

"Close your eyes," she whispered, her own lashes falling half-mast.

He did, and started when she pressed her hand to his face, cradled his jaw in her palm, which he hadn't been expecting. Her thumb skimmed across his bottom lip, her touch softer than silk, yet it left a blazing trail of heat in its wake. She explored tentatively, leisurely, and he had to force himself to keep his mouth closed, as she'd requested. Finally, with a sigh, her lips touched his, incredibly supple and pliant, and he nearly groaned at the sweetness of this simple kiss.

He'd been with his share of women over the years, the sex always satisfying and enjoyable...yet somehow his attitude about sex, and women, had become jaded. Somewhere along the way, he'd started taking that rush of sexual excitement for granted, instead of savoring the process, drawing out the pleasure until it was too intense to bear.

This simple kiss with Samantha reminded him of what was missing from his brief affairs, and made him feel like an untried teenager again, evoking in him that wondrous sensation of discovery. The spine-tingling rush of excitement made his heart thunder in his chest and his palms grow damp. He felt impatient, restless and feverishly aroused.

Growing bolder, she dragged her tongue across his

bottom lip, then sucked the plump flesh into her mouth and nibbled it with her teeth. She did provocative things to his lips, his mouth, that no other woman had—*without* using her tongue. She groaned, her breathing coming in soft pants, and his body burned with an incendiary fever. He couldn't remember ever being so turned on so fast, and he hadn't even touched her.

She pulled back abruptly, as if realizing just how erotic her kiss had turned. Her lashes lifted, revealing dark blue eyes brimming with desire. A flush of arousal stained her cheeks, and her breasts rose and fell with each shallow intake of air, full and straining against the bodice of her dress.

He slowly lowered himself back to his chair and watched her do the same. "That was the most *unchaste* kiss I've ever received."

She smiled, looking pleased with herself. "Yeah?"

"Oh, yeah." The woman honestly had no clue that she'd just turned him inside out with her innocent exploration. Picking up the deck of cards, he began shuffling them. "I think it only fair that you know I plan on demanding a few chaste kisses of my own."

A sassy, confident twinkle entered her gaze. "You have to win a hand first."

He did, presenting a flush over her three of a kind.

"Give me your hand," he said, reaching across the small table.

Confusion etched her expression, but she did as he ordered. He nuzzled her palm, then placed a light, warm kiss in the center.

She tilted her head, a small frown creasing her brow. "That's it?"

A slow, wicked grin lifted his lips. "What makes you think I'm done?" And with that, he dragged his tongue from her wrist to her palm and up the center of her middle finger.

She gasped, her gaze widening. Instinctively she tugged on her hand, but his hold was secure. Closing his lips over her finger, he sucked it deeply into his mouth and swirled his tongue along the length. She shuddered, and her hand went limp in his.

From there, the game became playful, daring and innovative. By silent agreement, they became creative, inventing ways to kiss without the conventional, tongue-tangling methods, awakening desires, but not fulfilling the slow, building ache he knew they were both experiencing.

For ninety minutes, his body remained in a constant state of arousal, his erection huge and near painful. Shifting on his seat to find a more comfortable position, if that was possible, he released a strained breath and dealt another hand of cards. Since he knew he couldn't stand much more of this torment without embarrassing himself, he decided it was time to end the game.

"Last hand," he called.

She met his gaze, her face beautifully flushed with all the sexy play over the past hour and a half. "All or nothing?" she asked brazenly. "Winner calls the shots."

He eyed her from across the table. He had no idea what she had in mind, but he didn't want to repress the sexy, desirous woman she'd been tonight. He could survive one more retribution. "All right."

Unfortunately, she lost the last hand so he'd never know what she'd planned. However, the disappointment reflected in her expression made him decide to give her a final payment she wouldn't forget anytime soon.

He moved his chair away from the table and crooked his finger at her. "Come over here and sit on my lap."

Without a doubt, his order surprised her. It excited her, too. He saw the eagerness in her eyes, saw the anticipation in the fluttering pulse at the base of her throat. Standing, she slowly rounded the table to his side. She wore a gauzy, peach-hued blouse with a low scoop neckline and pearlized buttons down the front, along with a matching skirt that swirled around her glorious, bare legs. It wasn't a sexy outfit by any stretch of the imagination, but he appreciated the way the material draped softly along her body and allowed him access to her smooth skin.

She glanced down at his lap, his raging arousal straining the fly of his jeans. A touch of humor and daring entered her gaze. "Are you sure about this?"

"You're the one who called all or nothing," he reminded her. But he also wanted to issue her a reassurance. "I want you to know you can say stop anytime and I will. And I promise you're safe on my lap, just as long as you don't squirm a whole lot, okay?"

A smile twitched her mouth. "Ladies don't squirm, not even when they're bored."

He lifted a brow at the underlying challenge. "Maybe I ought to see what I can do about changing that stuffy rule. Here's another promise for you. Though you might squirm, you won't be bored." Leaning back in his chair, he pointed to his lap for her to sit.

Drawing a deep, fortifying breath, she lowered herself to his hard thighs with mock primness, but there was nothing prudish about the way her bottom nestled against his groin. No, that was a pure, agonizing slice of heaven. Paradise beckoned in many forms, but the most appealing lay in lifting her to the table, spreading her wide and taking her right there.

Reining in his lustful thoughts, he focused on the task

ahead—a slow, simmering seduction. Adjusting one of her arms around his neck, he pressed the other to his chest, right over his steady heartbeat. "Keep your hands where they are unless I say you can move them."

She didn't say anything, but the acceptance in her luminous gaze spoke volumes. She wanted whatever sensual delights lay ahead.

Not one to rush things, he reached for the end of her braid and slipped off the band securing it. Leisurely he unraveled the strands, letting the anticipation build. When her hair was free and spilling in soft waves around her face and shoulders, he buried his hands in the silky, warm mass and groaned at the luxurious feel. "You have the most gorgeous hair," he murmured, massaging her scalp until a small moan slipped past her lips. "So rich and thick. The color reminds me of butterscotch."

"Mmm," she purred with pleasure, her body growing pliant.

Untangling his hands from her hair, he moved on to the next level of seduction. "Now, let's see. I have a few kisses to claim." He contemplated the situation for a few seconds before touching a finger to her lush mouth, which instinctively opened for him. "If I could place a kiss anywhere on your body, where would you like it to be?"

A damp gust of breath rushed out of her. "You choose."

"There's such a selection." He feigned indecision, drawing out the tension, leading her deeper into temptation. "I could kiss your mouth, of course, but I already know how sweet you taste, so I might want to try something different." His thumb brushed along her jaw in a tantalizing caress. "I can always press my lips to that sensitive spot just below your ear, or the pulse right here."

The hand on his chest curled into a tight fist, and the fingers at the nape of his neck slid into his hair—the only indication that she was as inflamed as he was.

His finger traced the scooped neckline of her bodice and dipped into her cleavage. His gaze holding hers, he slowly undid the buttons securing the front of her blouse, wondering just how far she intended to let him go before she called a halt to their provocative game. Until she did, he'd take her as high as she wanted to go.

"Or I could be creative and kiss your breasts." The front of her dress fell open, and he gently pushed the material aside. He brushed his knuckles over the plump swells rising from the cups of her bra, then used his fingers to pull the lacy webbing down so her breasts sprang free. She gasped as he bared her to his gaze, her hands automatically leaving their assigned posts to cover herself.

He caught her wrists before she could execute the move. Her eyes were wide and filled with conflicting emotions. "You ready to stop?" he asked gently, prepared to accede to her request.

She looked torn, possibly because she was enjoying something so decadent. She closed her eyes for a moment, and when she opened them again, he saw deep, dark desire, and a shameless need that transcended the brief uncertainty she'd experienced. She answered his question by putting her hands back on his chest and around his neck, leaving herself open to his touch, his gaze.

"Now, where were we?" he murmured. "Oh, yeah, your perfect, gorgeous breasts." He lavished praise, enjoying the flush on her cheeks as he reverently worshiped her body. "I could kiss them softly, or I could close my mouth over the tip and suckle your breasts, and flick my tongue over your tight nipples." His thumbs rasped over the beaded crests, and her head fell back on a throaty moan. She arched toward him, as if silently begging him to do just that.

His mouth watered for a taste, his body throbbed to take what she offered, but he restrained his own hunger, still intent on stoking hers. With fierce concentration, he moved on, finding the hem of her dress, and slipped his hand beneath.

Her breathing grew labored. So did his.

Dragging the material upward, he let it pool around his wrist while his fingers glided along her leg, then gently nudged her knees apart.

He met with initial resistance, those doubts again. "Just relax, sweetheart," he coaxed. "And if you don't like the way this feels, just tell me to stop and I promise I will."

She swallowed, her eyes bright with intense desire. "I do...like the way you make me feel."

"Then open up for me, and trust me." After a few patient strokes of his fingers, her tension dissolved and her legs eased apart, granting him access to forbidden territory. Holding her gaze, he ventured higher, to the soft downy skin of her inner thigh. "This is one of my favorite parts to kiss...right here."

Her teeth sank into her bottom lip, but that did nothing to hold back her low moan. *Damn.* He hadn't even touched her intimately yet and she looked close to un-raveling.

His fingers strummed over her quivering flesh, moving inexorably toward the very heart of her. "And right *here.*" He met with the silky, damp barrier of her panties, but didn't allow that flimsy obstruction to hinder his progress. He touched her, stroked her, creating a slow, tantalizing friction that made her cling to him. "Soft, teasing kisses, and long, slow laps with my tongue," he said, his voice low and ragged with need. "Should I claim my kiss that way, sweetheart? Would you like that?"

Sexual hunger touched her brow and widened her eyes. A whimper escaped her throat, her only answer. He felt that good girl-passionate woman struggle within her and wanted to push her a little closer to that wilder nature she fought so hard to keep under control.

"How about I stroke you here, just for the pleasure of it?" he offered, increasing the pressure of his fingers, his own body throbbing at the thought of giving her that kind of erotic release. "Just because it feels good and you like it. With nothing between you and my fingers…"

She closed her eyes, a huge shudder racking her body.

He kissed her cheek, slid his open mouth to that spot he'd told her about just below her lobe, and made her shiver. "Just say yes or no, sweetheart. The choice is yours."

Her lashes fluttered open, undeniable passion heating her gaze, and something more needy and desperate. Taking his free hand, she guided his palm to her breast, closing his fingers around the swollen flesh. "Yes," she whispered, a shameless wanton on his lap. "I want you to touch me, and kiss me, because it feels good, and I like it. I want you to give me pleasure."

The thick, full ridge of his erection swelled to enormous proportions against her bottom, pulsing with every heartbeat. A possessive emotion gripped him, along with the knowledge that he was about to unleash something wild and uninhibited in this woman.

Her bare, pouting breast filled his hand. Leaning forward, he planted a damp kiss on the smooth, rounded globe, ran his tongue over the crest, and finally took her nipple in his mouth and suckled her, hard and deep. With a soft, mewling sound, she lifted her hands and cradled his head in her palms...gasped sharply when he dragged his teeth across the tender tip.

Slipping his fingers beneath the band of her panties, he found her sleek, feminine folds of flesh. She was incredibly hot, deliciously wet and softly swelled. And responsive. He'd never known a woman so needy before, but then she'd been denied the most basic pleasure a man could give a woman for three long years.

She squirmed on his lap, and he fought to control his own urges. Knowing his restraint was near an end, he plowed his fingers into her hair, pulled her sweet lips to his, and gave her the openmouth kiss they'd denied each other earlier. His tongue thrust deeply the same time he pushed his finger into her tight slick sheath.

She stiffened at the invasion, her body clenching around his hand. He didn't stop or relent, but instead found an arousing rhythm with his thumb against that sensitive nub of flesh, using every ounce of his experience to drive her toward a blinding release. She was so primed that three strokes later she came apart in an earth-shattering orgasm.

He tore his mouth from hers, wanting to watch her as she climaxed. Her eyes, at first closed, flew open, staring at him with smoky astonishment at that first ripple of energy. And then the vortex hit, and she moaned and shuddered as she was completely swept away by the thrilling excitement he gave her.

When it was over, she sagged against him, spent and limp. She buried her face against his neck, her breathing ragged. Pure male satisfaction swelled within him, but his body screamed with tension, craving a sexual release that wouldn't be his tonight. Not ever. Not with Samantha. Because to make love with her meant branding his soul with emotions too powerful to contemplate—wants and needs that had no business invading his heart.

He could give Samantha physical pleasure, but he could never be what she needed in her life—a man who was constant and dependable.

That would be Tyler Grayson's job.

CHAPTER TEN

SAMANTHA FLOATED BACK to earth on a cloud of pure bliss. Her entire body hummed with sensual gratification. She felt deliciously satiated, wonderfully voluptuous, and more alive than she could remember being in a very long time.

With her face still resting against Nick's neck, she drew a shuddering breath. The scent of hot male skin filled her senses, making her dizzy, exciting her all over again. Her bared breasts tightened, aching for his insidious touch, the heat and pull of his wet mouth. Beneath the palm she pressed to his chest, his heart beat erratically. Against her bottom, his erection throbbed.

It was exhilarating to realize he wanted her just as badly as she craved him.

Very slowly, his fingers slipped from her body, sliding against still-sensitive flesh, making her gasp in electrifying awareness and arch toward that gradual withdrawal. Much to her disappointment, his hand moved down her thigh and out beneath the hem of her dress, leaving her empty, and still wanting. The incredible pleasure he'd just given her should have been enough, but like an addictive drug she'd been long denied, she wanted—needed—more.

She placed a hot, openmouthed kiss on his neck, then tasted his salty skin with her tongue. She felt him shudder, and the knot in her belly tightened. Her need climbed higher. Lifting her head, she met his dark gaze. With a brazenness long forgotten, she boldly skimmed a hand down his chest, over his taut abdomen, and fitted her palm over the arousal straining between them. Dampening her bottom lip with her tongue, she stroked him through his jeans, making him grow impossibly thicker.

He groaned, low and rough, and grabbed her wrist. But instead of pulling her hand away as she expected, he slid his fingers over hers, trapping her against that incendiary heat, making her squeeze him more snugly. "If you're not careful, you're gonna end up with more than the handful you've got right now."

If he'd meant to shock her, it wasn't possible. She was feeling entirely too shameless to be offended by his comment. Too hungry and needy. Curling her free hand around the nape of his neck, she brought his mouth to hers and initiated a deep kiss that quickly turned ravenous and skirted the edge of their control. That ache built again, making her restless and squirm in a very unladylike manner, until finally he dragged his lips from hers, his breathing harsh.

She trailed kisses along his jaw, to his ear. "Make love to me, Nick," she whispered huskily, even as she knew in doing so she'd be tangling them both up in something more complicated than a brief physical encounter. The only thing in her mind, her heart was the need to be a part of him. "I want you inside me."

He swore, then pulled her hand from his erection, his expression pained, as if he was barely hanging on to his restraint. "Samantha...sweetheart, we can't. I have no protection with me, and I won't risk you that way."

His excuse was rational and chivalrous, yet she suspected his denial went beyond having a condom handy.

She could see the reluctance in his eyes, the regret...the hunger.

Without a doubt, their desire was mutual. She was falling hard and fast and deep for him...in a way that should have scared her, but only made her more determined to experience that wild, thrilling ecstasy he evoked, the sensuality he'd revived.

He'd managed to deny her tonight, but he wouldn't be able to resist her for long.

"WHAT DO YOU THINK of this dress?" Samantha asked.

Sitting in one of the plush chairs set up in the lounge area of the exclusive boutique Samantha had coaxed him into, Nick eyed the outfit in question as she turned this way and that, in front of the three-way mirror. This was the third dress she'd tried on for him. Her ulterior motives for inviting him on this shopping expedition to find something to wear to tonight's dinner party finally dawned on him—she wanted to drive him completely out of his mind with unbridled lust.

He was almost there.

Every dress she'd modeled for him had been far removed from the tailored, conservative outfits she favored, and made him think of sex and sin. With her. In every way imaginable. And every time she returned to the dressing room to change, he mentally followed her inside, skimmed the short hem of the sexy outfit up her thighs, and gave in to the hunger that had been riding him hard since last night.

"Well?" she prompted when he remained silent for too long. "Do you like it?"

What wasn't there to like about a dress that zipped up the front for easy access and sheathed her heavenly body, from breasts to thighs, like a second skin? "It's pretty," he said, playing it safe.

She frowned. "That's what you said about the other two dresses." She glanced in the mirror again, as if trying to figure out why her outfit wasn't provoking the kind of response she was hoping for.

Pure willpower on his part, he thought.

"I have one more to try on," she said, her soft sigh tinged with frustration. "Maybe that dress will rank higher than 'pretty.'"

He shrugged with forced casualness. "Maybe."

Her determined expression didn't bode well for him. Turning around, she presented him with her tantalizing backside as she sashayed toward her dressing room and slipped inside the large cubicle. Releasing a tension-filled breath, he took a long drink of the soda the sales-lady had offered him. The cold liquid did nothing to douse his steadily rising temperature.

He was in big trouble with Samantha. Their escapade last night had unleashed a tigress intent on seducing him. Samantha fairly glowed, her newly awakened confidence showing in the subtle way she flirted and teased with him. And at every opportunity, she touched him, which was enough to make him burn with an agonizing need.

This Samantha was a much different woman from the reserved one he'd met at the bachelor auction a few weeks ago. Impetuous. Passionate. A gorgeous, alluring butterfly who'd burst from her stifling cocoon and wanted to rediscover and test the power of her sexuality—on him.

Last night she'd been clearly disappointed, but understanding, considering he could have made love to her a dozen other erotic ways. Today, she was tempting him with her private, provocative glances—forcing him to endure her new flirtatious behavior without allowing either of them to cross that imaginary line he'd drawn for himself.

Rubbing a hand along his jaw, he nodded politely to the saleslady as she crossed through the lounge area to Samantha's dressing room, a red dress and a shoe box in hand. Five minutes later, Samantha emerged in her latest attempt to make him drool, and he nearly had to swallow the saliva gathering in his mouth.

The dress was the most daring yet, with a neckline that scooped low to reveal just the right amount of cleavage. Judging by the thin straps crisscrossing her bare back, she was braless. The woman had a body that wouldn't quit, and the red stretchy material molding to her luscious curves enhanced every dip and swell she possessed. Strappy red heels completed the head-turning ensemble.

Though the conservative French braid she wore lessened the effect of sexy siren, it wasn't difficult to imagine her hair down around her shoulders, as it had been last night. Her eyes were a vivid shade of blue—bewitching and exciting.

She turned in a circle before him, giving him a full view of the stunning red dress that only a few women could wear with as much panache and style. "You like?"

Oh, yeah, he liked—too much. He sat in his chair calmly, knee crossed over opposite leg, trying like hell to hide the instinctive stirring in his groin. "I'm not sure it's an outfit your intended beau would appreciate."

He'd meant for his comment to yank her back to reality and remind her that Tyler expected a prudent lady who dressed practically, not a temptress who showcased her centerfold curves. Instead, her eyes shone with a reckless light and a smile flitted across that pretty mouth he'd ravished last night.

She turned to the saleslady with confidence. "I'll take the dress, and the heels." As she glanced back at her reflection in the mirror, a look of concern altered her features. With a small frown, she smoothed a hand over the panty line visible through the material clinging to her delectably toned posterior.

"Don't worry, a pair of thong panties will take care of the panty line problem for you," the saleslady assured her with a knowing smile. "And I have a large selection of red lacy ones. Why don't you go ahead and change, then I'll show you where they are."

Ten minutes later, Nick stood beside Samantha in the lingerie section of the boutique while she held up two of the skimpiest, sheerest panties he'd ever seen.

"I can't decide," she said, looking at him, a challenging light in her eyes. "Which pair do you like better?"

"I won't be wearing them," he replied humorously.

"Let me rephrase my question." She tilted her head and moistened her bottom lip with her tongue. "Which pair would you like to *see* on a woman?"

Images of Samantha in nothing but that wisp of red silk and lace filled his head. His blood heated, pooling low in his groin. Glancing at the thong panties in her hand, he bypassed both and selected a different pair made of red stretch lace so sheer she might as well not wear anything at all—which was an extremely intriguing fantasy, as well.

The thong strap was so thin, so dainty, the sexy undies dangled on the tip of his index finger. They were the most risqué of the bunch, and he'd picked them to shock her. "These would definitely play a starring role in my fantasies.'' His voice was low, as intimate as a caress, as dangerous as a naughty dare.

Her cheeks blossomed a becoming shade of pink. Just when he thought she'd relent, she called his bluff and added his selection to her other purchases.

He released a long, slow breath, which did nothing to ease the sexual tension gripping him. The knowledge that she'd be wearing nothing but those wispy panties beneath her dress tonight would no doubt plague his mind and keep his body in a constant state of arousal.

SAMANTHA PINNED HER HAIR atop her head in a loose topknot and pulled a few tendrils free to curl along her neck. The hairstyle softened her face and added to the sensual aura she'd so painstakingly created. The woman in the bathroom mirror was someone she'd hidden for the past three years, but never thought she'd see again. A woman who was sexy and secure, and who embraced life with an open heart.

Nick made her believe she could be that confident woman again, but only if she took chances. Risky chances that could pay off in spades, or destroy the opportunity to grasp a secure future.

She was beginning to realize she wanted both—stability *and* a man who accepted her for her true self.

Pushing a pearl earring into her lobe, she drew a calm, steady breath. For all the courage she'd spent the past hour mustering, her stomach rolled with a wave of anxiety. The cautious Samantha couldn't help but be a bit skeptical, and a whole lot nervous about the night ahead. Her intended was in for a traumatic shock. Samantha harbored no false illusions that Tyler would be impressed with her transformation. Tonight, she'd discover just what kind of emotional strength she possessed.

It all started with the woman in the mirror. A woman wearing a bold, sleek red dress like nothing she'd ever owned before. A woman who looked more like a femme fatale than a refined, conservative lady.

The *real* Samantha.

Slipping into her strappy heels with open toes, she smiled at her bright, strawberry-red toenails. She'd used the same vibrant color to polish her fingernails and had managed to find a matching shade of lipstick—Rebellious Red.

The name, and color, suited Samantha's purpose.

Tonight wasn't so much about defiance but rather the reintroduction of who she was—a confident, passionate woman.

Giving herself one last critical head-to-toe glance in the mirror, she grabbed her small red purse from the bed and headed out of her room and down the hall.

She met up with Nick at the stairs as he left his own suite of rooms. Her breath caught in her chest at the transformation in him. The man was stunning to begin with, but dressed in a navy suit that fit his build to perfection, along with that dashing eye patch of his, he looked every bit as aristocratic as Tyler Grayson—but not as stuffy. No, Nick radiated warmth, and a natural charm that began with the twinkle in his eye and curved his too-sensual mouth. His casual, laid-back attitude was honest and real, and very appealing.

"Nick Petrocelli?" she asked, feigning playful bewilderment. "Is that you inside that suit?"

He grinned and rolled his shoulders, as if the coat felt unfamiliar and burdensome. "Unfortunately, yes."

"Well, you look very handsome." She smoothed a hand down his silk tie, just because she wanted to touch him. Just because she wanted to see the flare of awareness darkening his gaze.

He didn't disappoint her. His smoldering gaze dropped to her mouth, taking in her full lips. "Red is a great color on you."

Splaying a hand on his chest, she felt the heat and hardness of his body through his crisp shirt. Every nerve ending she possessed tingled. Growing more comfortable in her new role, she leaned close to his mouth, teasing him with the promise of a kiss. "Who knows, it could be your color, too," she suggested huskily.

His dark brows shot up in surprise at her seductive comment, but before he could reply, she started down the stairs in her three-inch heels, leaving him to ponder that tantalizing thought.

She heard a low breath escape him, and smiled, maintaining her outward calm and poise. Then he followed her, remaining a few lazy steps behind. She could feel his gaze on her bare back, stroking along her spine, visually caressing the curve of her bottom as she gracefully descended the stairs.

Then he spoke, confirming her feminine intuition. "Either you aren't wearing any underwear, or those panties I picked out did the trick." His voice was low, and filled with male appreciation.

She glanced over her shoulder at him, affecting a sultry smile. "Hmm," she said, leaving him to wonder.

He was quiet for a few heartbeats, then finally said, "Tyler is certainly a lucky man."

Her steps faltered, and he reached out and grabbed her elbow to steady her. His touch branded her. The brush of his fingers against the side of her breast caused her nipples to tighten and ache. His mere presence excited her.

Regaining her composure, she glanced back at him, gratified to see his expression wasn't nearly as impassive as his words had been. "Who says I'm out to impress Tyler tonight?"

His jaw tensed ever so slightly. "You should be."

She wondered who he was trying to convince of that fact—her or himself? Truth be told, she wasn't out to claim Tyler's attention this evening, she wanted Nick's, as foolish as that liaison might be. She wanted to taste more of the passion and excitement he'd given her last night. And when he left her life in a week, she'd resume her role as the reserved Samantha, the woman Tyler expected for a wife.

With a sigh, she disengaged her arm from his grasp and continued her descent to the first floor. "Chances are, Tyler won't appreciate my choice of dress, as you suggested."

Choked laughter sounded from behind her. "Sweetheart, a man would have to be dysfunctional or dead not to appreciate that outfit and you in it."

His compliment stroked her feminine ego, especially when she remembered how remote he'd been at the boutique, and how frustrated she'd been that she hadn't been able to provoke a reaction from him. "So, then you do like the dress?"

This time, his smile was sexy-as-sin honest, his voice velvet and deep. "Yeah, I like your dress. You look…incredible."

His sincere praise was all she needed to inspire her for the evening ahead. She was out to please herself, but she wanted to impress him. With her head held high, she walked into the sitting room where she knew her grandmother would be waiting. And she was, along with Kathryn and Emily.

Kathryn gasped, her gaze widening in disbelief.

Amelia's body turned rigid with shock, her expression a comical sight to behold.

Outwardly, Samantha remained composed and unruffled. Inside, doubts tumbled through her as the oppressing silence in the room closed in on her.

Stick to your convictions. She silently chanted those words, drew strength from them.

Emily finally broke the quiet tension by approaching her. "Mama," she breathed in adoring amazement. "You look so pretty." She stroked her hand over her dress, awed by her mother's metamorphosis. "And you smell good, too."

Samantha smiled gently and caressed her thumb along Emily's soft cheek. "Thank you, sweetie."

Kathryn's initial shock ebbed into delight. "Samantha, you look absolutely stunning. I almost didn't recognize you."

"I have to agree," Amelia said evenly, her gaze sweeping the length of her granddaughter, a tight smile stretching her lips. "But you might want to take a sweater for later, just in case it gets chilly."

Amelia's subtle suggestion wasn't lost on Samantha—wearing a sweater would cover her up and ruin the effect of her dress. One of the things she'd always loved most about her grandmother was that she offered advice freely and candidly, but refrained from judging, leaving it up to the person to make the right decision.

Tonight, Samantha would let the passionate, confident woman in the mirror guide her. "It's a warm night, Grandmother," she said, softening her refusal with a smile. "I'll be fine."

Amelia said no more, but the uncertainty in her gaze spoke volumes.

"Since we're all ready to go, I'll have Victor bring the Rolls around to the front," Samantha said, dismissing the awkward incident. She took a moment to give Emily a hug and kiss, then headed out of the sitting room toward the foyer, a heady sense of power bolstering her spirits.

NICK COULDN'T REMEMBER the last time he'd felt so uncomfortable and out of place as he did at Tyler Grayson's dinner party. Everyone in attendance—and there were at least three dozen people—reeked of old money. The men had no qualms talking about their finances and net worth in casual conversation, and the women flaunted their husband's money in the extravagant jewels and designer outfits they wore.

He had absolutely nothing in common with any of these people, and though they were polite enough when Samantha introduced him, he got the distinct impression that this elite group of snobs were merely tolerating him out of consideration for Amelia. His eye patch had caused a certain amount of intrigue and interest from the single women in the crowd, but he'd headed off their flirtatious advances and come-ons.

The only woman that appealed to him was the one in the vibrant, head-turning red dress. The one who was off limits to him.

The small gathering of people around him making small talk for his benefit gradually dispersed for more important connections. Finding himself blessedly alone, Nick strolled to the buffet table and glanced at the array of food. He'd eaten shortly after they arrived, and though he'd feasted on the most delicious seafood, exotic delicacies and extravagant side dishes ever to grace his lips, he would have been happier eating a cheeseburger and washing it down with a bottle of beer.

He would have been happier if he'd stayed back at Cranberry Harbor with Kathryn, Victor and Emily.

Filching a few of the desserts on the table, he took his plate and found himself an inconspicuous corner where he could be alone and watch the party and guests, which he found more entertaining than the live band Tyler had hired for the evening. He took a bite of some kind of flaky chocolate pastry, and his gaze unerringly found Samantha. She stood with Tyler across the elegant ballroom, where he laughed and conversed with his guests—leaving her out of the conversation for the most part.

She looked miserable, and something near the vicinity of his heart squeezed tight. She'd been right. Tyler hadn't appreciated her new appearance—his tight frown had expressed his disapproval more than any words could.

Because Samantha had been invited to the dinner party as Tyler's date, decorum dictated she stay by his side. Nick had eaten dinner seated next to Amelia, who had remarked that it was a good idea Samantha and Tyler be seen publicly together, as a couple, to reestablish their relationship. Nick had verbally agreed, but deep inside he hadn't been able to shake the notion that Tyler was completely wrong for her. Samantha needed someone secure, without a doubt, but not a man who would stifle her creativity and passionate nature, as Tyler would.

He told himself Samantha's relationship with Grayson wasn't his concern, but his mind refused to process the lecture.

Finished with the melt-in-your-mouth pastry, he

licked the smudges of cream filling from his fingers. The
band played a slow ballad, and Nick watched Tyler escort Samantha out to the dance floor and pull her close.
While Samantha strained to put inches of space between
them, it seemed that after a few glasses of champagne,
Tyler had changed his tune about Samantha's dress and
wanted to feel her lush curves against him. He placed a
hand low on her spine, forcing her body flush with his
and establishing an illusion of intimacy that clearly made
Samantha uncomfortable. The more she seemed to resist,
the more pressure Tyler seemed to exert.

Jealousy and anger mingled, clawing at Nick like a
live thing. He couldn't squash the strong, territorial urge
to rip Tyler's arms off his body so he couldn't touch
Samantha. He was a cool, levelheaded cop, yet at the
moment he felt raw and savage—and a whole lot violent.

As if his own gamut of emotions wasn't enough for
him to deal with, Samantha's gaze found him, a silent
plea in its depths. *Aw, hell.* She wanted him to cut in on
her dance and save her from Tyler's stifling embrace,
but he couldn't, not without risking speculation about
their relationship, and possibly damaging her reputation.
She had to deal with these people, and their opinion of
her, long after he left her life and headed back to New
York.

Instead of the anticipation he usually experienced
when he thought about returning to his job, he felt an
odd twist of panic, as if he'd be leaving something behind more important than his position with the DEA.
Knowing how impossible and foolhardy it was to even
think in those terms, or allow his emotions to tangle up
the solitary life he'd created for himself, he banished that
thought right out of his mind.

The hardest thing he'd ever had to do was turn around

and walk away from Samantha at that moment, but he did. He needed to get the hell out of the ballroom, which had turned suffocating. Heading down a long hallway in search of the rest room, he tried to shake the strange tension gripping him.

Nick took care of nature's call, but had no desire to return to the ballroom and watch Tyler with Samantha. As he contemplated what he was going to do, he headed back down the hall and casually glanced inside an open door. He came to an abrupt stop, mesmerized by the collection of antique arms gracing the paneled walls and built-in shelves in the room.

Fascinated, he stepped inside. The interior smelled like rich cigars, leather and money. Within minutes, he was completely engrossed in the detail and excellent condition of the many swords, shields and daggers. Engraved plates described each of Grayson's investments, stating the name and origin of the collectible piece.

"I was wondering where you'd disappeared to."

Startled by Samantha's voice, he turned around, watching as she walked into the room, her heels clicking on the hardwood floor. "I had to use the rest room, and on my way back I saw all this stuff. It beckoned to my military background."

She smiled, the gesture tentative. "Mind if I keep you company for a while?"

If they didn't have a whole ballroom of people to contend with, he would have told her yes. But he had no desire to fuel gossip with a lengthy absence on both their parts. "That might not be such a good idea."

"Just for a few minutes, please?" Desperation tinged her voice. "I just need some time away from Tyler, and the balcony is too obvious a place to hide."

He rubbed at the back of his neck, indecision warring

within him. She obviously wasn't enjoying herself at this party, either, and he found he couldn't refuse her. "A few minutes," he relented. "And then we go back to the ballroom separately."

She nodded her gratitude, and like old friends, they perused the objects in the room, commenting on various antiques, sharing their thoughts. Time ticked by. Open doorways within the room led to other chambers, where more treasures abounded. Nick was having such a good time with Samantha that when he glanced at his watch a while later, he was shocked to realize forty minutes had passed, and he had no idea where in the huge mansion they were.

"We'd better get back before someone comes looking for us, if they haven't already," he suggested. Opening the main door to the room they were in, he encountered a hallway that split in two different directions. With Samantha following, he turned left, then left again, and down a flight of stairs. They came to a stop when the corridor ended with a closed door.

Curious, he opened it and flipped on the light. "Have a bottle of wine, why don't you," he muttered, amazed and impressed at yet another one of Tyler's private collections. Gleaming wooden racks against the walls held rows and rows of bottles of wine, more than Nick could count at a glance.

"This must be Tyler's prized wine cellar he told me about at dinner the other night," she said, crowding against Nick from behind to take a look for herself.

He ground his teeth at the fever spreading through his body. "I've never been in a wine cellar myself." And since he most likely would never get the chance again, and he needed to put some distance between him and Samantha, he stepped inside.

The room was temperature-controlled, set at a cool fifty-five degrees, according to the fancy gauge on the wall. Next to that was a mahogany-and-glass case displaying an array of fancy corkscrews. There was an ivory-handled one, another with mother of pearl and some with precious gems. The collection was definitely a pricey "look, don't touch" display.

Samantha entered, too, and the heavy door clicked shut behind her, making the cellar feel like a tomb. "It's chilly in here." She rubbed her arms in an attempt to chase away the goose bumps rising on her skin. Unfortunately, there wasn't much she could do about the erect nipples pushing against the front of her dress.

Nick pried his gaze away from the tempting sight. Hell, his body was generating enough heat for the both of them, and if they didn't get out of there, he was going to be inclined to share that warmth. "We've played around long enough. It's past time we got you back to the ballroom."

"You're right, of course," she said with a resigned sigh. She glanced at the delicate gold watch on her wrist. "Maybe we can make our excuses in about half an hour and leave."

"Sounds good to me." He grinned and reached for the doorknob, which made an awful grinding sound when he pushed it down. Tumblers snapped, dissolving the tension in the latch.

He swore, a sense of foreboding swirling around him.

"What's wrong?" Samantha asked, her expression concerned.

The corner of his mouth kicked up in a humorous grin, though there was nothing laughable about their situation. "The lock mechanism just broke. It looks like we're stuck in here."

CHAPTER ELEVEN

SAMANTHA STARED AT NICK, undisguised panic in her blue eyes. "Now what do we do?"

Remaining calm, he flashed her a reassuring grin. "We wait until someone finds us."

"Which could be *hours*." Her voice rose a hysterical notch. "You're a cop. Can't you think of something to get the door open?"

"I deal with criminals, not broken locks. You know I'm not much of a handyman." He strove for humor, anything to chase away the fright tensing her features. "However, if I had my gun with me, I could shoot the door open like you see in the movies."

She groaned, and her teeth began to chatter. Wrapping her arms over her chest, she hugged herself tight. "I'll freeze to death before someone finds us."

"Maybe you should have brought a sweater, after all."

A shiver shook her and raised gooseflesh on her arms. "I wasn't planning on getting locked in a wine cellar," she replied, her voice calming to a wry tone.

Taking off his jacket, he draped it over her shoulders. She smiled gratefully and snuggled into the warmth. "Thanks."

He eyed her long, bare legs. "You want my pants, too?"

"Not yet, though I appreciate the chivalrous offer."

Hands on his hips, he surveyed the impressive racks of wine. "Since we now have no immediate plans, why don't we share a bottle of wine and enjoy ourselves?" he suggested. "We could have our own private wine-tasting party."

She shook her head, though her eyes sparkled with mischief. "You're crazy."

"Just trying to keep us in good spirits." He grinned at his clever pun. "Get it? Good *spirits,* the wine?"

She rolled her eyes and flipped the collar of the coat up around her bare neck. "Yeah, I get it."

"So, you up for some wine? If anything, it'll help warm you up." He banished the more conventional way to generate heat—the friction of skin on skin.

"I suppose it couldn't hurt," she said, and shimmied with another shiver. "Though you don't strike me as the wine type."

"I'm strictly a beer kind of guy, but I'm not above broadening my horizons." He glanced back at the vast array of wines. "Red or white? Which do you prefer?"

"It doesn't matter. I'm not much into wine, either."

Another thing she and Grayson didn't have in common. Keeping that observation to himself, Nick closed his eyes and reached out, blindly selecting a bottle.

"What did you pick?" she asked, coming up beside him.

The perfume she'd worn was subtle, but no less arousing as it swirled around him, intoxicating him, making him think of every pulse point she might have dabbed that fragrance on.

With effort, he concentrated on reading the label. "This says Dom. Romanee Conti, 1995. Never heard of the guy," he said with a grin. "And it's only a few years old, so I guess it can't be too bad, or too expensive."

Since there was only one way to open the bottle, he retrieved the ivory-handled corkscrew from the display case and removed the cork. He sniffed the opening, then shrugged. The contents smelled like regular wine to him.

Samantha glanced around the small room. "There aren't any glasses."

"Then we drink it the old-fashioned way, straight from the bottle." He lowered himself to the parquet floor, bracing his back against the wall, then patted the smooth wooden surface beside him. "Come and sit down. There's nothing we can do until someone finds us. We might as well make ourselves comfortable."

After a moment's hesitation, she carefully lowered herself to the floor next to him and curled her long legs to the side. Like finely honed radar, his gaze automatically zeroed in on the smooth, tanned skin revealed as her already-short dress inched higher up her thighs. He thought about those red panties she was wearing...or not wearing, and felt an all-too-familiar tightening in his groin.

He forced his gaze to safer territory—her face, except her mouth made him think about how honey-sweet she tasted, made him fantasize about her lips and tongue and all those sensual delights he wanted to explore.

Wrapping his fingers around the bottle, he lifted it toward her. "How about a toast?"

She tilted her head engagingly, and a silky strand of hair slipped from her topknot and brushed across her cheek. "To what?"

"To an adventurous evening."

Her eyes crinkled at the corners, and she took the bottle from his grasp. "I'll drink to that." She swallowed a tentative taste of the red wine and, deciding she liked it, took a deeper drink.

She passed the bottle back to him, and he took a swig. The wine went down smooth, without the bitter aftertaste he'd expected. The alcohol warmed his belly and spread through his veins.

"And for being daring," he suggested, enjoying the delight in her eyes.

"Here, here!" She filled her mouth with more wine, leaving a pale red sheen of moisture on her lips he ached to lick off.

The toasts continued until they'd consumed the entire bottle of wine. "And for looking like such a knockout and making half the men in the ballroom drool like Saint Bernards," he continued, adding to their long list of excuses to hail.

She laughed, the husky, languorous sound filling the small cellar. "I did no such thing!"

"Did so," he countered.

Looking away, she tugged primly on the hem of her skirt. "I think I shocked everyone with my new appearance."

"Oh, without a doubt," he agreed.

She sighed, and apparently sufficiently warmed by the wine, she let his jacket slip off her bare shoulders. "There's a whole lot to be said for practical," she observed.

"Oh?"

She bit her lush bottom lip. "My new shoes are killing my feet with all those straps, and this sophisticated hairstyle is about to come tumbling down." She blew at the unruly strand against her cheek, which did nothing to tame it.

"Then kick off your shoes and let your hair down."

She glanced at him skeptically, though he could tell the idea intrigued her.

"It might be a while before anyone finds us, so we might as well make ourselves comfortable, right?" He tugged on the knot of his tie and loosened it, encouraging her to be just as relaxed.

After a moment, she slipped off her shoes, wiggled her cramped toes and groaned in relief. Then she reached up, pulled the pins from her hair and shook her head. The thick mass fell to her shoulders in a glorious disarray.

He swallowed back the thick knot of desire gathering in his chest, but couldn't stop the words that came to mind. "Men are suckers for women with long, thick hair they can bury their hands into." Especially him. "You shouldn't hide yours in a braid all the time."

Her cheeks flushed at the compliment, and she glanced away. Picking up the wine, she went to take a drink and frowned when she realized the bottle was empty. "Do you think we could have more?"

He could tell by the soft, hazy look in her eyes that she was feeling the effects of the first bottle. "One more, then I'm cutting you off."

Playing it safe, he opened the same vintage. Samantha's ladylike sips turned into long, easy swallows. Nick attempted to keep their conversation light and amusing over the next hour, and their minds off the sexual awareness that was simmering between them. Their situation was ripe with possibilities, and he'd even received a few subtle signals from Samantha that she'd welcome an advance, a kiss, a touch, or something even more intimate.

Resisting her took all of his strength.

Sometime later, a devious light brightened her eyes. "Do you know how to burp?" she asked, the question slow and lazy.

"Excuse me?"

She blinked drowsily, her expression serious. "You know, one of those deep, belly-rumbling belches men do so well."

He couldn't contain the laughter rising within him. "Yeah, I can burp like that." He'd learned that particular trick as a kid, living at Lost Springs with dozens of other rowdy boys. Boys would be boys, after all, and having contests to see who could belch the loudest and longest had been a favorite sport.

"Teach me how," she insisted. Just in case he had in mind to refuse her, she leaned close and looked up at him with those big blue eyes of hers. "Pretty please, Nick?"

He stared at her lips, scant inches from his, parted and curved into a beguiling smile. Oh, man, the night stretched endlessly ahead of him. "And what would you do with a very unladylike trick like burping?"

"Shock Tyler at the dinner table?" She giggled at the thought.

She was tipsy, and completely, utterly adorable. Amused at her request, and knowing it would keep them occupied for a while longer, he taught Samantha the fine art of drawing air into her stomach and releasing it in a loud belch. With practice, she expelled some of the finest, rudest burps he'd ever heard. The time between them was silly, filled with her fits of giggles and his low laughter.

A rattling at the door interrupted their fun. Her eyes rounded. "Someone's here," she said in a dramatic whisper, and scrambled to her hands and knees to stand.

More inebriated than he'd realized, she wobbled off balance, and he caught her before she toppled over. "You stay put," he ordered.

With a carefree shrug, she sat back down, let her head

loll against the wall, and continued practicing her belching.

Nick went to the door. "Whoever is there, we're stuck in here."

A pause, then a deep, distinctive angry male voice came from the other side of the door. "It's Tyler."

"The lock mechanism broke," Nick explained. "You're going to need a screwdriver to take off the lock and get the door open."

"Is Samantha in there with you?" Tyler demanded.

Nick pinched the bridge of his nose with his fingers, knowing he'd have some explaining to do about being in the wine cellar in the first place, let alone with Samantha as his companion. He wondered if Tyler would believe the truth, that they'd just been exploring and had wandered off in the wrong direction. They'd done absolutely nothing wrong or indecent.

One glance at Samantha's mussed hair, her flushed face and wrinkled dress, and he knew Tyler would think the worst.

"Yeah, she's in here."

The man on the other side of the door swore vividly, then there was silence as he left to retrieve the tools needed to get them out. Fifteen minutes later, Tyler managed to remove the lock and pry open the door. He stepped inside, flanked by two other men from the party, none of whom seemed to see the humor in the situation.

Tyler's frenzied gaze cut from Nick to Samantha, taking in her disheveled state. "Good God," he breathed, censure evident in his tone. "Everybody is now aware that the two of you have been locked in my wine cellar for the past two hours. Do you have any idea how this makes me look in front of my guests?"

"This isn't what you're thinking, Grayson." Before

Nick could explain what had brought them to the cellar, an innocent excursion, Tyler cut him off.

He pointed an accusing finger at Samantha. "You're drunk," he said.

Her brow wrinkled in thought. "I only had a few drinks of wine."

More than a few, but Nick wasn't going to argue her point.

Her spine straightened defensively. "I can still touch my finger with my nose." The pad of her index finger smacked her right between the eyes, and she frowned.

If the situation wasn't so dire, Nick would have laughed. She looked so indignant, and so damned cute.

Tyler disagreed with a snort. "This must be your doing, Petrocelli. I thought a cop had morals."

The two men still standing behind Tyler echoed his sentiment, glaring at Nick as if he was some depraved criminal.

"We did nothing wrong except drink a couple of bottles of wine, which you've got plenty of."

Tyler stalked to where Samantha still sat, picked up the empty bottles from the floor and read the labels. His curse was low and ripe and enraged. "You drank *two* three thousand dollar bottles of wine!" he bellowed, stomping his foot like a spoiled child.

"And they were good, too," Samantha drawled, complimenting Tyler with a deep, prize-winning belch.

That's my girl, Nick thought. Biting back his amused grin, he decided the cost of the wine was well worth the expression of comical disgust that flooded Tyler's expression.

SAMANTHA WOKE the following morning with the worst hangover she could ever remember—not that she'd suffered many, but this one was certainly a doozy.

With a low, agonized moan, she rolled to her side, away from the sun streaming in through her window, which only increased the pounding just behind her eyelids. Her mouth felt dry, as if someone had stuffed it with cotton, and she didn't even want to think about her stomach, which rolled like a storm-tossed sea.

She was never going to touch another glass of wine in her life.

Last night floated back to her in fragments. Tyler's dinner party. Getting locked in Tyler's wine cellar with Nick. Drinking too much. Learning to belch. Giggling. Tyler finding them. Nick helping her out to the car...and then nothing.

She caught the scent of something...tomatoes? The strong citrusy odor caused her stomach to rebel, and a pathetic groan escaped her dry lips.

"Come on, sweetheart, wake up," a wonderful, rich male voice coaxed. A cool hand caressed her cheek and smoothed her hair away from her face. "Just drink this and you'll start to feel better real soon."

She forced one eye open, and grimaced when she saw her rakish pirate hunkered by the side of her bed. She had to look as awful as she felt, and he looked as gorgeous as ever, his eye twinkling with sympathetic humor.

"Go away," she muttered, and attempted to draw the covers over her aching head.

He chuckled, low and deep, and pulled them back down. "I will, in a minute. But first you need to drink this."

She narrowed her gaze on the glass in front of her, filled with a thick, dark red liquid. Her throat closed up, her belly already refusing whatever it was he offered. "What is it?"

He grinned at her skepticism. "Trust me, you don't want to know, but I promise it'll help cure what ails you."

She moaned as another piercing pain seized her brain. "Just shoot me and put me out of my misery." She struggled to sit up, and the room spun. Glancing down, she was surprised to see that she was still wearing her red dress. Had Nick put her to bed last night? She couldn't remember that, either.

"Come on, drink this." He pushed the pillows against the headboard and eased her against them. "It's after eleven, and you need to get yourself in the shower."

She did as he ordered and drank his thick concoction in long swallows, desperately trying not to gag and make the situation worse than it already was. A shudder racked her body, and she sagged against the pillows.

She tried remembering more details about last night, but couldn't recall anything beyond Nick helping her out to the car and her collapsing in the back seat.

Dread filled her, and she looked at Nick to confirm her awful suspicions. "I passed out last night, didn't I."

"Yep." Merriment danced across his features. "As soon as I got you in the car, you let out a loud belch that stunned Amelia, and then you passed out cold."

She groaned in pure mortification, her cheeks burning with shame. "Did Amelia say anything to you on the ride home?"

"She was concerned about you," he admitted, but didn't reveal any details of their conversation.

The thought of disappointing her grandmother bothered her the most. "What have I done?" she moaned in dismay, and buried her face in her hands.

He pried her fingers away, and she met his compassionate gaze. "You had a little too much to drink," he said gently. "It happens to the best of us sometimes. Don't be so hard on yourself."

Unfortunately, the situation wasn't that simple for her. "I shouldn't have been that careless or impulsive. I *know* better," she said, self-condemnation lacing her voice.

She remembered Tyler's anger. If she'd acted more responsibly, this fiasco never would have happened. But she'd been feeling reckless and bold and so wonderfully impetuous...and now she had to figure out a way to repair the damage she'd done, to her relationship with Tyler and possibly to her reputation.

Most of all, this crazy incident proved that she couldn't allow herself to relax her control even one little bit. She was a woman of extremes, not moderation, just like her mother. She needed a staid man like Tyler to keep her from making such outrageous mistakes. And in return, Tyler would expect the decorous woman she'd attempted to mold herself into over the past three years...a woman who would always struggle with the need to experience excitement, desire and that thrilling rush of abandon, but who would not give in.

She closed her eyes and thought of forever abstaining from that exhilarating passion she'd recently rediscovered.... A passion she'd shared with Nick, a man who made her feel vibrantly alive, excited, and too reckless.

A man she was falling in love with, but who represented everything she'd denied herself since Justin's death.

"Hey, you okay?" Nick's voice was concerned. The fingers that brushed her cheek were achingly gentle.

Swallowing hard, she lifted her lashes, unable to stop the rush of emotion that constricted her chest. When had any man worried or cared about her? Never. But Nick's brand of tenderness was something she'd yearned for all her life. His touch was soothing, his deep voice understanding. He was a perfect combination of strength, gentleness and sensuality.

"I'll be fine." And she would be, for Emily's sake. Tossing off the covers, she moved to the edge of the bed, determined to make amends with Amelia, whom she no doubt had disappointed. "I think I'll take that shower you suggested."

With a nod, he straightened. "Good idea. I'll see you downstairs."

Forty minutes later, showered, changed and feeling more presentable, Samantha headed to the first floor and found everyone gathered in the dining area eating lunch. Kathryn had made chicken Caesar salads, mixed fruit and bread sticks. After drinking Nick's tomato concoction, she had to admit she felt halfway human again, and her nausea was gone, but she wasn't entirely sure she wanted to eat solid food.

Sliding into her chair, she smiled at the occupants sitting at the table, noticing Nick's warm smile the most. "Good afternoon, everyone," she greeted amicably.

"Hello, Samantha." Kathryn eyed her with a mixture of curiosity and amusement, making Samantha wonder if her aunt had seen her when she'd come home last night. Most likely she had. Unfortunately, Samantha couldn't remember if she'd walked into the house on her own, or if someone had had to carry her to her room. Since her memory remained blank, she suspected the latter.

Amelia stabbed her fork into her salad. "I'm glad you could join us for lunch," she said pleasantly.

Samantha's chest constricted as she glanced across the

table to Amelia. Much to her relief, there was no criticism in her grandmother's gaze. No, Samantha suspected Amelia knew how much self-condemnation her granddaughter was experiencing. Amelia wasn't one to compound misery or blame, and preferred to let one's conscience follow its own course, which was usually worse. Still, Samantha hated the fact that she'd disappointed Amelia.

Emily grinned up at her, her eyes sparkling happily, oblivious to her mother's inner turmoil. "You were a sleepyhead this morning, Mama."

Samantha placed a kiss on her daughter's brow and inhaled her sweet little-girl scent. "Yes, I was," she agreed.

Emily bit into a piece of chicken and chewed. "Mr. Nick said not to wake you because you weren't feeling well, so we went outside and played."

She cast Nick a grateful look for keeping Emily occupied this morning, and he acknowledged her with a subtle nod. "No, I wasn't feeling well, but I'm better now." Reaching for the bowl of fresh fruit, she put a spoonful on her plate, then added a bread stick, which was all her stomach could manage.

Lunch continued amid casual conversation about the garden party plans, which were coming along smoothly. With a soft, telling blush, Kathryn reported that the table diagram she and Victor had worked on was just about finished. Amelia expressed surprise that her daughter and Victor were working on the project together, but there was something in the older woman's gaze that seemed to approve of the growing friendship between the two.

As if by silent agreement, everyone skirted the subject of last night's embarrassing incident, and though Samantha was grateful for the diversion, she knew it was inevitable she address the issue. It couldn't be ignored, and she owed her grandmother an apology for her irresponsible behavior.

She waited until lunch was over and Kathryn and Emily were in the kitchen doing the dishes. She spoke before she lost her nerve, or Nick excused himself. It was important to her to let him know she regretted the incident and couldn't allow something so scandalous to happen again. "Grandmother, I'd like to apologize for what happened last night at Tyler's."

Amelia's gaze softened with the same gentle compassion that spanned the past twenty years of Samantha's life. "You don't owe *me* an apology, dear."

More than anyone, Amelia understood Samantha's internal struggle with the restlessness she'd inherited from Lucinda, and had always exerted patience with that shortcoming.

Samantha's hands twisted in her lap. "Getting locked in Tyler's wine cellar was an accident."

"I don't doubt you for a minute." Amelia's pale gaze flickered from Samantha to Nick, then back again. "Unfortunately, the incident did stir up some gossip, which stung Tyler's pride. I also know he wasn't happy about the loss of two very expensive bottles of wine."

Samantha winced, remembering very clearly the outrageous price of the wine she and Nick had consumed.

"I'm to blame for opening the wine," Nick cut in. "I'll pay for it."

"I've already handled the expense, Mr. Petrocelli." Amelia leaned back in her chair, her gaze unwavering as it met Samantha's. "I do hope you don't plan on teaching that burping trick to your daughter."

Samantha's face heated in embarrassment. "No, I don't."

"I'm relieved." She smiled faintly. "As for Tyler, you can apologize to him personally when he picks you and Emily up Tuesday to take you to the Seascape carnival."

"He still wants to see me?" Samantha wasn't sure how she felt about that. Her heart seemed to be torn into a huge mass of confusing, conflicting emotions. Her newfound feelings for Nick clashed within her, shaking up the very foundation of what she believed she wanted in her life.

"Of course he still wants to see you," Amelia assured her. "He's not happy about this mishap, but your apology will go a long way in restoring your relationship."

As always, her grandmother offered her advice, leaving the final decision up to her. And for the second time in Samantha's life, she found herself struggling between making the right or wrong choice.

CHAPTER TWELVE

WITH A DISGUSTED SIGH, Samantha dropped her paintbrush into a jar of solvent and started cleaning up her studio. For the first time ever, she found no solace in her painting. After lunch and her discussion with Amelia, she'd gone up to her studio in hopes of burning off the restless energy clamoring within her, but her efforts were useless. Her mind was too preoccupied with her fear of making the wrong choice again.

Once everything was cleaned and put away, she moved to the window overlooking the beach, trying to resolve her inner turmoil. Tyler was predictable and secure, just what she and Emily needed in their lives. Nick was exciting and reckless, everything that tempted her, but what she'd fought to resist since Justin's death. Nick had admitted he wasn't the committing kind, which should make Tyler's stability all the more appealing.

"Marrying Tyler is the right thing to do," she said aloud, as if hearing the words would convince herself of the fact.

"Tyler doesn't deserve you, and you deserve better."

Samantha whirled around at the sound of Nick's voice, her heart pounding in her chest. She'd been so caught up in her thoughts, she hadn't heard him enter her studio. How long had he been standing there, watching her?

He strolled farther into the room, moving slowly toward her, his gaze intense. "Last night proved that Tyler will never accept you for who you really are."

"Last night proved I can't trust my own judgment, and I can't allow myself to be impulsive and impetuous." Her voice ached with the knowledge. "I'm too much like my own mother, and I refuse to let Emily suffer because of my own selfish desires."

"Take a look around you, Samantha." He swept a hand around the room, indicating her provocative paintings. "*This* is who you are...a sensual, passionate woman. You always will be. Tyler might give you the security you and Emily need, but you'll grow restless with him, and possibly even resent him and your marriage because of it."

She shook her head, denying one of the fears that had been tumbling through her own mind but she couldn't bring herself to vocalize.

"You don't love him," he stated, stopping in front of her, so close she could feel the heat of him.

Lying to Nick would be ludicrous. "No, I don't love him, and there is no passion between us. But that's for the best, because I won't get so caught up in that wild rush of emotions that I forget the things that are most important to me."

Nick's gaze narrowed. "So you're just going to repress that part of you for the rest of your life, then?"

Samantha ignored his question. "I *need* stability," she answered instead, her misery tightening into a huge, painful knot inside her. "I never really had love with Justin, just passion, and look where that got me."

His nostrils flared, and he seemed to seethe with frustration. Unexpectedly, his hand shot out, curled around the base of her head and yanked her to him. His mouth crushed hers without warning, and her lips parted on a gasp of shock and surprise. His tongue thrust deep, claiming her, possessing her. She didn't resist.

He filled her with passion. He made her ache with desire. She softened and melted, responding with a hunger that equaled his own. When he finally dragged his mouth from hers, they were both breathing raggedly.

His features were dark, tormented and very vulnerable. "How can you deny *that?*" He bit the words out furiously, then turned and stalked out of the studio.

Knees still trembling weakly from his sudden assault, she touched her fingers to her wet, swollen lips.

With Nick, she tasted the forbidden passion she yearned for. With him, she hungered for that physical connection that fused hearts and souls.

With Nick, she'd fallen deeply, irrevocably in love.

THERE WAS ONLY ONE WAY to end the temptation, the madness, the craving and need she harbored for Nick. As for the love, she knew it was something she'd live with for the rest of her life.

Tying the sash on her ankle-length robe a little tighter, Samantha crept quietly down the corridor to Nick's suite. It was after eleven at night, the house was eerily silent, and she hoped that Nick was still up. If not, she planned to awaken him, though she was positive her unexpected presence in his room would put him on full alert. What she had in mind would no doubt shock him, and hopefully arouse him.

Considering she was about to blatantly seduce the man, she felt surprisingly calm and confident. She wanted him, and knew the desire was mutual. She wasn't going to take no for an answer. Tonight, she planned to make her intentions clear, verbally and physically. She'd even driven to the drugstore that afternoon to pick up a box of condoms so he wouldn't use that handy excuse, either.

She wanted this one night with Nick, wanted to indulge in the passion and desire she'd felt with him. She would take only what he would willingly give her. His body. Pleasure. Ecstasy.

She stopped at his closed bedroom door. Inside, she could hear the muted sounds of a late-night TV program. She remembered the way he'd kissed her that afternoon in her studio, so hungrily, so desperately. *So possessively.* By the time she was done with him tonight, he'd never forget her. She planned to brand him the same way he'd branded her heart and soul. He'd reawakened her sexual nature, and he was about to reap the benefits.

Without knocking, she boldly entered his bedroom, shut the door behind her and locked it with a soft "click." His gaze jerked to her in surprise, his expression cautious, his body tensing with an acute awareness that excited her all the more.

She couldn't blame him for being wary of her brazen entrance. He was sitting upright on the big four-poster bed dominating the room, his long legs stretched out on the mattress. The pillows propped against the headboard cushioned his back as he watched the TV in front of him. He was naked, except for a pair of striped boxer shorts. He wore nothing else to hinder the sight of all that glorious male flesh, from his broad chest to his flat belly, hard thighs and muscular calves. And she wanted to explore it all. He'd taken off his eye patch, and the light from the bedside lamp made his green eyes glitter with a sudden predatory zeal as he surveyed the hair that fell down around her shoulders and traced her curves through her cotton robe.

Something deep in her belly fluttered, and her pulse

quickened like liquid lightning through her veins. Pushing away from the door, she headed toward the television, not wanting any distractions for what she intended.

"What are you doing here?" he asked, watching her progress across the room, a frown marring his brow.

"I couldn't sleep," she said, her voice low and husky. "I kept thinking about the way you kissed me this afternoon, and the difference between your kisses and others I've—"

"I never should have kissed you like that," he interrupted gruffly.

"But you did." She snapped off the TV, throwing the room into more intimate shadows. "And I won't let you take it back, nor will I accept an apology for it."

He remained motionless, but his gaze was very direct, and arrestingly male. "Then what do you want?"

Her heart beat frantically beneath her breast at his question, not in fear, but in anticipation. Her taut, aching nipples grazed the soft cotton of her robe, and she imagined his damp mouth on them, soothing the tingling tips with his tongue.

Starting toward his side of the bed, she summoned a sultry smile. "I want to finish what that kiss started. I want to make love with you."

Nick blew out a harsh breath as he stared at the apparition approaching him—a sensual, desirable woman who had the ability to make him weak with a longing he'd sworn years ago he'd never succumb to again. Yet here he was, a drowning man with no life preserver in sight.

She wore her thick, rich hair down around her shoulders, a tumble of silk that beckoned to him. Her robe wasn't the sexiest thing he'd ever seen on a woman, but he was more interested in what it concealed—generous curves and soft, sleek skin he wanted to touch with his hands, tease with his fingers, taste with his tongue.

He nearly groaned at the mere thought. What she was asking for, he wanted more than his next breath. But she wasn't the kind of woman who gave her body casually, and he wasn't the kind of man who made promises...so why in the hell was he even entertaining the notion of making love with her?

He tried to end her seduction, grasping for the most logical excuse to end this insanity, yet not hurt or humiliate her in any way. "Samantha, I already told you the other night that I don't have any protection with me."

She stopped next to the mattress, an arm's length away. The determination in her eyes was unmistakable. "I won't take no for an answer, Nick." Reaching into the pocket of her robe, he heard a crinkling sound, then she presented a handful of foil packets, which she tossed onto the pillows next to him.

He cursed, feeling himself slipping deeper under her spell. And the thing was, he didn't want to escape, didn't want to send her away when he craved her so badly.

"I want you," she whispered, slowly untying her sash, then letting her robe part a few inches to tantalize him with a glimpse of her full, bare breasts and those skimpy red panties he'd picked out for her at the boutique. They framed her femininity in a delectable V, and were so sheer he could see the dense curls beneath.

A hot rush of blood made his manhood rise and throb. She noticed and licked her lips, nearly killing him with that sensual gesture. He didn't dare move, didn't breathe for fear of doing something completely uncouth, like jumping off the bed, pushing her against the wall and taking her without the finesse she deserved.

"Desire and passion," she repeated, and with a delicate shrug of her shoulders, the material slid down her arms and pooled around her feet, revealing all of her to his gaze without an ounce of modesty. "I want it all, and I want it with you. Just tonight, one night."

He sucked in a sharp breath at her words, at the heavenly body that was his for the taking. Had he ever seen such perfection before? If so, he couldn't recall. At the moment, the only woman in his mind, filling his senses, surrounding his heart, was Samantha.

There would never be another.

His heart thundering with the knowledge, he forced his gaze from her pale, full breasts to her face, now flushed with sexual excitement. Her eyes were dark with expectation, hungry for his approval. Still, he knew he had to be completely honest with her. "I can't make you any promises, Samantha."

"I don't want any promises beyond tonight," she said, understanding and accepting his terms. Sliding up onto the bed, she moved over him, straddling his lap so her knees bracketed his hips and her breasts swayed in front of his face, enticing him. "Just give me tonight, Nick."

He wanted to give her the rest of his life but knew he had nothing substantial to offer her. With a deep, internal shudder, he surrendered to her. "Tell me what you want."

Grabbing his hands, she placed them on the swell of her waist, just above the thin strap of her thong panties. "I want you to touch me...everywhere." Her fingers skimmed across his lips, and he nipped gently at the tips. "I want you to kiss me...everywhere." She slid her fingers along his jaw and around, to the nape of his neck...then drew his mouth slowly, inexorably to her breast. "And I want to watch you while you're doing it."

Her eyes only managed to remain open for a second, just long enough for her to watch his mouth claim her nipple. With the first stroke of his tongue across the hardened nub, the tentative grazing of his teeth over the tip, she shivered and tossed her head back, a sexy moan escaping her throat. Her eyes closed, and she arched into him, her thighs clamping around his hips instinctively.

With a whimper, she cradled him against her breast. He suckled her more fully, using the soft lapping of his tongue to increase her pleasure. He slid his hands up her back, drawing her closer, pulling her deeper into his embrace, fusing them in every way but the most primitive. Beneath her bottom, he swelled with a painful pressure, could feel the heat and dampness of her through his cotton boxers and her flimsy panties.

Her breathing turned erratic. She moved on his lap, rubbing against him rhythmically, searching impatiently for that searing release awaiting her. Knowing what she needed, he stroked his palms up her smooth, quivering thighs. Slipping his thumbs beneath the elastic band of her panties, he found her incredibly hot, exquisitely wet, and right on the edge of tumbling into a fierce climax.

With a languid stroke, and a firm tug on her nipple, he gave it to her. She bucked wildly against him, a soft, keening cry rumbling up in her throat. Dragging his mouth from her breast, he tangled one of his hands in her lush hair and crushed her lips to his just in time to swallow her breathless, seductive groan. The sound vibrated against his tongue, and his body absorbed the shockwaves of pleasure that racked her.

As she caught her breath, he buried his face in her neck, kissing, licking, and sucking on the soft, fragrant, sensitive skin of her throat, making her groan and begin that slow, rocking motion against his rampant erection again.

His nostrils flared with the savage need to mate with her, and he fought for control. She wanted passion and desire, and he'd just barely begun to show her the erotic, carnal pleasures still in store for her.

She was lethargic after her release and he took advantage of her pliable state. With a hand bracing her spine, he tilted her backwards, gently tumbling her to the mattress. She spilled onto the cool comforter like warm molasses, a soft, satisfied sigh soughing out of her.

He smiled down at her, at the sensual, arousing picture she made. Her hair was spread around her face and it cascaded over her shoulders, caressing the swells of her breasts. Her hands came to rest at the sides of her head, palms up and fingers slightly curled. Her legs were delectably splayed, her body his for the taking as soon as he removed that scrap of red lace.

The languorous, satisfied smile that curved her lips reminded him of a cat who'd just lapped a bowl of cream. Oh, he definitely intended to make her purr. Shucking his boxers, he moved between her spread legs.

She blinked lazily, admiring him through half-closed lashes. "You're beautiful," she whispered, soft reverence in her husky voice.

He grinned and reached for a foil packet on the bed, taking his own sweet time in appreciating her sexy curves and feminine treasures as well. "You stole my line."

Her gaze leisurely caressed his wide chest the corded tendons in his arms, and traveled to his taut belly. "You're so muscular, so perfectly made." She ventured shamelessly lower to his fierce erection. Her eyes widened in wonder, and she licked her dry lips. "All of you," she added breathlessly.

He groaned, feeling himself swell even larger, and struggled to sheath himself with a condom. "You're making this difficult, you know that?"

She laughed softly, playfully. "I'm glad."

Sufficiently protected, he hooked his fingers into the thin waistband of her thong panties and pulled them slowly down her endlessly long, slender legs, then tossed them somewhere behing him. Her thighs parted, her feminine folds glistening invitingly. She lay there so wantonly, waiting, fully expecting him to mount her. But he wasn't done touching her, stroking her, or tasting her on his tongue...

Leaning down, he kissed the inside of her knee, skimmed his open mouth toward that sweet spot so close, so tempting. She sucked in a startled breath, but didn't resist him. Her hand reached down and clenched strands of his hair in her fingers as he nuzzled the silky, sensitive skin of her inner thigh. As he kissed, and licked, and sucked his way to that treasure trove of delights awaiting him, her tense muscles gradually relaxed, allowing him free access.

When he finally reached his destination, he cupped her bottom and tilted her closer. His warm breath washed over her seconds before he kissed her sweetly, leisurely, wanting this to be perfect for her. But she was impatient and needy—she wasn't giving him the time he'd wanted to explore and discover every pulse point, every erogenous zone. She was so damn sensitive, so responsive, so uninhibited that the moment his tongue rasped her tender, engorged flesh she whimpered and began to convulse.

He groaned even as his tonge delved deep, pushing

her higher before allowing her to free-fall into that downward spiraling climax. A lusty cry broke from her, and her back arched off the mattress as she twisted wildly beneath his sensual siege.

Before the orgasm ebbed he slid over her, nudged her thighs wider apart with his knees, and stretched her arms above her head with his hands. He kissed her with the same searing hunger that was within him.

Beyond mindless, his initial driving thrust was deep and strong. She sucked in a sharp breath as he invaded her body so abruptly, and he moaned as her inner muscles clamped him tight. She was primed, wetter than the mouth he kissed, yet she felt incredibly small and snug, reminding him just how long it had been since she'd been intimate with a man.

Gloved in velvet heat, he throbbed within her, his mind urging him to move. He continued to kiss her deeply, waiting for her to relax and soften around him. His patience was rewarded. Her fingers curled around the hands that pinned her, and in gradual degrees her body melted like rich, warm honey. Instinctively, she wrapped her legs around his waist and tilted her hips for him, drawing him deeper, until he was buried to the hilt and he had no idea where he ended and she began.

Being fused as one was a heady sensation. He lifted his head so he could look into her hazy eyes and watch her face flush with the passion he gave her. His hips pumped a slow, lazy rhythm at first, the long, meausured strokes that pushed them gloriously higher until there was no place to go but back down.

This time, they tumbled off the steep precipice together. With the sweet taste of her on his tongue, the womanly scent of her filling his senses, and her name a ragged cry ripped from his throat, he lost himself in the incredible, selfless pleasure she gave him.

And he knew in that moment that he'd never be the same again.

THANK YOU.

Those were the last words Nick remembered Samantha whispering to him before she'd slipped out of his room and returned to hers sometime in the early morning hours. He'd made love to her with all the passion and skill he possessed, and in return she'd given him the most satisfying night of his life, emotionally and physically.

He didn't want her gratitude, dammit, he wanted... Oh, hell, he wanted *her,* and she wasn't his to take.

With a ruthless curse, he rolled to his back and glanced at the empty side of the bed Samantha had occupied only a few hours ago. The red panties she'd left on the pillow reassured Nick that the previous night hadn't been some kind of dream, but an incredible, unforgettable reality with the most passionate woman he'd ever known.

Picking up that scrap of red lace, he breathed deeply of her scent—and wanted her all over again. They'd made love in imaginative, erotic ways that had made her blush, yet she'd never once told him no, wanting to experience ecstasy in its purest form.

At one point, she'd crawled over him, reached for his eye patch on the night stand and slipped it on. Then his lady pirate had proceeded to plunder his body in ways he'd only ever fantasized. Her silky hair had caressed him from neck to ankles, her hands had discovered nerve endings he hadn't known existed, and her lips and tongue hadn't been the least bit shy about exploring his body as he had hers.

And sometime during the night, she'd touched him in that dark place he'd shut down years ago. His heart. His soul.

She'd kept her promise and hadn't asked for anything beyond passion and desire, yet he was the one who suddenly wanted, needed more. But the fact remained—he had nothing to give her in return.

Furious with himself for letting the entire situation wreak havoc with his heart and emotions, he got out of bed, dropped to the floor and punished his satiated body with a double set of push-ups.

A few more days and he'd be gone from Cranberry Harbor. A few more days and his life would return to the empty nothingness it had been before Samantha.

It couldn't be any other way. He knew that. Accepted it. And hated it.

CHAPTER THIRTEEN

"YOU'RE A BRAVE MAN, Petrocelli," Victor said, his heavy Russian accent filling the interior of Nick's Blazer as they drove back to Cranberry Harbor after attending to personal business in Portland.

"What's life without a little risk?" Briefly taking his gaze off the stretch of highway in front of them, Nick glanced at his companion and grinned. "Just remember, you were an accomplice."

Victor's mustache twitched with a smile. "A willing one, I admit."

Nick was joking, of course. He'd never hold Victor accountable for something that had been one hundred percent his idea—a ploy that would no doubt make Samantha upset at first, then force her to rethink her future with Tyler. Smuggling one of her "lovers" paintings out of the house that morning without her knowledge had been daring and difficult, but Kathryn and Victor had helped him by managing to keep Samantha and Emily distracted long enough for him to carry the canvas out to his car and tuck it in the back seat.

On the pretense of running errands for the garden party, he and Victor had driven to an exclusive art gallery in Portland that Nick had queried about the possibility of taking Samantha's paintings on consignment. After viewing only one of her paintings, the gallery owner had enthusiastically agreed not only to represent her, but to exhibit her work in a local art show.

After watching Samantha blossom the past week and a half, and experiencing the depth of her sensuality when they'd made love, he was hoping that she might be ready to embrace the woman she truly was—and no longer cling to the woman she thought she should be. Nick knew she'd never attempt a venture as bold on her own. This was his gift to her, her one opportunity to realize she could live a full, adventurous life doing what she loved, painting, yet still maintain the stability she needed. That she could be true to herself, *and* the passionate woman that made her so unique.

Through her paintings, she had the ability to reshape her life and future.

Nick had no doubt that convincing Samantha of her own internal strength would be his most difficult challenge. Lucinda's neglect had left insecurities that wouldn't be easily breached.

But he had to try. For Samantha, and Emily, too.

Arriving back at Cranberry Harbor, Nick parked the Blazer in the garage and slipped from the vehicle, excited about sharing his news, but apprehensive on other levels, as well. There was always the possibility that Samantha wouldn't appreciate his presumptuousness with her artwork.

After retrieving the painting from the back of his car, Nick shook Victor's hand, sealing the male camaraderie they'd established. "Thanks for all your help."

"It was my pleasure, and Kathryn's, too. She adores Samantha, and is genuinely pleased that there is a man in her life who appreciates her many talents." His words were teasing, but his gaze was serious.

Nick arched a brow. "Samantha is a gifted artist. Any man can see that."

"And what about the chemistry between the two of you?" Victor asked candidly. "Will anything come of that?"

Glancing up at the monstrosity of a house in front of them, Nick sighed. Although he longed to make love with her again, he knew he'd spend the next few days resisting her. Nothing could come of them being together. He shook his head regretfully. "I'm afraid not. We're worlds apart, Kislenko."

"Only if you put those worlds between the two of you."

Nick laughed. "Oh, you're a fine one to talk. What about you and Kathryn? How long will the two of you continue to sneak around?"

Victor didn't appear at all surprised that Nick had figured out their secret. "Not much longer, I hope. I'm not getting any younger, and I want what every man wants. I want a home of my own, and Kathryn for my wife."

"Not every man is cut out for marriage," Nick said, dredging up his own personal credo.

"Every man needs a good woman to complete his life. Even you, Nick Petrocelli." Victor's smile held a lifetime of wisdom. "Kathryn will complete mine."

Who will complete yours? The question was left unasked, but unmistakably there.

"Good luck," Victor said, the simple words encompassing more than just Nick's meeting with Samantha.

They went their separate ways, and Nick tried not to think about the prospect of Samantha completing his life. The notion was not only ridiculous, but impossible. Still, the thought haunted him, made him yearn for something he knew wasn't his to take.

He found Samantha in the kitchen with Kathryn and Emily. The three of them were standing in a row as they worked together to make apple tarts. Kathryn rolled the dough and formed the shells, Samantha sliced the apples and dipped them in a sugar-cinnamon mix, and Emily arranged them on the unbaked crust.

Samantha's gaze met his, filled with a multitude of emotions that made him feel whole, complete...until she glanced down and saw the painting he held. Her expression turned wary.

"Hi, Mr. Nick," Emily said cheerfully, her face smudged with flour. "I'm making yummy apple tarts."

He glanced at the little girl, watching as she wiped her sticky fingers down the front of the pint-size apron she wore. "I love apple tarts. Be sure to save me at least half a dozen, okay?"

Emily's engaging grin warmed his soul. "I'll put extra apples in yours."

Forcing himself to move across the kitchen, Nick came up to Samantha's side, very aware of Kathryn's expectant gaze on him. She knew where he and Victor had gone and was anxiously awaiting the results of their impromptu trip into Portland.

He smiled, hoping against hope that he'd done the right thing. "I have a surprise for you."

Samantha looked skeptical. "Oh?"

"I didn't want to say anything, just in case my inkling didn't pan out."

Very carefully, she sliced into an apple and began cutting it into sections. "What inkling?"

He could feel the tension rising in him. As a DEA agent, he had no qualms about charging into a room full of drug dealers to make a bust, yet one beautiful, sweet woman had the ability to reduce him to a jumble of nerves. "That you're an incredible artist, worthy of the backing of a high-profile gallery that wants to exhibit your work."

Out of the corner of his eye, he saw Kathryn smile.

Samantha's hand stilled, and she put down her paring knife. "What, exactly, are you saying?"

Setting the canvas down, he withdrew his wallet and pulled out a business card, which he held toward her. "Have you ever heard of Brensen's Art Gallery?"

She wiped her hands on a terry towel. "Yes. I've been there before, just to browse." Tentatively, she took the business card. After verifying the name, she glanced up at him, a slight frown forming on her brow. "They're quite exclusive."

"I know," he said softly, and smiled, his own excitement bubbling to the surface. "I took this painting to their gallery today. After seeing only one of your paintings, they want to represent you and sell your work. They want to exhibit your lovers collection in a local art show."

Realization finally dawned on Samantha, except she didn't express the exhilaration he'd been hoping for. Instead, she looked shocked and appalled.

But before she could reply, Kathryn drew her into her embrace for a quick hug. "Oh, Samantha, this is wonderful news! I'm so happy for you!"

By the time Kathryn let her go, Samantha was shaking her head in fierce denial. "I can't do this."

Nick released a deep breath. "I've already told them yes."

"You had no right to do that without my permission," she said, staring at him as though he'd betrayed her. "My paintings are not for public viewing. You of all people should know that."

"They're unique, and sensual, and beautiful," he said, telling her exactly what viewers would see. "Your paintings and the lovers you create are an extension of you."

"They represent who I *was*," she argued vehemently, her blue eyes filled with emotional anguish. "And they remind me of who I can never allow myself to be!"

She was so very wrong. But she was so distraught, there was no way she would listen to reason.

"My goodness," Amelia declared, entering the kitchen. "What's going on in here? I can hear the two of you arguing all the way down the hall."

Samantha tensed, a look of dread shadowing her features. She made no reply, and neither did Nick or Kathryn.

"Mama's going to sell her paintings," Emily announced brightly, repeating information she'd heard.

"No, I'm not," Samantha said firmly, her gaze cutting to Nick. "Nick made assumptions he shouldn't have."

Amelia's gaze turned curious. "And what's this I heard about lovers you create?"

Mortified by her grandmother's question, Samantha looked away. After a moment, as if realizing that Amelia would figure out her secret sooner or later, Samantha whispered, "They're in my paintings."

"What are?" Confusion laced Amelia's voice as she looked at Samantha, then Nick, for an answer.

Nick kept his mouth shut, knowing it was up to Samantha to admit the entire truth about her paintings to her grandmother.

"Shadows and silhouettes of lovers," Samantha finally said, her cheeks pink with embarrassment. Picking up the painting Nick had brought in with him, she lifted it for her grandmother to see. "They're right here." With obvious reluctance, she pointed to a cluster of boulders on her seascape and the entwined image of her lovers.

Amelia's gaze narrowed as she studied the picture. "Oh, my," she muttered, her brows rising in shock. "I had no idea."

"I know, and I'm sorry. I never intended for you to find out." Samantha's voice was thick with misery, her gaze glittering with a wealth of other emotions. "And don't worry, my paintings will never make their way into an art gallery."

With that, she set the painting down, turned and disappeared out the kitchen door that led to the backyard.

Amelia sighed as she watched Samantha go. After a moment of silence, she transferred her gaze to Nick, something akin to resignation touching her features. "It seems my granddaughter is more talented than I'd realized."

He nodded, knowing this astute woman understood Samantha's internal struggle better than most. But did she truly recognize the significance of her paintings? "Yes, she is," he agreed, then headed out the back door, too, in search of Samantha.

He found her sitting in the gazebo in the rose garden. Climbing the stairs, he took the bench seat opposite her, not surprised when she wouldn't look at him or acknowledge his presence. "Samantha...the last thing I'd ever want to do is hurt you. I took that painting to Brensen's because I wanted to do something special for you."

She turned accusing eyes on him. "You wanted to do something *special* for me?" she repeated incredulously.

"Yeah." Leaning forward, he braced his forearms on his knees. "I wanted to show you that you can be the sensual woman that you are, and still lead the life you want to. The two don't have to be exclusive."

Choked laughter escaped her. "Not with my paint-ings. Displaying those pictures is something the reckless, impetuous Samantha would do."

"But that woman is a part of who you are," he said gently. "Not someone to be ashamed of."

Her voice rose an angry notch. "I have a daughter to think about, Nick, and that doesn't include me doing something so frivolous and self-centered. Once word spread about my paintings, this secure environment I've created for Emily would be threatened. People talk, and I wouldn't want any kind of gossip to hurt my daugh-ter." She drew a deep breath, but it did nothing to calm her. "Three years ago when Justin died, I made a prom-ise to myself that I'd never do to Emily what my mother did to me. I swore I'd never again put my needs above Emily's. Accepting Brensen's offer caters too much to my reckless nature. One taste of that excitement, that success, and I risk losing sight of what's really important to me. It's happened before, and I can't let it happen again. I live with the constant fear that I'll become as unstable and capricious as my mother, and Emily will ultimately suffer."

He shook his head. "I've never met Lucinda, but just from what you've told me, you're nothing at all like her. She might have been a passionate, impetuous woman who didn't think of anyone but herself, but you're self-less, and warm, and caring. Unfortunately, Justin took advantage of those qualities, and as a result you now question your judgment about everything. There's noth-ing wrong with being cautious, as long as you don't let it control your life."

Nick stood and slowly crossed the gazebo to where she sat, trying not to analyze how that statement could apply to his own life. He'd been cautious since the day his mother had died, and he'd let that wariness control his life.

Stopping in front of her, he pushed that disturbing notion aside. "You need to believe in yourself, Samantha. Believe in who you are. That doesn't mean you'll forget about Emily, or what's best for her. If anything, it'll give you the strength to fight for what is the right thing to do, for both of you."

She glanced up and bit her bottom lip, looking so lost. Tears mingled with the uncertainty shimmering in her eyes. "Maybe I don't know who I am anymore," she whispered in a tight voice. "And maybe I don't know what the right thing to do is anymore, either."

He ached to wrap her in his embrace and offer her assurances, but knowing he didn't have that right, he reached out instead and touched the lone tear that slipped from the corner of her eye and rolled down her cheek, tenderly wiping it away. "Maybe it's time you found out, before you make another mistake with Tyler."

Knowing there was nothing else he could say to convince her of her internal strength, he turned and headed out of the gazebo.

"ARE YOU SURE YOU'RE feeling well?" Tyler asked, his tone slightly exasperated.

Samantha pulled her gaze from the passing scenery as they drove back to Cranberry Harbor after spending a few hours at the Seascape carnival. After too much sun and junk food, Emily had fallen asleep in the back seat of Tyler's BMW, the two small stuffed animals he'd won for her pushed aside.

What should have been a fun outing had been stressful for Samantha, upsetting for Emily, and clearly frustrating for Tyler, who didn't have the patience to deal with a little girl's whims. Tyler's inability to relate to children caused Samantha concern and made her wonder exactly what kind of father he'd be...maybe not the warm, loving one she'd envisioned.

She dredged up a smile that felt stiff on her lips and answered Tyler's question. "I'm fine."

He slanted a glance her way. "You've been quiet and distant all day, and haven't said much in the way of adult conversation. Other than your apology this morning for the fiasco at my dinner party, you haven't been too accommodating."

Accommodating. The word itself sent a disturbing shiver down her spine. "I just have a lot on my mind with the garden party coming up." A lie. She hadn't stopped thinking about Nick and the conversation they'd had yesterday about her paintings and her future and being true to herself. She kept telling herself that displaying her art wasn't a practical, or responsible choice, that marrying Tyler was, but her heart wasn't listening to her head.

Her explanation seemed to soothe him, and he allowed a smile to grace his features. "Ah, Amelia's biggest charity bash of the year," he said with too much enthusiasm. Reaching across the console separating them, he placed his hand over hers. "The event would be a wonderful time to announce an engagement, don't you think?"

Her breath wheezed out of her. "Excuse me?"

"An engagement," he said simply, and without emotion. "A proposal. You and I getting married." When she remained quiet, he went on. "Surely this doesn't come as a surprise, considering our shared past. I know things didn't work out between us the first time I proposed, but this time can be different."

She pulled her hand from under the intimacy of his, extremely uncomfortable with the direction of their conversation. "I'm not sure we really know each other anymore."

His fingers tightened on the steering wheel and his brows drew into a frown. "Our families have been friends for years, Samantha."

"We've barely started dating again," she pointed out evenly, though her stomach churned with anxiety. "We've both changed over the years. Don't you think we should take more time to see if we're really compatible?" So many doubts had begun to swamp her since her conversation with Nick; she needed time to sort everything out.

"I don't need any more time to know that you'd make a good wife and mother for my children. I find you quite suitable, Samantha," he said, making her feel like a brood mare he'd chosen. "You have qualities I find very desirable in a woman."

Desire. He knew nothing of it, and he certainly didn't inspire the exciting sensations that came with the emotion. Unbidden, thoughts of her breathtaking night of lovemaking with Nick flitted through her mind, warming her. He was the kind of lover she'd always craved, giving her free rein to explore her own sexuality and indulging in his own hunger for her. She feared she'd never experience that kind of passion again. Not with anyone but Nick. And in a few days, he'd be gone forever.

Tyler turned off the highway, heading toward Amelia's mansion. "Between both of our families, I think we're a fine match," he said, apparently fighting for his cause. "We both want the same things, Samantha," he continued. "I want a family and I'm sure you want more children."

Oh, she did, more than anything. But would that be enough with a man she didn't love? A man who seemed to have little tolerance for Emily. She tried to draw in a deep breath, but she felt so smothered that her lungs burned with the effort.

"We don't love each other, Tyler," she said, remembering Nick's words. She was beginning to wonder if she could settle for less.

"Love happens in time," Tyler assured her, the voice of reason. "I'm sure once we begin to share intimacies, our feelings for each other will evolve in due course."

She didn't think that was likely, not when she'd already given her heart to another man. What Tyler was suggesting was impossible.

In that moment, a startling revelation shook her deeply. She'd promised Nick that if she could have just one glorious, passionate night with him, she'd never ask for anything else. She'd lied. To Nick and herself.

She wanted forever with him, as impossible as she knew that fantasy was. Nick hadn't told her he loved her, hadn't given her any indication whatsoever that he wanted anything beyond their brief, but sizzling, night together. And she had no right to expect more, because she'd always known he wasn't the kind of man to take on another wife and a child. He was independent and had something far more exciting waiting for him in New York that she couldn't compete with. His job.

He was reckless, exhilarating and all wrong for her.

And she loved him.

"The garden party isn't for another few weeks," Tyler said, cutting into her heartbreaking thoughts. "In the meantime, just think about my proposal, Samantha."

"I'll think about it." Day and night, she knew his proposal would haunt her.

A week and a half ago, she'd been so certain that staid, dependable Tyler was everything she wanted in her life. Now she couldn't push a disturbing question from her mind: was Tyler really what she *needed?*

UNABLE TO SLEEP after her mentally exhausting day with Tyler, and troubled by the ensuing thoughts about Nick that had been tumbling through her head, Samantha slipped on her robe and padded downstairs to make herself a mug of hot tea. She entered the kitchen and flipped on the light—and spied Kathryn coming down the back stairway. Her aunt started with surprise at being caught, her eyes widening with dismay.

Samantha frowned when she saw the suitcase she carried.

Panic flashed across Kathryn's features. "Samantha, what are you doing down here? It's past eleven."

Her aunt's anxious tone clearly indicated that she'd expected everyone to be in bed. "I couldn't sleep and came down to get something to drink." Samantha gestured to the paisley-print luggage in Kathryn's grip. "What are you doing sneaking down here in the middle of the night with a suitcase?"

Kathryn hesitated for a few heartbeats, then finally met Samantha's gaze. "I'm leaving."

Samantha's stomach dropped to her toes. "You're what?"

Kathryn's nervousness dissipated, and a becoming blush stained her soft cheeks. "Victor and I, we're eloping."

Reeling from Kathryn's unexpected announcement, Samantha could only stare at her aunt. She'd known the two had been dating on the sly, but she hadn't realized just how serious their relationship had turned.

"I love him, Samantha," she said, the emotion she spoke of evident in her voice and her expression. "I've been alone for too long, and he makes me so very happy. Happier than I've ever been. He's the man I've waited for all my life."

"But you can't just leave and...*elope*. What about an engagement, a wedding?"

"I'm too old for all that fanfare," Kathryn said, dismissing the idea of a traditional ceremony. "Besides, I find eloping incredibly romantic. It was Victor's idea."

"Does Amelia know?" Samantha asked.

"I left her a note, which she'll find in the morning." Kathryn offered her a reassuring smile. "We'll be back before the garden party, I promise."

"She'll be stunned, as I am."

"I'm sure, initially," Kathryn agreed impishly. "But I'm hoping she'll be happy for me. I'm nothing without Victor. He completes me, and he's all I need and want in my life."

Kathryn's words touched a sympathetic chord in Samantha and tugged on her heart.

A tender light entered Kathryn's gaze. "No matter what happens, always know that I love you and Emily with all my heart."

A lump of emotion wedged in Samantha's throat, and she embraced her aunt in a warm hug. "Oh, I love you, too, Aunt Kathryn," she whispered around the ache in her chest. "And I'm so happy for you and Victor."

When they broke apart, Kathryn touched her gently beneath the chin, her touch maternal and affectionate. "In a lot of ways, you've always been like the daughter

I never had, and because I care so much about you, I want you to be happy, too."

The automatic reply of "I am happy" sprang to Samantha's mind, but she bit back the lie. The truth was, she was miserable, confused and torn between doing the responsible thing or allowing passion to be her guide in rediscovering her true self. The only certainty was that she'd fallen deeply in love with a man who didn't seem to need anyone or anything.

As if sensing the direction of her thoughts, Kathryn offered a compassionate smile. "I waited years for love to find me. Follow your own heart, Samantha. It'll lead you in the right direction. You've got so many years ahead of you, don't throw them away on a man who won't appreciate your sweet nature, or a marriage that is less than what you dream of. You deserve much more."

Samantha clung to every word of wisdom Kathryn spoke, respecting her aunt for taking her own personal chances with the man she loved. In that moment, Samantha knew she'd risk the life she'd created for herself for the one man who filled her heart with confidence, laughter and an overwhelming love sweeter than anything she'd ever known.

She'd gamble everything for Nick, but would he do the same for her? Would he make a place for her and Emily in his solitary life, or reject the love she offered and leave Cranberry Harbor without a backward glance?

The risk was a heavy, emotional one, reckless and impulsive, but she had nothing left to lose—except her heart, and a future married to a man she didn't love.

Tyler was what she thought she wanted, but she *knew* Nick was the man she needed.

The back door to the kitchen opened, and Victor

leaned inside, his questioning gaze traveling from Samantha to Kathryn.

Kathryn smiled, her expression revealing adoration for the man who'd swept her off her feet and intended to marry her. "I'm afraid we've been discovered."

"I'm happy for both of you," Samantha said, quick to reassure Victor.

"Thank you." Relieving Kathryn of her suitcase, he picked up her hand and pressed a sweet kiss on her knuckles. "Are you ready to go, my love?"

Kathryn's blush deepened. "Oh, yes," she breathed, secure in her feelings for Victor and the life they would share together.

Samantha hated to interrupt the tender moment between them. "Can I see you two off?" she asked.

Victor's eyes twinkled with mischief. "You may, but I plan to push my car past the main gates before starting the engine so we don't wake Amelia. And we don't have time for you to run upstairs and change."

Samantha had forgotten that she was still wearing her robe over her nightshirt. Considering everything was decently covered, she didn't mind. If this was the only wedding her aunt was going to have, Samantha wanted to be part of it. "Then I'll just come outside to wave goodbye."

He held the door open wide for them. "Let's go."

Before they could shuffle out of the kitchen, a deep male voice stopped them. "Hey, how come I wasn't invited to the party?"

The guilty trio turned to face Nick, and Samantha's breath squeezed out of her lungs. He was wearing the same old jeans and T-shirt he'd arrived in almost two weeks ago, a sinful grin gracing his lips. She met his warm, intimate gaze and swallowed hard. The connection between them was undeniable, as were the emotions neither had spoken of.

She would, tonight...and risk everything.

Victor explained their plans to elope, and Nick insisted on helping the two lovers make a clean getaway, sharing a private joke with Victor about being an accomplice and owing the older man one.

A full moon hung in the sultry night sky, the only illumination to guide them, but a romantic one at that. The two men pushed Victor's vehicle down the drive while Samantha walked beside the car and Kathryn steered, looking as giddy and excited as a schoolgirl. Too soon, they were out of the main gate and far enough away from the house to start the vehicle without disturbing the sleeping occupants still inside. Samantha shared a last-minute hug with Kathryn, and Nick shook Victor's hand, wishing the couple an eternity of happiness.

And then they were gone, leaving Samantha and Nick standing in the darkness of midnight.

"We'd better head back to the house," Nick suggested, pushing the tips of his fingers into the front pockets of his jeans. She nodded her agreement, and they walked silently back toward the imposing structure that had been her haven since the summer her mother had dropped her off and never returned for her.

Once inside the house, they climbed the stairs side by side. Samantha glanced at the man beside her and thought of everything her aunt had said to her about love and dreams, and especially following her heart. Right now, and forever more, her heart would be full of love for Nick.

"That was very romantic, don't you think?" she

asked softly, wanting to break the quiet tension that had settled between them. "I'm happy for her, and Victor."

"Honestly, so am I," he admitted, his voice low and deep, but reserved, too. "I don't think I've seen two people so in love."

Stopping at the third-floor landing, she placed a hand on his strong arm before he could head down the hall toward his room. *Just look at me, Nick, and you'll see how crazy in love with you I am.*

He did look at her. He looked deeply into her eyes as no other man had, and she ached to say the words tumbling around in her brain. Feeling uncertain, she decided to *show* him.

Reaching up, she touched a hand to his face, cradled his stubbled jaw in the palm of her hand and met his dark gaze unwaveringly. "Nick...I want to kiss you."

He grasped her wrist, but didn't pull her hand away from his cheek. "Samantha, we shouldn't—"

She didn't allow him the chance to refuse her. Leaning into him, she curled her free hand around the nape of his neck and pressed her mouth to his, parting his lips with the subtle pressure of hers. With a low growl that rumbled up from his chest, he responded, unable to deny her. Pushing her against the wall behind her, he met the silky thrust of her tongue, kissing her thoroughly, hungrily...like a man starved for the taste of his mate.

His hands crushed her hair, angling her head, her mouth, for a deeper, more desperate kind of kiss. She obliged him willingly, her craving for this man insatiable. She knew it would always be so. He seemed to want her just as much, and that knowledge bolstered her courage to lay her heart bare, to tempt fate with this man who made her feel complete.

She was the one to break the kiss, but he buried his

face in her neck, his breath hot and damp against her skin. His body, pressed intimately to hers, was hard, feverish and undeniably aroused, branding her with a stunning heat. He kissed her throat, tugged her sensitive flesh between his teeth—claiming her in a primitive kind of way.

She wanted him deep inside her, filling her body and soul with all the indescribable sensations only he evoked. But she needed more than his body, more than the incredible pleasure she knew he could give her.

She wanted—needed—his love. Her life, her future hinged on that one simple, so very complicated emotion.

Threading her fingers through his hair, she gently pulled his head back until she could see his face. His gaze was bright and luminous with need, yet his expression was anguished. He struggled as she struggled—wanting something he feared was completely forbidden to him.

She was his for the taking, and she summoned the words to tell him so. "I love you, Nick Petrocelli," she whispered, and knew she would until the day she died.

As if she'd doused him with cold water, he abruptly let her go and stumbled backward. He swore, the words sharp and succinct.

His reaction wasn't what she'd been hoping for and made her chest constrict with dread. Shoving her unease aside, she reached out, attempting to bridge the emotional and physical distance that suddenly separated them. "Nick?"

"Don't, Samantha," he demanded, his words low and angry—at her or himself, she couldn't be sure.

Swallowing past the tightness in her throat, she risked her heart, her future on the one man who'd given her the confidence to believe in herself. Now she believed in *them*, and set out to prove it. "Don't what, Nick?" she asked softly. "Don't love you? It's too late, I already do."

His jaw was set in denial, but the powerful emotion in his gaze gave her hope, and the fortitude to be more reckless than she'd ever been in her life. Allowing the true, passionate Samantha to emerge, she grabbed a handful of his T-shirt and pulled him down the corridor toward his room.

Before dawn broke over the horizon, she'd love him so completely there would be no doubt in his mind as to the depth of her feelings for him.

CHAPTER FOURTEEN

NICK KNEW HE SHOULD HAVE issued a protest at Samantha's bold plans to seduce him, and he had every intention of doing so. But as soon as they stepped into his bedroom and she flipped on the light, locked the door behind them, then turned those sultry blue eyes on him that seemed to eat him up in a glance, he knew he'd never be able to resist her.

Without preamble, she pressed *him* up against the wall, and he didn't even try to deny what he wanted so badly. Her mouth crushed his in a deep, hot, wet kiss, which he returned with equal fire. She skimmed her cool hands beneath his shirt and broke their kiss to pull it over his head. He caught her gaze, bright with that recklessness she tried so hard to suppress. It fueled his hunger, and made him just as impatient and restless, more so than he could ever remember being.

He tugged at her robe and let it fall to the floor, then yanked her nightshirt off, too, leaving her gloriously naked except for her panties...which she didn't give him the chance to remove. Her mouth and hands were suddenly everywhere, and all he could do was delve his hands into her silky hair and lose himself in the pleasure she was so determined to give him.

Her soft breasts pressed against him, and her mouth grazed his neck. From there, her lips trailed tantalizing, biting kisses down to his chest. A moan rumbled up from his throat when she laved his nipple with her tongue and teased the tip with her teeth. The muscles in his belly contracted involuntarily as her fingers followed the path from his navel to the waistband of his jeans, then lower, cupping and caressing him until he was hard and aching. Her mouth wasn't far behind, her tongue wicked and provocative, her breath hot when she finally knelt before him and placed a damp, openmouthed kiss against the erection straining the fly of his jeans, then nipped at him gently.

He sucked in a fierce breath as a surge of liquid fire shot to his groin, making him throb against her mouth. Before he could recover from that assault, her fingers worked the button on his jeans, then lowered the zipper and freed him. He shuddered at the relief, then groaned low and deep when her fingers circled the hot, hard length of him. Her thumb brushed over the sensitive tip, and he looked down just in time to see her lips part for him....

His chest heaved, and his hands tightened in her hair, keeping her just out of reach. "Samantha..." Her name was a husky warning.

She tilted her head back and glanced up at him. Her eyes glowed with soft sexuality, silently begging to let her have her way with him. "Let me love you," she whispered. "Please."

Her words wrapped around his heart, stealing his emotional restraint, as well as his physical control. There was nothing left for him to do but surrender. He wanted her too much, needed her more than was wise.

She took him in the heat of her mouth, and too soon, he was on that sharp edge. He didn't want to tumble over that mindless cliff without her, so he pulled her back up, smothering her flimsy protest with an anxious, eager kiss that inflamed them both. Somehow, someway, they made quick work of their remaining clothes. Somehow, someway, they made it to the nightstand for one of the condoms she'd left behind the other night, then the bed. When they fell onto the mattress, it was Samantha who demanded to be on top, and he let her straddle him and be the aggressor because it freed him up to pleasure her in a dozen different ways. He lost himself in the texture of her skin, her feminine scent, the womanly curve of her hips, her sleek thighs.

With a sultry smile, she guided him home, sheathing the length of him with her incredible heat, then rode him in a rhythm that was as wild, uninhibited and just as giving as he knew her heart was. He caressed her breasts, stroked a hand down her belly until the honeyed heat of her slid against his fingers like liquid fire…all the while reveling in how bold and beautiful she was.

He watched her first climax roll through her like a languid wave, stealing her ragged breath and making her arch urgently toward his pleasuring fingers. Her breasts, so lush and full, tightened and peaked above him; her thighs quivered against his hips. With a low moan, she fisted her hands on his belly, let her head fall back and her eyes flutter closed. A soft, keening cry erupted from her throat as she convulsed around him.

Before she could recover, he rolled her beneath him, wrapped her legs tight around his hips, and drove into her, frantic and frenzied. He couldn't get close enough, deep enough. She evoked those desperate feelings, and something more elemental that he feared…a need and longing he'd spent his entire life denying.

He told himself to slow his urgent pace, wanting this moment to last, wanting to commit everything about her to memory…. But he was too greedy to go leisurely, too hungry to take his time, and the pleasure gripping him was too acute, frighteningly so.

He plunged harder, deeper, faster. Wrenching his mouth from hers with a fierce, agonizing groan, he buried his face against her throat, suckled the soft skin of her neck and breathed harshly in her ear, urging her higher.

Her body responded with a series of tremors that started deep within her, and coaxed him to let go with each successive gliding thrust.

"I love you," she whispered, just as that soaring need pushed her over the brink.

It was those three little words that broke the tenuous threads on his control and finally allowed his own searing release to consume him. He followed her over that summit, and let out a guttural groan as emotions he'd kept barricaded for too long flooded free—anguish, ecstasy, longing, need.

And too much love.

HE COULDN'T STAY. He had to go. Just as soon as he fabricated an excuse about his abrupt departure to Amelia, whom he still owed two more days according to the auction agreement. He had to get out of Samantha's life. After last night, it was imperative that he leave, before things got any more complicated.

Harsh laughter escaped him. Who was he kidding? What was going on inside him transcended complicated and bordered on sheer insanity. With a low curse he shoved more clothes into his duffel bag, his mind forcing him to acknowledge what his heart already knew. His denial was fierce, an instinct born of self-preservation.

But the stunning truth remained.

He loved Samantha.

But he'd never have her.

She didn't belong in his dark world and his solitary life. He had nothing to offer such a vibrant, talented and passionate woman as Samantha. He'd stifle her. He might be able to match her passion, but he didn't have it in him to give her the emotional security she craved.

In time, she'd grow to hate him, as Camille had.

And then there was sweet Emily, who deserved a full-time father, not a part-time parent who put his job above family. A man who risked his life, the safety of everything he held dear, every time he strapped on his gun and stepped into the ominous underworld where he worked. She needed brothers and sisters, and love and laughter surrounding her. She needed a father she could believe in, depend on, and trust to always be there for her.

He couldn't be those things; being a cop was all he knew. Fighting for justice, putting himself on the front line—that was his life. He liked the energy of his job, the adrenaline rush of the danger he faced, the excitement and intellectual challenge of bringing down some of New York's most nefarious crime lords.

And just as soon as his sight was restored and he was back with the agency again, active in his duties, he'd forget all about loving Samantha.

Or so he tried to convince himself.

"I WAS CERTAIN TODAY couldn't get much worse, what with Kathryn eloping with Victor instead of letting me give her a proper wedding," Amelia said with a weary sigh. "And now you're leaving."

Nick shifted in the stiff, uncomfortable chair he sat in opposite Amelia in her library. "I'm sorry to cut my obligation short, but I need to get back to New York sooner than I thought.''

Amelia studied him thoughtfully, her astute gaze telling him she didn't believe his excuse. "I'm thinking your departure has more to do with Samantha."

Unwilling to admit to his personal, *intimate* relationship with Samantha, he opted for a vague response. "I think my presence has served its purpose."

Resting her hands over the head of her ivory-handled cane, Amelia nodded her agreement. "Samantha certainly has blossomed from your attention. In fact, I've seen a side to her I haven't seen since just before she married Justin."

Nick couldn't ignore the twinge of guilt he experienced. "I know the incident at Tyler's dinner party got out of hand, and I didn't have the right to take her paintings to Brensen's—"

"I'm not criticizing you, Mr. Petrocelli, just making an observation. These past two weeks have been very enlightening for me as far as Samantha is concerned, to say the least." A slight smile softened her lips. "You know how shocked I was to discover those lovers in my granddaughter's paintings."

Sensing the other woman's need to talk, Nick made no reply.

"I have to admit that curiosity got the best of me, and I've made a few trips up to Samantha's studio to browse through her collection of paintings. After taking a closer look at her other works, I found something besides those shadowed lovers."

"Which was?" he prompted, curious himself.

"The impetuous, vibrant woman Samantha used to be, before she married Justin." A frown furrowed her brow.

"And I'm afraid, in some ways, I'm the one responsible for stifling her."

Nick knew Amelia only had Samantha's best interests at heart, just as much as Samantha wanted to show her grandmother that she was responsible and level-headed. "She doesn't want to disappoint you, like Lucinda did."

"Aah, my wayward daughter," Amelia said, nodding. "Yes, Lucinda was stubborn, fiercely independent and always such a free spirit who was determined to do as she pleased, even at the expense of others. My husband and I were very strict with her, and hindsight being what it is, I believe that Lucinda rebelled to the extreme because we were so restrictive."

Regret and resignation mingled in her tone, then gradually ebbed into something more melancholy. "Then along came Samantha, my first granddaughter. I loved her from the moment I held her in my arms. When she came to live here at Cranberry Harbor when she was a child, I tried not to be restrictive with her the way I was with Lucinda. I only wanted her to think about her choices and make the right ones. She was always reasonable and responsible, until Justin. He wasn't a healthy decision, but one based on romantic excitement and impulse. I know Samantha wasn't prepared for that relationship, and Justin's relentless pursuit of danger. Yet on some level, I think she believed she was destined to repeat the same cycle as Lucinda."

Which was why Samantha was cautious when it came to trusting her own judgment, he knew. But hadn't she opened up to him last night by giving him her heart, her love? She'd trusted *him*, and he'd failed her. Resorting to his own safety tactics, he'd let go before things spiralled beyond what he could control. Amelia continued. "All I want for Samantha is someone who can appreciate her passionate nature and impetuousness without threatening it, someone who can also give her and Emily the stability they both need.''

A brow rose incredulously. "And you believe that's Tyler Grayson?"

"At one time, I believed so," she admitted. "But I want Samantha to make the right choice for *her*. Whether it be Tyler, or another man. Ultimately, I want her to be happy. I want her to be in love, as any woman should be."

Nick refrained from informing the older woman that Samantha *was* in love, with a man who could give her passion but not security.

Amelia's gaze scrutinized him, as if trying to search deeper than the surface of his cool facade. She was making him extremely uncomfortable. "What I want is for her to trust her judgment again. I can't shelter her forever. I would prefer that if she decides to marry again, she make that decision with her heart and not her head, as she did with Justin. She thought she loved him, but their relationship wasn't based on the kind of mutual respect and trust that comes with true love."

Nick drew his hand along his jaw, trying not to think just how much this conversation echoed the problems of his first marriage—the lack of respect and trust and true love. Everything he'd now gained by loving Samantha.

Glancing at his watch, he feigned surprise at the time. "I need to get on the road." He waited for Amelia to stand, then did the same. "The permanent scholarship to the Lost Springs Ranch for Boys still stands?" he asked, needing to make sure that donation was secure.

"Of course it does. You did exactly what I asked you to do. You flattered my granddaughter and built her self-confidence. We'll see what happens between Tyler and her." Amelia smiled, a teasing light in her eyes. "And hopefully, one of these days I'll get myself a great-grandson."

A small gasp sounded from behind them. He and Amelia turned at the same moment, finding Samantha standing in the half-open doorway to the library. The shock and disillusionment reflected in her features revealed that she'd overheard part of their conversation, enough to know that he'd been assigned as her personal assistant with ulterior motives.

Never would he have believed he would fall in love with her.

"Samantha…" Wanting to ease the same anguish he felt squeezing his own heart, he stepped toward her, needing to explain and apologize for the simple plan that had backfired on both of them.

She whirled around and left before he could say anything more.

"Aw, hell," he muttered. Then he turned and followed her. He had to make her understand that he'd never meant to hurt her.

SAMANTHA HEADED UP to the sanctuary of her studio, anger and frustration bubbling within her. It wasn't directed at Nick, but herself, for believing that last night might have made a difference with him. She'd been reckless and risked her heart, and lost the gamble.

Despite hearing that Nick's duties at Cranberry Harbor had started as a flirtatious escapade, she *knew* she'd touched a part of him last night. She'd felt the love in his touch, seen those tender emotions reflected in his gaze. Yet just as she'd learned to suppress her passion after Justin's death, Nick had learned to deny his own emotions. There was nothing left she could do to reach him, or prove the depth of her love for him. For as much as the man advocated she be true to herself, he seemed to harbor a few fears and vulnerabilities of his own.

Crossing her studio, she stood before her current painting, letting the landscape and the secrets within soothe her battered heart and soul. Without a doubt, Nick had coaxed her out of the staid, reserved persona she'd cultivated over the past three years, and it had felt so good to leave it behind. Emily deserved a reliable mother, but there was a new strength blooming within Samantha, a forgotten belief in herself that made her want to try balancing her passionate nature with the responsibility she'd acquired since Justin's death. It was a frightening notion, one that could alter the course of her future.

Samantha heard Nick's footsteps on the stairs, and although a part of her was dying inside, she found the strength to face him with a calm that belied her inner turmoil. She wouldn't beg or plead with him to stay, and deep inside, she knew she didn't have the right to make that kind of selfish demand, not when he had his own life in New York.

"You've come to say goodbye," she said, meeting his gaze, which was filled with the same uncertainties and misery swirling within her.

"Yes." Nick stopped a few feet away, not trusting himself to touch her. At the moment, all he wanted to do was pull her into his arms and kiss her. He craved that one last taste, that connection, but knew it wasn't his to take.

"Where are you going after you leave Cranberry Harbor?"

Her tone was so emotionless, they could have been

talking about the weather. They had important issues to discuss, but for now, he played along. "I'm driving back to Lost Springs to make sure everything is okay with Lindsay, then I'll be heading back home, to New York, to start laser treatments on my eye."

She nodded, the gesture annoyingly polite. "So you can return to your job," she stated.

"Yes." Rubbing at the taut muscles bunching the back of his neck, he forcibly shook off the irritation bristling up his spine. How could she be so impassive when his insides were churning with a burning dread beyond anything he'd ever known? "My lieutenant can probably assign me to a desk job until my full sight is restored and I can go back into the field. Pushing paperwork isn't my favorite thing, but it'll be better than sitting at home." *Where thoughts of you will surely drive me crazy.*

Finally, she glanced at him, a sad smile on her lips. "I hope you'll be happy, Nick," she said softly, sincerely.

"I *want* you to be happy, Samantha," he said, his voice low and gruff.

She gave a small shrug that fell short of the nonchalance he suspected she was striving for. "I'll be fine."

Her vague tone made his gut tighten. "I want to explain what you heard in the library earlier—"

"There's no need to explain," she said, cutting him off. "I understood everything perfectly."

"I never meant for things to go as far as they did."

She had never looked so fragile. "I don't regret anything that happened between us, and I blame you for nothing." She folded her arms over her chest, as if trying to hold herself together. "You never made me any promises, Nick, and I had no right to expect them, or ask for any in return. I knew that. I was just hoping you might feel the same way about me. If I didn't take that chance last night and tell you that I loved you, I'd always wonder what could have been.''

What could have been. Her simple words held such a powerful message, one that hinted of fate and destiny. He tried to resist its pull, but it was stronger than his will. The declaration he hadn't been able to bring himself to speak last night tumbled from his lips before he could stop it. ''I *do* love you, Samantha.'' The words were rusty but undeniably honest.

This time when she smiled, the gesture held a hint of feminine intuition, as if she'd known. ''But not enough to trust me and what we've discovered together.''

''I don't trust myself.'' He jammed his hands on his hips, frustration welling within him. ''My job is my life. It's all I know. And when I get caught up in my work, I neglect things that are important to me. I don't trust myself not to neglect you or Emily.'' He swallowed back the growing knot in his throat. ''I'm too much like your first husband. I'm reckless, I like the thrill my job gives me, and I can't give you the kind of life you need.''

''Then this is for the best,'' she said, her voice resigned. ''And we'll both do what's comfortable and secure, and I'll have to be happy with that.'' Her gaze met his, searching past the surface to deep, soulful places. ''What will bring you happiness, Nick?''

The question clawed at him, forcing him to acknowledge the fact that he didn't know what in his life brought him contentment and satisfaction. Ever since the day he'd left Lost Springs and set out on his own to join the Marines, his goals had been clear, and he had pursued them, to the exclusion of all else...including the woman he'd married.

He'd believed his position with the Justice Department would bring him the greatest satisfaction, and on some level, it did. Physically and mentally, he'd thrived on the excitement and challenge of his assignments. But now, having had forced time off from the stress and pressure of his job, he realized he'd grasped that day-to-day high to distract him from the emptiness of his life. Emotionally, he was far from happy, fulfilled or gratified.

He realized he had no acceptable answer for her.

When the silence stretched too long between them, she moved to the nearby table and picked up her sketch pad. Fingers lightly caressing the cover, she met his gaze. "I want you to have this."

He stared at the tablet she extended toward him, confused. "It's your drawings."

"But the pictures belong to you," she said simply. "I want you to take this with you, so you'll never forget how profoundly you affected my life."

He didn't want to take the pad of sketches. He'd already glimpsed at what the tablet contained—pictures of him. Content. Peaceful. He didn't want that constant reminder of what he was giving up. But neither could he refuse this one connection to her. Reaching out, he took her gift, but knew it would be a long time before he gained the courage to take another look at the pages within.

"I'll never forget you, Nick Petrocelli," she whispered, her voice quavering. "And someday, maybe those drawings will help you answer the question I just asked."

CHAPTER FIFTEEN

NICK STARED INTO the black depths of his coffee, wishing for something stronger than caffeine to numb his memory of the two feminine faces that had haunted him on the fourteen-hour drive back to Lost Springs from Cranberry Harbor. Branded forever on his mind was Samantha's expression, which contained a mixture of resignation and futile hope after she'd given him her sketch pad to take with him. As long as he lived, he knew he'd never forget the heartbreaking image, or the fact that he'd blatantly walked away from the most generous, selfless woman he'd ever met.

If that hadn't been crucifying enough, his final visit to Emily to bid her goodbye had damn near torn his heart from his chest. The six-year-old had clung to him and sobbed, begging him not to leave. He'd tried to console her without making promises of seeing her again, knowing full well they would never come true.

He'd retrieved his duffel bag after that emotional encounter and headed out of the sprawling mansion, anxious to escape the doubts and insecurities swirling within him. Then he'd made the mistake of glancing up at the windows flanking the front of the estate one last time, and seen Emily with her hands and face pressed to the glass, tears streaming down her soft cheeks.

He'd heard her faint cries, *Don't go, Mr. Nick. Please, don't go,* and forced himself to keep on walking to the garage and his Blazer, the ache in his chest tightening to awful proportions.

Over a thousand miles later, the crushing pressure hadn't abated one iota.

With an irritable growl, he glared at the sketch pad he hadn't let out of his sight since the moment Samantha had given it to him. It sat on the table next to his elbow, beckoning him to open it and flip through the pages....

He touched the cover, trailing his fingers over the smooth surface, his heart pounding with an excruciating blend of apprehension and anticipation. His thumb caught beneath the stiff cover, lifted it...

A creak from the living room stopped him. A moment later, Lindsay entered the kitchen, surprise lighting her face when she saw him sitting at the table. It was barely five-thirty in the morning, but she was dressed in jeans, a blouse and boots—ready for the day ahead. The few days he'd spent here before the bachelor auction he'd learned her schedule started an hour and a half earlier than the boys' morning routine, which gave her precious time alone to plan out the day.

"Hey, Nick." She crossed the kitchen to him, and he stood, accepting her warm hug. "When did you get back?" she asked.

He lowered himself to his chair and watched as she retrieved a mug from the cupboard and poured herself a cup of the coffee he'd made. "A little bit after midnight. I used my key and crashed on the couch for a few hours." And he'd woken up with Samantha on his mind, and a deep, endless ache in his heart. "Since it was so late, I didn't want to wake you."

Smiling, she approached him with the hot carafe of coffee and refilled his mug. "I wasn't expecting you until at least tomorrow."

He ducked his head sheepishly. "I suppose I should have called."

"Nonsense," she chided. Picking up a box of frosted doughnuts from the counter, she brought them, and her coffee, to the table and took the chair across from Nick. "You're welcome here anytime. No reservations necessary. This is your home, too, Nick."

Home. Despite being an orphan, he'd always felt as though he'd belonged here, at Lost Springs Ranch. A part of him always would. Since the day he'd left to join the Marines, he'd lived in many houses and apartments, but none warm and comfortable enough to call "home." He supposed it was the people who lived in the dwelling that made a simple house a home, filling the rooms with love, and life, and laughter, as his aunt and uncle had done here at Lost Springs.

That's what was missing from his apartment, he knew, and why he suddenly dreaded the thought of returning to New York and the emptiness that awaited him. There was no love, or life, or laughter to anticipate. No, he'd left all that behind with Samantha.

Lindsay's blue eyes brimmed with curiosity as she reached for a doughnut. "So, what happened with you as Amelia Bainbridge-Campbell's personal assistant?"

Nick recounted his two weeks at Cranberry Harbor, from Amelia's scheme to bolster her granddaughter's confidence and Nick's part in her ploy, to Samantha's relationship with Tyler and their impending engagement, and finally, his abrupt departure from Oregon and his return to Wyoming. The tale left him feeling more desolate and miserable than ever.

Perception glimmered in Lindsay's gaze, and she smiled softly. "You've fallen for Samantha, haven't you?"

There was no denying the truth, so he didn't even try.

"Yeah, I have," he admitted, then went on to issue the same argument with Lindsay that he had with Samantha about his job, his life-style. "I can't be what Samantha and Emily need in their lives. I've got a job that isn't conducive to making a happy, secure marriage."

Lindsay offered him no sympathy. "You insist you can't give Samantha what she needs, but you're not even willing to try."

"I learned what I'm capable of giving in a relationship, and not giving, with Camille," he replied with heated frustration. "And I got nothing but a divorce for my efforts. I refuse to put Samantha or Emily through that."

"Relationships are about compromise, Nick. Give and take, and it goes both ways." She eyed him perceptively. "Maybe you couldn't give Camille what she needed because she demanded more from you than she gave in return."

"Or maybe I wasn't willing to sacrifice things that were important to me for the sake of our marriage."

"Maybe," she conceded. "What *is* important to you, Nick? Your job? Or a woman who completes your life and gives you more excitement and thrills than chasing bad guys?"

He honestly didn't know anymore, but something still held him back.

She met his gaze and said softly, "Or maybe you're afraid of needing Samantha too much."

A chill slithered down his spine. "What are you talking about?"

"My parents raised you after your mom died, but you've never needed anyone or anything in your life. You've always been independent, relying on no one but yourself. Maybe depending on Samantha, and needing her, scares you a little bit, too?"

His jaw hardened as he steeled himself against her words, but he couldn't ignore the truth that slammed into him—the truth he'd known all along. Lindsay had pried open a twenty-year-old fear and laid it bare, forcing him to acknowledge the fact that he'd spent his entire life avoiding attachments because of the most basic, maternal one he'd lost so abruptly as a child.

When he said nothing, she sighed and carried her cup to the sink and rinsed it out. "I've got some paperwork to do in my office before the rest of the ranch wakes up." She came up behind him and placed a warm, understanding hand on his tense shoulder. "Find some kind of compromise, Nick. A middle ground for both of you. If Samantha loves you enough to risk her future, maybe you ought to try and do the same for her. Don't throw away this chance to be happy because you're afraid of needing someone."

And with that, Lindsay was gone, her words echoing in his mind, prompting him to confront the emotions he'd buried for twenty long years.

Picking up Samantha's sketch pad, he faced his greatest fears, and his greatest hopes. The pages within the tablet were filled with pictures of him, some of which he'd seen the day he'd come across her sketch pad in the attic. But there were new ones, too, of him alone, playing with Emily, and even a sketch of him sleeping in his bed—had she captured his image after they'd made love? The blissful smile curving his mouth suggested she had.

Every picture reflected the fact that he *needed* Samantha in his life. It showed in his eyes, his expression, his smile. He couldn't ignore the truth. She gave him something no one else ever had—peace, inner calm and a sense of security.

He'd been running for too long, searching for something to fill the vast emptiness within him that even Camille hadn't been able to touch. He'd honestly thought his exciting, dangerous job had fulfilled his needs, but now he knew differently. It had merely been a diversion.

His future was with Samantha, and Emily. Together, they'd be a family. Together, with compromise, mutual respect and trust, they'd make it work—he knew he couldn't live the rest of his life without Samantha and Emily. They completed the man he'd become. A man who needed Samantha's love and understanding, her fire and passion.

She completed him.

With that knowledge lightening his heart, his mind whirled with plans. Amelia's garden party was two weeks away, which gave him time to reevaluate his priorities and prove how much he loved Samantha and wanted her and Emily permanently in his life.

He'd start with a call to his lieutenant to issue his resignation from the force, then look into relocating to Portland, Oregon, where Samantha could pursue her dreams of painting, and he could find a job that would still keep him active, yet ensure he came home every evening to his wife and family.

And then he'd go and claim what was his: Samantha and Emily.

SAMANTHA'S STOMACH TUMBLED with a combination of anxiety and exhilaration as she drove closer to Portland and the first step to the new future that awaited her.

She was taking one of the biggest risks of her life. She might have lost Nick, but she refused to lose her identity, as well. During the past week and a half since his departure she'd done a lot of soul-searching, and many paintings, in an attempt to get back in touch with herself. She'd mulled over the many conversations she'd had with Nick about her past, and the one point that remained foremost in her mind was the one he'd made to her that afternoon in the gazebo—ultimately, she had to believe in herself, in who she was. And that belief would give her the strength to do what was right for her.

His advice had gone a long way in bolstering her confidence. She knew and accepted exactly who she was...Lucinda's daughter, passionate, sensual and determined. But she also realized she possessed qualities her mother hadn't. While Samantha craved excitement and enjoyed the freedom of being impetuous, she was responsible first and foremost. And being responsible meant doing the right thing, for her and Emily.

She could no longer blame herself for her tumultuous marriage. Initially, she'd been caught up in the excitement Justin offered, but her expectations in a husband, in a marriage hadn't paralleled his. Too late, they'd realized they wanted different things. While she'd craved hearth, home and a family, Justin had continued to chase thrills, deliberately destroying any chance at a marriage based on love, respect or trust.

She'd made one mistake with Justin; she wouldn't compound her errors with another loveless marriage to Tyler. She deserved better than that, and so did Emily.

That revelation had enabled her heart to free other emotions, resolve other worries. She was taking charge of her future.

Though her heart ached at the thought of going on without Nick, she knew she'd never forget him. He was in every landscape she painted, every dream that stole into her mind in the darkness of night. He was the reason she trusted herself again; she only wished he could trust his own emotions, as well.

After parking her car in front of Brensen's, Samantha

stepped out and drew a deep, fortifying breath. She smoothed a hand down the front of her linen skirt, then made her way into the gallery. The rich smell of oils and the colorful canvases sparked an excitement deep inside her.

This was her future. She knew it, without a doubt. And she'd made the right choice…for her.

"May I help you?"

Samantha turned and faced the woman approaching her. "Hi, I'm Samantha Fairmont," she said, introducing herself, pleased when the woman's eyes lit up with recognition. "I'd like to talk to you about your offer to exhibit my collection."

THE DAY OF THE GARDEN PARTY dawned bright and clear. With an abundance of confidence and a new lease on life, Nick strode across the lawn toward the tables set up around the extravagant rose garden, his gaze briefly taking in the elegance of Samantha's planning. Everything had come together with such flair and panache. The tables were set with fine linen, silver and china rimmed in gold. Centerpieces of tulips adorned each table. An orchestra played a light selection of music while guests milled around, enjoying the rose garden, conversation or the appetizers that were passed around.

People turned to look at him, glancing from his eye patch to his black jeans and casual knit shirt, but he paid them no mind as he continued to search the large crowd of people for a woman with rich butterscotch hair, eyes bluer than the Wyoming sky he'd left behind, and a smile that had remained in his heart since the day he'd left her.

After today, he vowed they'd never be apart again.

Amelia stepped up to a podium that had been set up beneath an awning draped in vines and roses, looking pretty in a peach chiffon dress. Her smile was radiant. The crowd quieted when she tapped the microphone, their attention focused on her.

Nick stopped his progress through the mass of people out of respect for Amelia's speech, but his gaze continued to scan the attendees for Samantha. Frustration swept through him when he couldn't find her.

Amelia greeted her guests and talked about the charity that would benefit from this special event. Then she gestured to a couple standing near the podium, her gaze glimmering with maternal pride. "I also want to take this opportunity to announce my daughter's recent marriage to Victor Kislenko, and the wedding gift I'd like to give both of them."

Nick smiled when he spotted the newlyweds. Victor puffed out his chest like a lucky groom, and Kathryn blushed like a new bride as a round of applause and congratulations ensued. When the audience quieted once again, Kathryn continued.

"My daughter loves to cook, and I know she's always wanted to open a bed-and-breakfast of her own. I've decided to give her and Victor Cranberry Harbor for that purpose, with the stipulation, of course, that she continue to host the annual garden party. And I hope, of course, that she'll allow her mother to stay on as a permanent guest!"

Kathryn squealed in delight at her mother's generous gift, and hugged Victor exuberantly.

And that's when Nick saw Samantha, standing next to the couple with Tyler Grayson by her side. She looked beautiful in a knee-length, deep purple dress that tastefully displayed her figure. Her hair flowed around her shoulders in a lush fall of soft curls, and her eyes sparkled for her aunt's happiness as she joined the crowd in their applause.

Abruptly, Tyler grasped Samantha's hand and pulled her toward the podium. Her eyes widened in surprise, and she reluctantly followed him. Nick started forward through the throng of people, a sense of dread growing within him. He wasn't about to let Grayson beat him to a proposal that belonged to *him*.

Samantha tried stopping Tyler, all to no avail. "Tyler, I don't think—"

He cut her off and spoke into the microphone. "Everyone, I have an announcement to make, as well—"

"So do I," both Nick and Samantha said at the exact same moment.

Samantha gasped as Nick's loud, firm voice captured everyone's attention. Unerringly, her shocked gaze found him in the audience, and she gaped at him incredulously. Then her expression softened and changed, reflecting a myriad of emotions—surprise, hope and a thrilling excitement that chased away the momentary bout of uncertainty that had gripped him.

"Mr. Nick!" Emily exclaimed, bolting from where she'd been standing next to her aunt Kathryn, her frilly party dress swirling around her coltish legs as she ran toward him. "You came back!"

Knowing there was nothing he could do to stop the little girl's exuberant welcome—not that he wanted to—he caught her in his arms and accepted her warm, loving hug.

"I missed you so much!" Emily gave him a big, smacking kiss on his cheek that had a few of the nearby women issuing sentimental "aahs." "Don't ever go away again."

Nick closed his eyes and absorbed what he'd nearly lost. Home. Love, life and laughter. It was all here, waiting for him. "Not a chance, kiddo," he whispered.

Tyler cleared his throat into the microphone, interrupting the sentimental moment and prompting Nick to state his business. He set Emily back down and whispered for her to go back to her aunt.

Straightening, he met Samantha's gaze and smiled lazily. "By all means, ladies first."

Taking a deep breath, Samantha approached the microphone and smiled at the audience. He could tell his presence distracted her, as did the reason for his impromptu visit. But she managed to put on a professional demeanor that belied the nervousness he saw in the depths of her eyes.

"This garden party wouldn't be a success without your generous donations, and I'd like to thank you all for your support," she began, her voice poised and sure. "I've recently taken up a cause of my own, and hope that you will all support my endeavor in raising money for the Lost Springs Ranch in Wyoming, which is a foster home for troubled young boys."

Murmurs rippled throughout the crowd, and Amelia looked astonished at Samantha's statement. Nick smiled, and continued to watch the woman he loved.

Her gaze scanned the crowd, avoiding him. "In order to raise funds for this cause, I'd like to announce that I'll be having my first art showing at Brensen's next month, and half of the proceeds will go to Lost Springs Ranch. Today, though, I'd like to present an original, one-of-a-kind painting of mine, and propose a silent auction, in which *all* the proceeds will go directly to the Lost Springs Ranch."

With the self-assurance of a woman reborn, she stepped to a nearby easel Nick hadn't noticed until that moment. She pulled the sheet from the canvas, revealing one of her seascapes. Without a trace of embarrassment, Samantha pointed to an obscure silhouette in the breaking waves and disclosed the secret of her shadowed lovers to everyone present.

As Nick glanced at the expressions of the guests around him, he caught glimpses of surprise, delight and interest. There was none of the criticism he knew Samantha had once feared. Even Amelia and Kathryn looked elated with Samantha's renewed confidence. His own chest swelled with a wealth of emotion.

The only one who didn't seem happy about Samantha's artistic ability was Tyler. When she returned to the podium, he expressed his displeasure in a low whisper that the microphone picked up. "We didn't discuss this, Samantha."

She smiled sweetly, though the look in her eyes brooked no compromise. "There's nothing to discuss."

As if to support her claim, a man in the crowd yelled out, "I'll bid ten thousand dollars for the painting!"

Party-goers gasped, and Samantha laughed, her eyes dancing with pleasure. "It's a silent auction, sir, but I'll be happy to open the bid at ten thousand dollars."

A flurry of excitement coursed through the crowd as buyers expressed their interest.

Samantha's gaze met Nick's, and she suddenly looked uncertain again. His heart thumped in his chest, and an awful thought crossed his mind—now that she'd embraced her potential, what if she no longer needed him in her life?

Tyler frowned at Nick, his annoyance at the unexpected turn of events nearly palpable. "And *your* announcement, Mr. Petrocelli?"

Despite his inner doubts, Nick approached the podium, his gaze locked on Samantha, the woman he intended to spend the rest of his life with. "I'd like to announce my engagement to Ms. Samantha Fairmont."

Samantha sucked in a startled breath, her eyes rounding in disbelief.

"You can't do that!" Tyler said, his face flushing indignantly.

"I believe I just did." Fishing a diamond solitaire engagement ring from his front pocket, Nick dropped to one knee before Samantha, took her left hand in his and slid the band onto the proper finger. "Samantha Fairmont, will you do me the honor of becoming my wife, and the mother of my children?"

She bit her bottom lip, and overwhelming tears brimmed in her luminous eyes. Reaching out with her free hand, she cupped his jaw in her palm. "Oh, Nick," she breathed. "I didn't think you were coming back."

It wasn't quite the answer he'd hoped for or expected. "I love you, Samantha. And I *need* you. I need the way you complete me, and bring love and laughter into my life. Don't make me spend another day without you in it."

"I love you, too," she whispered, her voice tight with emotion.

"Oh, for goodness' sake, Samantha, tell the man *yes*," Amelia said with mock impatience.

Samantha gave him a watery smile, though her eyes were bright with joy. "Yes, I'll marry you and be your wife and the mother of your children."

Tyler sputtered a protest, but the resounding applause echoing around them drowned him out. Nick's gaze landed on Amelia, who smiled her approval at the happy couple.

"I want a great-grandson, Petrocelli," she said with a decisive nod.

"Yes, ma'am," he replied with a grin.

MUCH LATER, AFTER THE PARTY was over and the house had settled down for the night, Nick slipped into Samantha's bedroom. She was waiting for him, and eagerly ran into his embrace. His arms slid around her back, drawing her body flush with his. He smiled at her as she entwined her arms around his neck, seemingly needing the warmth and intimate contact just as much as he did.

"I've waited all afternoon to do this," he said, his voice rich with feeling. "I'm so proud of you. What you're doing with your collection of paintings is generous, and selfless, and now everyone knows exactly what a beautiful, talented woman you are."

Her smile was radiant as she smoothed her palms down his chest. "You're to blame for that, of course."

His brows rose. "Me?"

"Yeah," she said with a sigh, her busy hands tugging the hem of his shirt from his jeans. "You made me realize I can't hide who I am, so I've come to accept the passionate, impetuous woman I've always been. And I *like* who I am."

"That's the woman I love and need, so I don't ever want you to change." His blood heated as her fingers touched his bare belly. Unable to resist her slow seduction, he skimmed his hands up to the zipper at the back of her dress and slowly drew it down, trailing his fingers along the silky skin he exposed. When he reached her bra, he unclasped it, then continued on his tantalizing journey.

He smiled when she shivered. "You're everything that's been missing from my life, Samantha, and I'm through using my dangerous job as an excuse to hide from my own emotional insecurity."

"Ah, your job." Soft lips pressed a kiss on the side of his neck. "I guess since I'll be marrying you, this means I'll be traveling from New York to Portland for the art shows I've committed myself to at Brensen's."

He pulled the sides of her dress and the straps of her bra down her arms, and trailed a string of kisses along her bared shoulder, breathing deeply of the soft, feminine scent he'd missed so much. "Nope, there's no need for either of us to travel far, not when we'll be living in Portland."

She drew back, catching the front of her dress against her chest before it could fall to the floor. Her confused gaze searched his. "But your job with the Justice Department…"

He shrugged, not regretting his decision for a moment. "I resigned."

She shook her head, her thick hair tumbling around her shoulders. "But law enforcement is what you love."

"It is," he admitted, using the tip of his finger to playfully tug the material bunched around her breasts, aching for a glimpse of her. She held tight, wanting more answers.

He gave them to her. "But I love you and Emily more. See, I spent the past two weeks doing a little reevaluating of my own. And in order for us to make our marriage work, it's going to take compromise. And compromising means giving up something for the other person, but still gaining something in return. Giving up my position with the DEA means I'll be gaining a wife I can't live without, and a little girl I absolutely adore."

She worried her bottom lip. "I don't want you to grow bored or restless, or feel restricted in any way."

He knew she was expressing concerns she'd experienced in her marriage to Justin. "Ah, sweetheart, you give me all the excitement and thrills I can handle, and once I've had my eye surgery, I'll be doing investigative work for the district attorney's office in Portland. The job will keep me active, but I'll be home every evening for dinner, and long, lazy nights of making love to you."

A fire burned in her gaze and flushed her skin, and he tried not to let all her blatant sensuality distract him.

"I'm finished being reckless with my life," he promised, skimming the back of his knuckles along her cheek, down her throat, over the ring he'd placed on her finger that made her his. Now he wanted to brand her in a more elemental way. "I have you and Emily to think about, and the family we're going to have together. I did this for me, as much as for you."

Her smile was radiant with love, and a soul-deep happiness. "Since we're compromising here, I guess that means I've got to give you passion and desire in return."

He grinned. "Oh, yeah," he murmured, and watched as she released the bunched material. Her dress and bra flowed down her body and pooled around her sandaled feet. He dragged his gaze up, and groaned at the vibrant, deep purple lace panties she wore.

Then all he could do was surrender as she undressed him, heating him with her loving caresses and her soft lips. Once they were both naked and inflamed, she led him to her bed. When they finally lay face to face, skin to skin, he looked down at this woman who'd made his life so complete, so perfect, and knew the unending need and love he felt for her wasn't a weakness, but a strength.

As they joined their bodies, their souls entwined, as well. With a smile on their lips, and their hearts filled to overflowing, they began their life together.

And nine months later, Amelia's first great-grandson was born.

continues with

THE $4.98 DADDY

by

Jo Leigh

Jarred McCoy returned to Lightning Creek to clear his conscience. Being sold to twin six-year-old girls for the grand sum of $4.98 was not in the plans at all! Neither was getting roped in to helping their mother restore her family ranch house. Neither was falling for Beth Cochran and her irresistible family. But Beth was not in the market for a superhero, no matter what her daughters thought!

Available now.

Here's a preview!

BETH WAVED until she couldn't see Sam's Jeep anymore. Just the cloud of dust that took its time settling back down to earth. She went to the side of the house, to the ladder. "Jarred," she called, looking up to the edge of the roof.

"Yeah?"

"Can you hold the ladder, please? I'm coming up."

His head appeared over the jagged edge of some shingles. "You don't have to. I've got things under control."

"I want to."

"That's okay. You just rest. I've got it."

"Don't be silly. It'll get done twice as fast if I help."

"All right," he said grudgingly. He took hold of the ladder, steadying it for her slow climb. When she got to the top, his strong arms pulled her to safety.

He turned away abruptly, going back to the row of shingles he'd been working on.

This wasn't exactly how she'd pictured things. Had he forgotten already? How he'd held her in his arms? How his kisses had made her weak in the knees? How desire had made them both crazy?

Or had she gotten things wrong again?

No. This time, she wasn't going to doubt herself. He'd kissed her, and kissed her hard. She hadn't made that up. She had seen the heat in his gaze, and felt the need in his muscles.

Sam had said something to him. That's what happened. Sam had seen them kissing, and he'd given Jarred hell for it. She should have figured that out right away. "Jarred?"

"Yes?" He didn't look at her, or even stop using the electric nail gun.

"I don't know what Sam said to you, but I want you to know I'm not sorry we kissed."

He stopped. Jerked his head up so fast she thought he might lose his balance. "What?"

"I know Sam must have read you the riot act, but that's only because he thinks of me as a sort of surrogate granddaughter. I don't think he thinks of me as a...well, as a woman."

"He doesn't," Jarred said, not as a question, but as a slightly bewildered statement.

"I think he's just trying to protect me. That's all. He knows what I've been going through this past year. How hard it's been. He doesn't want me to get hurt."

She waited for Jarred to say something. To stop staring at her like that. As if he couldn't understand a word she was saying.

"What I'm trying to say is that it's okay. You don't have to worry about it. I realize that things got a little out of hand, that's all. We kissed. No big deal. I...I mean, it was a big deal. I liked it. A lot. But it wasn't a big...deal."

Jarred's eyes narrowed. His mouth turned down into a frown, which deepened into a scowl.

"I'm sorry," she said, her face heating with embarrassment. "I didn't mean anything by that. I just didn't want you to feel—"

"Beth," he interrupted, his voice as sharp as the edge of a knife.

She stopped, leaned back, thought about dashing down the ladder and wondered if she could do it without killing herself.

He mumbled something under his breath. "Beth," he said again, "I'm not leaving tonight."

"Oh?"

"I'm not leaving until the house is done. Okay? Happy now?"

She couldn't have been more shocked. He was going to stay until the house was done? But he had another life. A business to run. Oh, God, that meant he'd be here for months. Living here, under the same roof. Day after day after day.

"I'll call tonight. Have my things sent out here. Then I'll go over the plans for the house again, and I'll figure out what needs to be done."

"You will?"

He nodded. "I'm not going to leave until the last coat of paint is dry. And that's final."

"I see," she said, finally coming out of her shocked stupor. Finally hearing everything he said. "I'd like to know one thing," she said.

"Yeah?"

"Who invited you?"

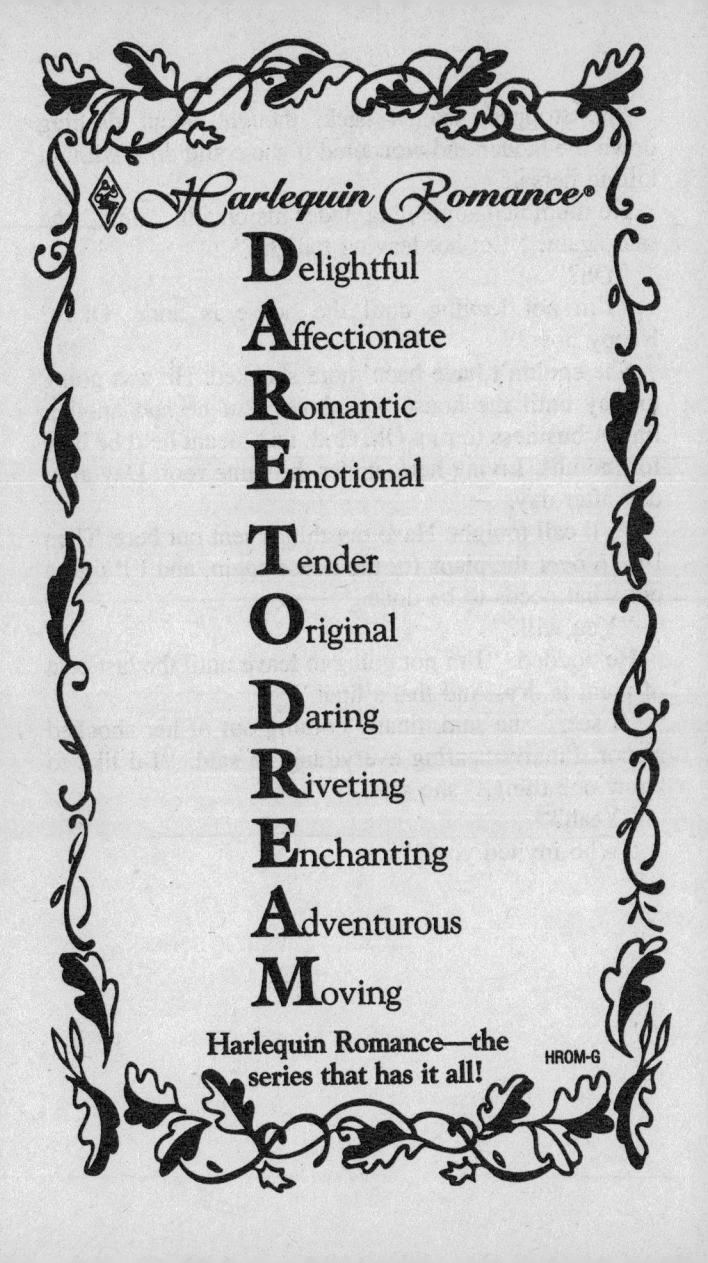

HARLEQUIN  PRESENTS®

HARLEQUIN PRESENTS
men you won't be able to resist
falling in love with...

HARLEQUIN PRESENTS
women who have feelings
just like your own...

HARLEQUIN PRESENTS
powerful passion in
exotic international settings...

HARLEQUIN PRESENTS
intense, dramatic stories that will keep you
turning to the very last page...

HARLEQUIN PRESENTS
The world's bestselling romance series!

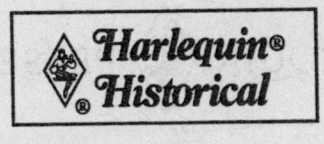
Harlequin® Historical

From rugged lawmen and
valiant knights to defiant heiresses
and spirited frontierswomen,
Harlequin Historicals will
capture your imagination with
their dramatic scope, passion
and adventure.

Harlequin Historicals...
they're too good to miss!

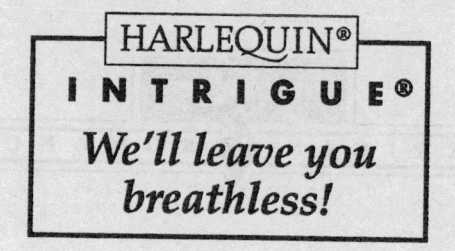

LOOK FOR OUR FOUR FABULOUS MEN!

Each month some of today's bestselling authors bring
four new fabulous men to Harlequin American Romance.
Whether they're rebel ranchers, millionaire power brokers
or sexy single dads, they're all gallant princes—and
they're all ready to sweep you into lighthearted fantasies
and contemporary fairy tales where anything is possible
and where all your dreams come true!

You don't even have to make a wish...
Harlequin American Romance will grant your every desire!

Look for Harlequin American Romance
wherever Harlequin books are sold!

HARLEQUIN SUPERROMANCE®

...there's more to the story!

Superromance. A *big* satisfying read about unforgettable characters. Each month we offer *four* very different stories that range from family drama to adventure and mystery, from highly emotional stories to romantic comedies—and much more! Stories about people you'll believe in and care about. Stories too compelling to put down....

Our authors are among today's *best* romance writers. You'll find familiar names and talented newcomers. Many of them are award winners—and you'll see why!

If you want the biggest and best in romance fiction, you'll get it from Superromance!

Available wherever Harlequin books are sold.